ROCKAWAY BRIDE

PIPPA GRANT

INTRODUCTION

Kidnapping the bride seemed like a good idea at the time.

Her fiancé stole my fortune, so I stole his woman.

Tit for tat. Or tat for tit. However you want to look at it.

The one thing I didn't expect?

Willow Honeycutt, preschool teacher, boy band super fan, is completely crazy.

And somehow she's turned the tables on me.

Now, she's holding *me* hostage, and she won't let me go until we hit every item on her sparkly new, completely insane bucket list.

And that last item?

That last item might cost me more than any fortune.

It very well might cost me my heart.

Rockaway Bride is a romping fun romance between a down-on-his-luck rock star and a boy band-loving preschool teacher, complete with a road trip, handcuffs, and fun with nuns. This romantic comedy stands alone with no cheating or cliffhangers and ends with a rockin' awesome happily ever after.

1

WILLOW HONEYCUTT (AKA a bride on the verge of a breakdown)

WHEN I WAS little and dreaming of my wedding day, I always pictured myself with a Mohawk, a tie-dyed fluffy wedding gown cut off at the knees, biker boots, and dashing out the back of a chapel in Vegas to peel off into the sunset on a Harley.

Mostly because I was secretly in love with Davis Remington, the youngest member of the boy band Bro Code, who had tattoos and sometimes shaved parts of his head and made headlines once when he crashed a Harley, and he was just *hot*, and I assumed that's what his wedding would be like, and also that I would be his bride, because he was *only* a few years older than me.

Not that I ever told my mom that. As far as she knows, I always loved Tripp Wilson—you know, the big brother of the group, who was more years older than me and therefore only a silly girl crush—because that helped her sleep at night, and I knew how much she worried.

About everything.

Being a single mother in the city is *hard*. So I kept my dreams of marrying a boy band bad boy to myself, I got good grades, I got scholarships for an early childhood education degree and then a job teaching preschool. Meanwhile, Mom married the king of a small Nordic country—yes, seriously—and I stayed in New York and joined a band where we cover our favorite boy band songs and mostly play juice bars some nights and weekends, and tomorrow I'm having the fairytale princess wedding in a palace, exactly like every girl dreams of.

Except me.

And tonight, while I wander the stone hallways of Skyr Castle in my mom's adopted home country of Stölland, where I'm supposed to be getting my beauty rest after the rehearsal dinner, at which my soon-to-be mother-in-law kissed up to the king so very blatantly that even the palace mice were embarrassed for her, I'm trying really, really hard to convince myself that my regrets and doubts are a result of this wedding's lack of Mohawk, tattoos, biker boots, and getaway Harleys.

And that my regrets and doubts have nothing to do with Martin.

My fiancé.

Whom I'm marrying.

In eighteen hours.

Eighteen.

Hours.

Eighteen hours until my life and my freedom and my future are forever sealed in the bonds of marriage.

To Martin.

I'm going to throw up.

I breathe through the nausea and turn a corner, passing one of those knight thingies that are in the corners of ancient stone castles everywhere, except this one is all suited up in Viking armor instead of metal armor, so it has a vicious-looking helmet with horns on top and some weird protrusion covering where a person's nose should be, a shield portraying the Frey family coat of arms, which has a killer sheep carrying a spear and an ax and eating a whale on it—royalty is so weird—and a bearskin rug where a breastplate should be.

Bearskin coat?

Whatever.

The point is, I turn the corner on knees and legs which are rapidly melting to the consistency of slime, wishing I had a paper bag, and I find myself face-to-face with three real Viking princes.

My stepbrothers. Who, thankfully, are all in jeans and casual dress shirts instead of Viking armor, because that truly would be the end of me for the night.

"There's the lovely blushing bride," Gunnar, the oldest, says.

"Blushing?" Manning, the youngest, scans me up and down, smiling as he always does. "I believe the more appropriate adjective would be *hyperventilating*."

"You two fuckers are bloody useless," grumbles Colden, the grumpy one.

All three have this quasi-British accent that would be intriguing if any of them were tatted up, owned motorcycles, and *not* my stepbrothers.

Colden shoves a wine bottle into my hand. "Drink."

Stölland's national beverage is mead, and I learned the night before my mom's wedding to the king several years back that I don't tolerate it well.

I take the bottle and glug off the top without asking for a glass, because he's right. I need a drink. And I've known my stepbrothers long enough to know that when one is handed a bottle, one drinks off the bottle.

Which is awesome tonight.

Tonight, I need all the drinks.

"Maybe this won't be so bad," Gunnar says to Manning, who nods his agreement while they both watch me swig.

The two of them are nearly the same height, both with thick brown hair tinged with red in the sunlight, both with pale blue eyes, and both fathers now, though Gunnar—the crown prince—is always clean-shaven, whereas Manning, who's so far down the line to inherit the crown that he's been given permission to live in the States and play professional hockey basically until he's too old to play anymore, almost perpetually sports a short beard around his never-ending smile.

He's madly in love with the perfect woman for him, and they have the most adorable baby together. Of course he's smiling.

Oh, god. Oh god oh god oh god.

The possibility of having Martin's babies is suddenly so real that my ovaries have just offered themselves as tribute to a cryogenics experiment. And possibly performed some sort of self-freeze.

I take another fortifying gulp of honey wine and pray it stays down. "What won't be so bad?" My voice comes out high and panicked like I've been sucking helium, only worse.

Colden sighs. He's shorter than his brothers by a couple inches, with hair much darker, almost the same shade as mine. I'm told he resembles their long-departed mother. And I know firsthand he prefers the company of sheep to the company of people.

"The night before the wedding talk," he answers.

My face goes so hot my brains melt out my nose. Or so it feels. "Uh, guys, I don't think—"

Manning laughs. "Not *that* talk, dear Willow, though if you need pointers—"

Gunnar silences him with a sneak attack headlock. "We were referring to the *if you need to run, we'll make it happen* talk. Family tradition. Though I do believe this is the first time we'll actually mean it."

My heart skips a beat.

Or maybe four beats. "I can't run," I object. Or try to. The words get stuck, and I have to swallow them down with another healthy swig of mead before I try again, when the words once again get stuck.

"You can, you may, and you should," Colden replies.

Manning twists and flails, attempting to get out of Gunnar's headlock, which would be way more entertaining if the mead in my belly wasn't churning like a tsunami of bad idea bubbles and over-whelming doubts.

"We've bought you a ticket," Manning says between grunts and twists.

"A ticket to *where*?"

"New York, but we can change it to anywhere," Gunnar replies. He's grinning now, clearly enjoying the hell out of getting the upper hand on Manning, who should be the strongest of the bunch since he plays professional hockey.

My stepbrothers are all over-muscled Viking goobers.

And I might possibly love them more than I love peanut butter cups right now.

"Do you truly wish to marry Martin?" Colden asks.

My tongue swells. I rub it over the roof of my mouth and I gag.

"Exactly as we suspected," Gunnar declares. He releases Manning, who springs just out of reach of the eldest Frey brother. "Come, Willow. We've a plan."

I stomp a foot and I sway. Whoa. That mead is *yum*. Am I supposed to be drunk this fast? I don't remember getting drunk this fast last time. Although, I suppose not eating anything at the rehearsal dinner might've been part of the problem. I kept sneaking my food to the dog when my bridesmaids and mom weren't looking.

"I'm going to marrrrr—" I start, but I can't finish. While my step-brothers watch expectantly, I take another drink off the bottle, and I try again. "I want to marrrrr—"

All three of them continue to stare at me.

"Fudge you all!" I say.

Gunnar and Manning smirk.

Colden sighs again. "We can order him beheaded instead," he offers.

"And his mother too," Manning agrees.

"But not the dog," Gunnar says. "Viggo's rather taken with the dog. I daresay the dog may not make it back on the plane to the States."

"You can't steal people's pets!" Which is a phrase I'm capable of saying. Whereas I can't make myself say I want to marr—marr —*fudgesicles*. You know. Do that thing. That ceremony.

With Martin.

I swallow half the remaining bottle of mead in four gulps. My eyes burn. My throat's on fire too. But the alcohol is warming my belly and defrosting my ovaries, and I'm starting to breathe better.

"When you're king, you can do anything," Gunnar tells me with a shrug.

"*You're not the king.*"

"But I will be one day. And then my son will be someday after that. Which isn't the immediate issue, my lady. The immediate issue is canceling your wedding."

"I know none of you are Martin's biggest fan," I say, pointing the bottle at each of them, "but he—he—we've been together for *seven years*. That's like…like…a llama caw wedging."

I get two matching squints and another sigh.

"A common law wedding?" Colden translates.

I point the bottle at him. "Seventeen points for House Coldendorf!"

The three of them share a look.

Or maybe the five of them share a look. Why are there two Mannings and two Gunnars and only one Colden?

I should've eaten something for dinner.

And not used that secret passageway Manning showed me in my

chambers—palaces don't have *bedrooms*—to slip away from my bridesmaids tonight.

My bridesmaids wouldn't be getting me drunk and trying to talk me out of doing...the thing...tomorrow.

Or maybe they would. They're not Martin's biggest fans either, and I'm almost positive last month's book club topic was runaway bride books for a reason.

I squeak as a thought hits me.

"Did my friends tell you to do this?" I demand.

They share another look. "The throne room," they say together.

"Oh, no, are the sheep in there?" I whisper. "They can't be. Not yet. The sheep don't invade the palace for washings until the washing day."

"For weddings until the wedding day," Manning helpfully corrects.

I point at him. The one of him on the left, I mean. "You told me so when I helped you herd them inside before Mom married King Tor."

"Bloody bastard, I knew that was you." Colden catches Manning with a punch to the arm.

Gunnar leaps between them. "Later," he says.

"Fight! Fight! Fight!" I chant. And then I giggle. Because I'd *way* rather watch Vikings fight than get marr—marr—marrrrr—*fudgebuckets*.

"We possibly should've skipped the mead," Manning says cheerfully.

"The mead's tradition," Gunnar replies.

"For the *men* in the family," Colden points out.

"For everyone," Gunnar argues. "Merely because there hasn't *been* a royal female born in the palace in two hundred years doesn't mean the females should be excluded."

"She's not technically royal," Manning observes.

"She helped you herd sheep. She's family."

Colden twitches his fingers at me. "Hand over the bottle, Willow."

I pull it to my chest. "No trucking way."

Am I drunk?

Maybe.

But I'm also seeing something very, very clearly.

I've been with Martin for seven years. I know all of his eighteen cats. I know his birthday, his family's birthdays, the gate code for his family's Long Island estate house, that he's allergic to soy and works too much, that the diamonds his mother wears in public are replicas of family heirlooms because she's terrified the plebian masses will breathe wrong or steal the real pieces, and that he has some insecurities that come from not being loved enough as a child, which is why it took him six years and an anti-anxiety pill to propose.

But I don't know that I love him.

I mean, I *love* him. But I don't think I'm *in love* with him.

He's the outward physical manifestation of the perfect husband—successful financial blah blah something, animal lover, upper-crust family, respectful of my boundaries—and he's also boring as h-e-double hockey sticks.

And he never comes to my band's performances, whereas my bandmates' boyfriends are always there.

Over dinner one night last week, I told him about Beatrix Clara Clementine trying to prove she could fly by leaping off the top of the slide on the playground at the preschool where I teach, and he had no idea who I was talking about.

Beatrix Clara Clementine joined my class *last August*, and on her first day, she tried to practice being a submarine in the bathroom sink, which was the first of no fewer than ten instances this school year where we had to call an ambulance for the child. It's *June* now. She's been in my class an entire school year, and he still doesn't know who she is.

I don't even know what Martin does for work anymore. We used to talk about stuff like this, but he switched companies to work for his uncle a while back, and now it's all *I don't want to talk about work.*

And we haven't had sex in *four months.*

"We've a secret stash of mead in the throne room," Manning tells me. "No sheep, I promise."

"Better fucking not be," Colden mutters.

"If there are, it was the Berger twins," Manning replies. With a smile. Of course.

I hug my mead tighter to my chest. "I'm taking this to bed," I tell my stepbrothers.

All three—five?—of them study me closely.

They might be Viking goobers, and they might've gotten stuck with a stepsister who has no interest in any of this royal business, but underneath it all, they're good guys.

They've been good to my mom. They've been good to me.

And it's sweet that they care.

But me getting marr—marr—*dang* it.

It is none of their business.

They can't tell me what to do. They can't tell me *how* to do it.

"May I escort you back to your chambers then?" Gunnar asks.

I shake my head, which makes something slosh between my ears, and not in a completely unpleasant way. There are enough guards milling about that if I get lost, someone will point me in the right direction. And since Mom's so popular here, and everyone says I look just like her, there's little chance of me finding myself with a battle ax to the throat or anything if they think I'm actually an intruder.

"Pass along any messages for you?" Manning offers.

I shake my head again, and there's more wooziness.

Woozy is good. Woozy is fun.

Colden's frowning the biggest. He pulls me in for a hug, which is surprising, because I really did think he only liked sheep. "We have your back for anything you need, Willow."

Gunnar grabs me next "Didn't sleep a wink the night before my own wedding," he says. "But I didn't have the choices you do."

Right.

Because his marriage was arranged. Short-lived, but arranged nonetheless.

Whereas mine isn't.

They're right.

I can call this off. If I'm not sure, and I'm *not* sure, then I *should* call this off.

I need to talk to Martin.

Maybe after I take a walk.

2

─────

Dax Gallagher (aka a fallen rock star)

Hangovers and halibut don't mix.

Check that.

Hangovers, halibut, and *handcuffs* don't mix.

I groan, gag on the heavy scent of raw fish, and lift my hand to rub my eyes while the world dips and bobs around me. Except my hand weighs twice as much as it did yesterday.

Because it's attached—with handcuffs—to an arm.

I jerk upright, my head screams a protest, metal digs into my wrist, and a feminine shriek to my left makes my whole skull crack. Gray light filters into the cold, cramped storage room from a high round porthole, and I'm barely able to make out the shape of a slender woman with dark hair crouched in the small space beside me.

Handcuffed to me.

Shit.

Fucking shit on a shithorse.

I groan again.

She shrieks again.

"Stop," I growl. "Or I'll tape your fucking mouth shut."

Yeah, I'm a prince among men.

"Who are you? Where am I? Oh, no. Martin."

She groans, last night's bad decisions sucker punch my gut, and the world bobs and weaves—or maybe that's the boat—and shoves me against her.

"Shut up." Fuck fuck *fuck*. My skull feels like there's a meat cleaver attempting to separate it into two halves—the idiotic half and the impulsive half—and my brain has yet to catch up to her first two questions.

Neither of which I'll be answering.

"The wedd—wedd—*oh!*" she shrieks. She yanks on the hand-cuffs. "What's this? Who are you? Why are we—*oh my god*. Did I kidnap you? Oh, *duck*, please tell me I didn't kidnap you. It was the mead, I swear. Come on. Get up. Let's see if we can get out of here."

The boat pitches, she shrieks that unholy sound again, topples onto me, and now my stomach's getting in on the whole body rebellion act my head started.

The boat. We're on a boat. *Fuck*, what was in that shit I drank last night? Something cursed and unholy, apparently. I dabbled in some heavy, dark shit in my early twenties before I wised up and decided I wanted to live long enough to enjoy my success—haha, so fucking *funny* today—but I don't ever remember a morning after like this.

Another layer of dread flops onto the pile of shit that my life has been decaying into the last two months.

Maybe it *wasn't* the mead.

No. I'm not going there. Not buying into that bullshit. The last two months—all just coincidence. *Life*.

Not fucking black magic.

There's no such thing as black magic.

Might be such a thing as karma though.

The princess tries to stand, pulling my arm with the handcuffs, and I smirk despite myself, because while handcuffing her and getting her on this boat might have been an impulse—and possibly I did those in the opposite order? I can't remember—I'm realizing it puts me in control.

And I need to be in control.

"Sit down, princess. You're not going anywhere."

Finally, a full three seconds of silence.

But it comes with a heavy scrutiny. My eyes are adjusting to the low light, which means hers probably are too. I can make out a deli-cate bone structure. Full cupid's bow lips. High cheekbones. Feath-ered brows. Big eyes, though I can't tell the color. Simple pearl earrings in ears just a little too big. Dark hair just brushing the tops of her shoulders. A light sweater over tiny tits that are lifting with each rapid breath.

She could be a fucking fairy princess.

Which doesn't matter. What matters is that she's my ticket to getting back what's rightfully mine.

Her eyes go round, and she squeaks again. "You're Dax Gallagher."

Six months ago, that meant something. Shit, six *days* ago, that meant something. I give her an ugly smile. "And you're fucking annoying."

I don't know anything about kidnapping someone, but I know we're not going to be friends.

She sniffs at me like she's blaming me for the fish smell, then glances around. We're leaning against cold storage boxes, probably stuffed with fish and hopefully not hiding anything else, with just enough room in here for the two of us, a door, and that porthole. There's not much to see.

"Why are we on a boat?" she asks.

The boat. Why were we on the boat? Drinking and kidnapping did *not* mix. I had a good reason for the boat when we boarded.

Right.

So her thieving asshole of a fiancé can't come storming the castle to rescue her. Though I was honestly probably more concerned about her stepbrothers.

Of *course* the weasel was engaged to a fucking king's stepdaughter. "Quit. Talking."

"I have to pee."

Fuck.

Should've taken the dog instead.

I shift and reach into my pocket for my phone. One call—and a fucking handful of painkillers and two days of sleep—and everything will go back the way it was supposed to be. Little Miss Fairy Princess will be swapped back for what her dipshit fiancé took from me, I'll do whatever the fuck the label thinks we need to do to get the band back on top, and I'll hire a whole damned team of PIs to find Danger.

My drummer going missing is the last straw in this hexing —*karma*, whatever—bullshit. I'm putting an end to it.

Now.

I open my phone, hit the contact and dial, but it immediately disconnects.

"Why are you calling Martin?" the princess demands. "Does he have something to do with this? Ohmygosh, does he know I was running? I didn't mean to run without telling him. Oh, no. My mom. I need to call my mom. What am I going to tell my mom? The parade. They'll have to cancel the parade. And oh my gosh, *my mom*. She's been waiting to be a grandmother for *six years*. Not that she's ever pushy about it, but I can just tell. And she likes Martin. I think. I mean, I know a lot of people don't, but Mom does. Or at least she doesn't actively *dislike* him. But I can't marry him. *We don't love each other*. Would you marry someone you didn't love? Never mind. Three divorces. I know. I read *People*. I'm allowed some vices, okay? But I'm not going back. I'm not marrying him, no matter what you two are planning. And I need to call my mom."

"Why can't you go two seconds without opening your fucking mouth?"

She tilts her head. "Wait...I didn't kidnap you. You were in the meadow. You asked me if I wanted to see the northern lights. But it's June. You can't see the northern lights in June."

The privileges of being rock royalty.

Sometimes you know the right people to get into the right castle grounds.

Even if your own crown is tarnished and mangled from being run over by a semi-truck overloaded with horse shit.

"How much did you have to drink last night?" I ask her while my cell phone defiantly informs me that I have no signal. *Fuck*.

I look back at the princess. She was weaving and bobbing more than this boat when I found her frolicking with the sheep, which saved me an ass-ton of time trying to find her inside the palace walls.

Not that I can talk. I was doing my fair share of weaving too.

Pretty fucking sure we wouldn't be here if I hadn't been.

Whisky never gives the best ideas, and whatever that bartender gave me last night was stronger than whisky.

She grimaces. "Waaaaaay too much."

"Then shut. The fuck. Up."

She blinks. It's a whole eyeball blink, slow, like she's practiced how to make her eyelashes dance with her cheeks just right to convey a mix of sexy as hell and too innocent for her own good.

My dick stirs, and I snarl. She's engaged to a cockroach. Probably involved in half the shit he did.

She doesn't get to be innocent.

Or sexy.

I rise and yank on the handcuffs holding us together. "Get up, princess. We're finding a cell signal, and I'm getting the fuck rid of you."

For the first time since she started babbling, she makes a sound that's not a head-splitting shriek.

This one's a tiny gasp.

Like maybe she's finally realized she's being held captive, and I'm fucking pissed, and we're on a boat.

I yank on her arm again to get her off her ass and moving.

And because I'm hungover, I don't see what's coming next.

Namely, her fist.

Right to my junk.

I woof out a gasp of my own and double over. My vision goes triple. *Fuck*. My balls feel like someone's trying to chop them off with a rusty flaming hacksaw. My already unhappy gut heaves.

She grips me by the hair and shoves me against the coolers. They rattle behind me, a wave of fish gut smell lands on my tongue, I gag again, and she knees me in the family jewels.

This time I see it coming, and I'm almost able to block her. "*Fuck. FUCK!* Stop!"

She tries for a right hook, but since her right hand's tied with mine, she can't get it. Before I can subdue her, she gets me under the ear with another left hook.

"Christ on a fucking crackpot, *stop*."

She weighs less than my last wife's stupid dog, and she's beating the shit out of me.

The haze in my head clears—though the cleaver remains—and I lift my left hand, block her next punch, and spin us until *she's* the one trapped against the fish coolers. I wedge myself between her legs to keep her from racking me again.

"My stepbrothers are going to *kill* you," she says.

"They have to get to me first, princess." It strikes me that there's something odd in her statement, but I can't quite process what it is.

"I *hate* killing, I *hate* it. I don't even kill spiders for my friend Zeus, but I'm going to watch my stepbrothers kill you and feed you to a sheep and I'm going to enjoy every single minute, and then I'm probably going to throw up, because it'll be disgusting, but *you kidnapped me on my wedding day,* you—you—you *gas mole.*"

More brain cells are waking up.

My most prized possession—yes, I mean my thunder down under—is still aching like a bitch. I'm not certain yet I won't toss the sewage still swimming in my gut. My head is screaming every time I smell fish, the boat rocks, or this annoying as fuck woman even *looks* at me, but I'm suddenly painfully aware that I'm pressing my body against soft female flesh.

Soft, *angry* female flesh.

Her fiancé is a toadstool. She should be the same. Toadstool fuck-wits deserve each other. "You said you're not marrying anyone today."

She visibly gulps, but she doesn't break eye contact. I have at least six inches and probably fifty pounds on her. I know where we are. I know *why* we're here.

She doesn't.

Supposedly.

Yet she persists in trying to stare me down.

"When my stepbrothers are finished with you, the Berger twins will be next," she says. "And then you'll have my friends to deal with. Sia, Parker, and Eloise are more terrifying than my stepbrothers and the Berger twins combined. Especially Sia and Eloise. I mean, Sia *is* a Berger, and Eloise is just…Eloise."

I snort. Which is honest to god chutzpah on my part, because I'm roughly acquainted with the Berger twins and have seen Stölland's princes.

"Big words, little princess. But there's one problem. If your fiancé doesn't cough up what he owes me, your friends and family will never get close to either one of us again."

Even more chutzpah. I don't have a fucking clue what I'll do if the weasel doesn't pay up. I don't murder women.

Fuck, I don't *kidnap* women.

Except today.

Desperate times, desperate measures.

And she came with me willingly.

For the record.

"What does he owe you?" she demands.

"Don't play innocent. You sleep with the devil, you know what the devil does."

She flinches and tries to knee me again, but I block her and smile.

An ugly, ugly smile. "I don't want to hurt you, princess. But I'll defend myself if I have to."

The boat jerks to a stop before she can answer, we're both pitched sideways, and she comes up swinging again.

Christ, I just want a bed, a Dr Pepper, and a big greasy plate of onion rings on top of my painkillers.

And my drummer to be found. My bassist's finger healed. My lead guitarist's tax problems solved. And my keyboardist's divorce to get easier.

No more crazy one-night stands followed by threats.

No more falling record sales.

No more of that unsettling feeling every time I hit the studio or write a song.

And for my last memory on a stage to be something better than being chased off by shitting pigeons.

Oh, and also, *I want my fucking money back.*

The door swings open, knocking me in the back, and a sailor stops in the doorway. He's not the same guy I paid off last night with my last grand to get on the ship.

That sailor was younger and happy with the cash.

This one?

He looks at me.

At the princess.

Back to me.

"Docked. Get off." He eyes our hands.

The handcuffs.

I wink at him.

Takes a whole fuck-ton of effort to wink at him.

"Who are you?" the princess demands.

He looks her up and down again, like he's trying to decide if she's in a bad spot and if he really wants to get involved, or if she's in a bad spot and he wants to help me with whatever I'm planning on doing to her.

Fuck. Again.

I don't want to get off this boat, but I don't want this asshole calling the police or the royal guard or whatever the fuck they have in this sheep-obsessed country. Probably get picked up by something wooly with a badge.

And that's the best of the scenarios I'm coming up with, based on the way he's looking at the princess.

I grab her by the wrist and tug.

"Pleasure doing business with you," I say to the sailor.

He looks at me expectantly. "She stays," he says. "*You* get off."

I lean down to his level. He smells like rotting fish, his eyeballs are hard as flint, and I might be hungover and aching in the nut sack, but there's no fucking way I'm leaving my bounty behind. The rational, home-grown Texan in me wants to beat the ever-loving shit out of the sailor on principle for the implication that he's going to keep her as his own captive to do as he wants.

But I'm not a rational, home-grown Texan.

I'm a fucking rock star who just kidnapped the fiancé of the man who robbed me of my entire fortune.

"This one's *mine*," I growl. "And I will remember your fucking face until the day I die, so don't you *dare* do anything fucking stupid."

I shoulder past him.

Or try to.

He steps in my path and grabs for the princess. "Stay, little sheep." The beefy, toothless, menacing dude leers at her.

She gasps, spins, and the next thing I know, she's twisted us so that we're holding the sailor with our cuff chain to his throat. She's anchored herself against the storage boxes and is pushing him against the wall beside the door. He gags and pulls at the cuff chain, but she twists her wrist harder.

"A little help," she grunts at me.

I put my feet on the guy and tighten the chain too.

Belatedly.

Because I can't believe she just pulled that move off.

The boxes shift behind our weight, and more fish smell wafts out.

"We're getting off this boat," she announces to the sailor. "And I'm *also* going to remember your face *forever*. And if you *ever* look at one single woman wrong again, I'll personally see to it that every guard in Stölland hunts you down until they find you, and that you'll be laid out, naked, in front of the palace while chickens peck at your peewee. Understand?"

I choke.

I was with her until *peewee*.

The sailor's turning red.

She twists again, shoves him into the coolers, and yanks on the handcuffs. "Run!" she shrieks.

She drags me out the door. Two more sailors look up at us, surprised, like they didn't know we were stowing away.

It's not a large boat, but when she flings a leg over the railing, I pull back. "Whoa, princess—"

"*Jump*," she orders.

I'm not—oh, *fuck*.

Here comes sailor number one, and he is *pissed*.

I fling a leg over the railing too. "Count of three—" I get out before she's leaping.

It's maybe six feet to the rickety dock. We land in a tangled mess, mostly because she pulled me down, but she's back on her feet and tugging on my wrist before I can catch my breath.

Who the hell *is* this woman?

"Run," she orders again.

Brilliant plan. I need to find somewhere to stash her, get a cell signal, and make my ransom demand.

Shit, this is getting real.

But there's one problem.

One *major* problem.

I look around quickly as we dash off the dock. At the massive coastline. The flat land. The sand and beaches breaking up the green rocky ledges. No houses in sight. No other docks beyond the one that's groaning like it's going to crumble under our feet any minute.

No sheep either.

We're not in Stölland anymore.

And I don't know where the fuck we are.

Willow

I, Willow Elizabeth Honeycutt, do solemnly swear that I will never, ever, ever, ever get involved with another man in my entire life for as long as I shall live.

Which will apparently be *not very long*, if the look on that creepy boat guy's face was any indication. I've lived in the city my entire life. I might be *nice*, but I'm not innocent, and even if I had been, some of the training the king requested I take with his guards when Mom married him reinforced the idea that there are *not nice* people in this world.

People who are also *not right*.

But right now, I'm really glad the king made me take that training. And I'm equally glad that once we got over the first hill, we stopped, peeked back, and saw the boat heading back to sea.

So now I'm sitting here, having peed in the sand *in front of a bleeping rock star*, catching my breath and debating if hyperventilating should be my first course of action, or if I should smash in Dax Gallagher's head with one of those rocks dotting the landscape first.

Honestly, the rock's losing the battle, because as long as I'm handcuffed to him, I'd have to drag his unconscious—or dead—body along with me to go find help, and all my bobby pins are back at the castle waiting for my wedding hairdo, which I won't be getting.

Holy moly.

I'm not getting married today. Not wearing my dress. Not saying vows. Not taking a carriage ride through the capital. Not spending the day celebrating with Mom and the king and my stepbrothers and my friends.

Yet another sign not getting married is a good idea—I'm more upset at the idea of missing a party with Mom and my friends than I am about not marrying Martin.

But I can't think about that right now, because we're not in Stölland anymore. I don't know what country we're in, but it can't be too far from Stölland.

Too far being a relative term.

I glare at Dax's intricate dragon sleeve tattoo on the arm tethered to mine while he curses at his phone, which is apparently not getting any signal.

Surprise, surprise.

This could've gone so differently. He could've come charging up the aisle as Mom and King Tor were giving me away, hollering that he'd secretly loved me since the night he saw my band cover Toto's "Africa" the one and only time we let Eloise pick our entire set list, begging me to escape with him on his Harley, shave my head, get a brow piercing with a unicorn stud, and tattoo his name on my rear end, but *no*.

He's never been to one of our shows, he doesn't love me, and he's not *rescuing* me from my wedding.

The day I meet one of the biggest rock legends of my generation, he stinking *kidnaps* me, claiming he'll *give me back* to freaking *Martin* once Martin gives him...something.

Men.

Just *men.*

I should be terrified on top of irritated, but I can't quite work up the effort. Which is clearly one more sign that calling off the wedding is a good idea.

Or else it's a sign about my ability—or disability—to judge danger.

I don't *think* Dax will hurt me, but then, I don't know him. Not really. I simply know *of* him.

Dax Gallagher, lead singer for Half Cocked Heroes. Legendary for his raw, gravelly voice. His tight, hard body. The tattoos. The drinking. The women.

The talent.

He's sin in denim and ink, seduction and danger in a sound wave.

And he's currently holding me hostage.

Or so he thinks.

Maybe *I* should hold *him* hostage.

See how he likes *that*.

He throws his phone on the grass and yanks on my arm. I yank back. He's not big and beefy like my friend Sia's hockey-playing brothers, who are identical twin tanks on skates, but he's still stronger than I am. Considering his lean physique, he's actually freakishly strong.

Strong enough to drag me by the handcuff through the dewy grass.

Or maybe I just lost that much weight from not eating so well the last six weeks. Wedding stress isn't for wusses.

I flop onto my back. My arm's twisted weird, my wrist is getting chapped where the metal keeps rubbing it, my shoulder aches with every tug, and my ivory pants are probably getting grass stains up the yin-yang, but I refuse to get up.

I haven't worked with preschoolers for six years to not know how to be as non-compliant as possible.

"Christ on a fucking kum-twat," he barks.

"Did you just mock kumquats? Or was that an honest mistake? How would you feel if *Dax* was corrupted and suddenly everyone thought you were a vegetable called *yax*? Or better yet, how do you think a carrot would feel if it suddenly had to be called a *Dax*?"

I also haven't worked with preschoolers for six years to not know how to be annoying.

My tactics are clearly working, because he looks like his brain's about to erupt like a volcano and launch his bloodshot eyeballs clear out over the hill and into the sea.

Sea? Ocean? Bay? Gulf?

I have no idea where we are, and so I have no idea what that body of water is.

I do know what the dark things on the horizon are though.

Those are clouds.

Dark, menacing, *going to drench us until we die of element exposure* clouds.

"Of the two of us, princess," Dax sneers, which is stupidly hot and seductive, like when he sneered in his music video for that song that was supposedly about his second ex never getting better than what she had with him, which also shouldn't have been hot and seductive, because *ego*, "you're not in any position to be a smartass."

"Because you have a secret army of ninjas about to storm the beach in their magic helicopter? You're a terrible kidnapper. You don't even have tape for my mouth. And you lost the keys to the handcuffs, didn't you?"

"You need to shut up," he growls. His dark hair is unkempt and wild, his stubble two days past five-o'clock shadow, his biceps bunching as though he's barely keeping his temper in check.

"You need to let me go," I counter.

I probably should get up. I want to find a cell signal as well. And also a phone. So I can call my mom and apologize for missing my wedding. Apologize for not being sorry that I'm missing my wedding and for feeling this weird relief that probably means I should've called this off months ago. Apologize for stranding her with Martin's mother.

Which is honestly probably my biggest faux pas of the day.

"I'm not letting you go until your thieving fiancé hands over what he owes me," he informs me. Still snarling in that gravel-thunder voice that makes the hair on the back of my neck stand on end.

Maybe I should be worried about my safety.

I'd really like to see my mom again. My friends. My kids at school.

Yes, fine, I'd even miss my stepbrothers if Dax Gallagher murdered me here on the shore of...wherever we are.

And I should probably want to see Martin, to apologize for basically leaving him at the altar, and to ask him why he never told me he knew Dax Gallagher, because Martin *knows* I love music. Except maybe Martin was protecting me because he knew Dax was actually a kidnapping crazypants.

"Whatever it is you think Martin owes you, I can almost certainly promise you that he doesn't have it. He can barely take care of himself some days. I don't know why you think he'd be capable of deviously robbing anyone else."

His expression goes hard as petrified lava, his hair goes two shades past midnight and starts to smoke, and the dip in my belly tells me I might be wise to shut up.

Before he decides I'm too much trouble and he murders me.

But if he murdered me, he'd have the same problem I'd have if I murdered him. We're still attached with handcuffs, and I'm a little out of practice at getting out of them without a key.

Also, as noted before, all my bobby pins are back at the castle, so even if I did clearly remember how to spring myself from hand-cuffs—seriously, that training the king sent me to was fun, if also a bit terrifying—I'm ill-equipped to follow through with the knowledge.

"I don't know why you thought kidnapping me was a good idea," I continue. Let's face it. If he were going to murder me, he probably would've done it about the time I hammered him in his privates.

Or possibly that psychological phenomenon of feeling like I know him since I know *of* him, and the subsequent feeling that I'm moder-ately safe with him, is going to totally get me killed, because my mom's not here, my friends aren't here, my stepbrothers aren't here, and I'm feeling weirdly…free.

Gloriously free. "Martin doesn't want me, and even if he did, he's not *the riding in on a white horse to save the day* type, so this was a very poor plan on your part."

Probably.

I didn't exactly talk to him about calling off the wedding, but I can imagine he's pretty upset with me right about now.

I really should've talked to him.

Dax studies me. In addition to the bloodshot redness in his eyes, there are dark smudges beneath, adding a haunted quality to his rugged features. I don't know what he drank yesterday, but it was clearly something stronger than that bottle of mead my stepbrothers gave me.

Or possibly it's just that my liver still works like it's supposed to.

"He'll pay for you," he growls.

The hairs rise on my arms now, but I lift my chin anyway and try to fib my way through this. "No, he won't. He doesn't want me. I'm too much trouble."

He smirks.

I smirk back, though my heart's racing faster than a cheetah. "And now I'm your trouble."

He smirks harder, which is unfairly sexy with all that just-tumbled-out-of-bed look.

I don't think I *can* smirk harder. But I try. Even though I doubt it makes me sexy at all. "And you've never seen trouble like me."

"No, princess. You've never seen trouble like *me*."

"Is that a challenge?" Something sparks in my heart, a burst of adrenaline shoots through my veins, and the idea of being a challenge—oh, could this be *fun*.

He laughs.

He actually *laughs*.

Because I'm sweet, innocent, preschool teacher Willow who never curses, who takes carrots and celery in her lunch every day, and who dutifully never misses a band practice, a day of work, or a Sunday afternoon family dinner at Martin's family's.

Martin *won't* pay for me. Whatever Dax thinks he has, there's no way he has it. Not Martin. Martin has eighteen cats and can't tell his mother *no* for anything—including letting his mother bring *her* dog that he's *allergic to* come to *our* wedding in *Stölland*—and just last week scared himself walking into the bathroom late at night and catching his reflection walking back at him.

Also, when's the last time I got to be trouble? The night I helped Manning let the sheep into the palace aside. Of course.

Is there something truly, *truly* wrong with me if I confess that being kidnapped is *way* better than marrying Martin today?

Dax isn't exactly Davis Remington—Bro Code will always be my teenage music love, and there's nostalgia there that I'll never shake—but he *is* the bad boy of rock 'n' roll.

And—handcuffs aside—being here, in the hills beyond a random beach, with nothing but rain approaching and the crash of the surf rolling through my ears and the wet grass beneath me—it's like I'm *alive*.

Free.

Untethered.

And it's scarily intoxicating.

"*Heeee-maw!*"

We both jerk toward the noise, which basically means he drags me another half-foot on the ground.

A donkey with one floppy ear crests a grassy hill behind us. It eyeballs us. He's gray, with shaggy fur, a white snout, a crooked ear, and an overbite.

He bares his teeth at us and paws the ground.

He's a donkey bull getting ready to charge.

"Fucking hell," Dax mutters.

"I bet that donkey's trouble too," I offer. Helpfully.

He cuts a laser-sharp glare at me. "Shut up."

"Do you know where we are? Because I'd think you would've planned for us to be somewhere with a cell signal if you wanted to make a ransom call."

"Shut. *Up.*"

This is *fun*.

I really hope he doesn't kill me. He's truly a terrible kidnapper. If I were doing the kidnapping, I would've brought rope and tape and definitely a voice scrambler and probably a taser and—and I probably shouldn't continue on with that train of thought.

Both for my own peace of mind, and for knowing that *I'm* not the psycho one here.

Though I am seriously considering psychological warfare. What if I *could* convince him that I hold the upper hand, and he has to do what I tell him to?

Also, *who am I*?

Holding a rock star hostage is *not* me.

Though I'm not opposed to singing for him to see if he thinks it would be worthwhile for my band and me to cut an album.

For fun.

To give to our families for Christmas.

Oh, heck. We'll just do it anyway. Sia—our keyboardist—is dating a billionaire. He'll pay for it.

The donkey *hee-maw*s again. Slobber drips from its lips when it bares its crooked teeth at us.

I scramble to my feet.

The donkey growls.

Dax steps between me and the donkey. "Fucking dimwit," he hisses at me. "Stand still. You want the fucking thing to charge us?"

"You shouldn't say *firetruck* so much," I chide. Mostly to get his goat. My friends *firetruck* all the time. I don't mind profanity, I just don't use it myself because of my job. "You never know when a kid might overhear you."

"It's a fucking *word*, and I'll fucking use it however I fucking want."

"You know the next step after extreme cussing is promiscuity and too much drinking." I have no idea if that's true, and I don't really care if that's how he wants to live his life, but I'm sure a lecture will irritate him. Mostly because, if the tabloids are true, he already imbibes in both booze and women. Frequently.

His shoulders bunch, and he grunts. "That's also known as fucking *living*."

Oh, snap. He's got me there.

The donkey brays again. I peek around Dax and watch it take two wobbly steps toward us, snout flaring.

"Is it going to charge us?" I whisper.

"I don't have any fucking clue."

"Now you're just *firetrucking* to irritate me, aren't you?"

"You realize I've kidnapped you and you're in a shit-ton of fucking danger?"

"My stepfather's a king. You hurt a single hair on my head, and he'll use his political connections to make you disappear no matter where we are in the world. Besides, if you were going to hurt me, you'd be throwing me to the donkey instead of protecting me from it. And how do you know *I'm* not in charge here? Maybe I'm going to hold you hostage until you get me a helicopter to France so I can see the Eiffel Tower."

Seriously, I don't know where this is coming from, but I haven't had this much fun in *ages*. There's a dam bursting free inside me, and crazypants Willow is whirling out to play.

He steps aside and shoves me in front. "You know what? Fine. You face the donkey."

The donkey eyeballs me. It takes two more menacing—albeit woozy—steps toward us.

Dax's grip on my shoulders tightens. "Fucking fuckwit shitballs," he swears. And suddenly he's between me and the donkey again. "When I say run, you better run your ass off," he orders. "Now, move. Slowly. Toward that hill to the right."

He's watching the donkey, which means he doesn't see the ridiculous smile blooming on my face.

He's right.

I've been kidnapped.

A sane person would be a little worried.

However, I haven't felt completely sane since the moment my future mother-in-law—no, since *Martin's mother* suggested that his entire family, including cousins and aunts and uncles, be invited to the palace every other Christmas at the very least, since I was taking Martin away from the family.

Like we weren't planning on continuing to live in New York. Close enough to visit *every single day*. If you don't mind some traffic or congestion on the subway. And where—oh, ducks.

Where all my stuff has just been moved into Martin's apartment.

I shake my head. Not going to think about it.

"Stand *still*," Dax hisses.

The donkey gives a full-body shudder and trots at us. Snorting. *Mee-haw*ing.

"*Damn* it," Dax mutters.

"I told you I was trouble." I don't know who I am or why I'm talking so much. This isn't me. Truly. But there's something about this weird *freedom* that's making me insane.

"*Go*," Dax orders.

I turn.

He turns.

We crash into each other and topple over in a mangled mess of arms and limbs. The handcuffs jerk at my right arm. Dax scrambles to his feet and tugs on the handcuff. "Get up. *Get up*."

I'm halfway to my knees when the donkey headbutts him, pitching him face-first into the grass.

My arm jerks along with him, yanking my shoulder. I try to cover my head and drop as low and small as I can go, but I'm struggling to get control of my cuffed arm, and the donkey's right on top of me, breathing heavy, snorting, and—

And then he licks me.

The donkey *licks* me. Right on the arm.

I shriek.

He snuffles my armpit and licks my arm again.

Just like a dog would.

"Heyo, Beezers, whamcha gah yeah?" a voice calls.

The donkey brays.

Dax leaps to his feet again, the donkey snorts and headbutts him, then lips my arm and nuzzles my hair.

"Stand still!" I order Dax. I grab the chain on the cuffs with my left hand and pull it, because if I don't, he's going to yank my arm again, and then I'll have to nail him in the peanuts again, and I'm not really into causing anyone pain if I don't have to.

Though if I do have to cause someone pain, I won't lose a lot of sleep about it being Dax.

"Eh-yo?" the voice says, along with something else in a thick accent I can't entirely understand. A woman crests the hill. She's stout, with bushy, gray-streaked hair tied back in a knot and flyaways circling her head. Her boots are sturdy, her overalls clean, her blue eyes deep-set, and as she gets closer, I can make out laugh lines at the corners of her eyes and mouth.

The donkey gives one last snort at Dax before trotting back to the woman.

"Hi," I call. I try to wave with my right hand, remember the handcuffs, and switch to my left hand. "We're lost. Can you help us?"

Her weathered brow furrows. She looks from me—on my knees in the damp grass—to the handcuffs, to Dax, and back to me.

I can't imagine how I look after all the drinking, the boat ride, the wind, and the donkey attack.

As for Dax, his tats are on full display down his arms, he's in a jet black T-shirt with a coiled snake on it, his dark stubble is almost thick enough to count as a beard, and his raven locks are long enough to be whipping wildly about in the sea wind.

He's a pirate come to pillage and plunder.

I wonder if the people here—wherever here is—would recognize an American rock god?

The woman's curious eyeballs collide with mine. Curious, and more than a little concerned.

I could tell her the truth. That he kidnapped me, and I need her to call local law enforcement to take him into custody and get me in touch with my mom.

"We need a boat," Dax tells her.

I punch him in the leg. "Hello, *manners*," I say. "You're nobody here."

A muscle ticks in his jaw. Cold, hard amber eyes bore into me, as though he needs to remind me that while he might try to save me from rabid donkeys, he's the one in control.

Like he *owns* me because he thinks Martin owes him something.

He's just as irrational as a preschooler.

And he's starting to really tick me off.

I punch him in the leg again before rising to my feet. I smile at the woman. And I have a very nice smile. It's sweet. Nonthreatening. Reassuring.

That's me.

Sweet. Compliant. Such a dear.

Barf.

"Stölland?" I say.

"Och, aye." She nods and points out to sea. I'm guessing that's north based on the hazy sunshine coming through the clouds to the right.

Which means we're…in Scotland?

I've always wanted to see Scotland. My friend Parker—she's the guitarist in my little band—and her boyfriend, Knox, have us all doing a monthly romance book club, and now I'm so addicted. I've been reading Scottish historical romances like crazy—last month's runaway bride books excepted, of course, and—and that's not the point.

But *Scotland*.

Highlanders. Loch Ness. The Shetland Islands.

"Shetland?" I ask her, pointing to the ground.

She nods and pats her pony.

"We need a phone," Dax snaps.

She scowls at him and says a mouthful of something I don't understand, because her accent is thick and she's speaking so quickly, but she's stepping toward Dax like she, too, is going to slug him.

Plus the donkey's getting riled up.

Dax thrusts long fingers through his wild hair and opens his mouth. I clock him in the ribs before he can talk. "Phone?" I ask the woman, making the universal sign for talking on a telephone.

She eyeballs my handcuffs again.

I smile and thrust my hips, simulating doing the hibbity-jibbity, then shrug sheepishly, which might be a move I learned from my friend Sia, who's always banging her boyfriend at work. "We got carried away. He can be annoying, but he makes up for it."

"Aaah." She nods knowingly.

Dax growls.

But he can't argue with results.

The lady tips her head over the hill. "Come on then."

4

DAX

THE PRINCESS IS TOO CHARMING for her own good.

She's also too fucking *hot* for her own good.

Christ on a biscuit—when she thrust her hips, I thought I was going to lose my damned mind. It was like watching Snow White doing a porno.

Except I've seen that flick, and it didn't do anything for my dick.

Not like Little Miss Princess's moves did.

And *that's* what the fucknoodle was engaged to, whereas I have three ex-wives who all wanted *something* from me.

Because that's all I'm good for.

Being *something* for *everyone*.

Not anymore. I'm *done*.

The princess drags me along the path with the Scottish lady to a thatched-roof cottage not far from the sea, the donkey trying to bite me anytime I yank back on the handcuffs. More donkeys graze in a field, some twitching their ears when we walk by. Other cottages dot the rolling green landscape. The clouds are gathering quicker.

"We're getting a fucking boat and we're getting out of here," I growl at my captive.

Who's not intimidated by me *at all*.

"Do what you want," she replies cheerfully. "I'm getting a bobby pin and having lunch with Ilsa. I've never had a real Scottish meal before. Have you? Oh, you probably have, haven't you? But I'd bet not in a real Scottish home. Not one this small and charming, anyway."

"What the hell is *wrong* with you?" I demand.

The donkey takes a nip at my ass.

Willow—yes, I know the princess has a name—lifts a perfectly plucked dark brow. She has grass stains all over her linen pants, a tear in her pink cardigan, and her nipples are poking through her silk camisole, and yet she manages to look like fucking royalty.

"Quite a lot, actually," she says. "Maybe you should've done your homework better."

I did my fucking homework. She's a preschool teacher. Sings in some two-bit band that covers boy band pop music. Supposed to be marrying the twatwaffle who stole my fortune *right now*.

And she's not broken up about it at all.

I might be screwed. My whole band might be screwed.

Because she might be right.

The asswipe might not pay to get her back. *Fuck.* Just *fuck*.

I should've stuck with the original plan. Go see the king. Tell him what his stepdaughter was marrying.

But she was there. In the meadow, outside the castle.

And she was so fucking pretty. And she said *hey, I know you. You're some musician, right? Wanna come play my washing?*

She bent over laughing, and fuck me, but that laugh went straight to something in my soul, and in that moment, I decided I'd be damned before I'd wait to talk to some king.

I was taking matters in my own hands.

Ilsa says something in her thick accent, Willow laughs, and I'm dragged along into the surprisingly bright cottage. Thick wood planks line the floor, handmade quilts hang from the walls, and sturdy, simple furniture pieces are positioned throughout the blended kitchen and living area. Everything inside is functional and classic and probably handmade.

Reminds me of my pop's place back home in Texas.

My gut tightens again.

I have to get my money back.

I've spent half a lifetime building my fortune. Working my ass off. Missing too much back home.

And now that Dad can't work anymore with the arthritis getting too bad, I need to take care of him the way he took care of me.

Need to take care of my band too.

If I even have a band anymore with everything falling to shit. I can't even write songs without a restlessness gnawing at my gut anymore. And that started *before* the one-night stand and all the other crazy misfortunes piling up.

Ilsa gestures us to sit at the modest wood table, and she steps into the back room.

I stay standing.

Willow pulls me toward the cabinets.

The donkey's outside, so I don't hesitate to tug on the cuffs. "Let's go. I saw a car in back."

"We have no money, no passports, and no map. Absolutely not."

Dammit. She's not wrong.

But we found one person on this beach. We can find another. "I said, we're leaving."

She rifles through a drawer. I tug again, and she digs in her heels. "I'll scream if you don't stop that, and then Ilsa's going to come out here with a shotgun and blow your head off. But she'll probably let the donkey in first."

I got the wrong woman. That's the only possible explanation.

The dipshit always talked about his fiancé like she was an angel made of cotton candy. Not like she was mouthy and fearless and a pain in the ass.

My phone still isn't registering a signal.

I yank on her again, and this time, my whole arm flies back, handcuff dangling, and I smack my wrist against the table. "*Fuck*."

Willow dangles a needle at me, as if to say, *yep, I picked the cuffs* as Ilsa emerges from the back room with a hatchet.

Jesus. Could this thing go more wrong?

"Sit," Ilsa says to me, very clearly, gesturing to the table.

"Thanks, Ilsa, but I got it." Willow holds her hands up. The red marks on her right wrist make me flinch. "Although, maybe you shouldn't put the ax away *just* yet."

Ilsa's brow furrows as though she doesn't understand. My nuts are in fucking hiding. "Put that away," I order.

"I'm so sorry to ask this," Willow says sweetly to Ilsa, *so fucking sweetly that it has to be fake*, "but could I borrow your phone?"

"No," I growl.

Ilsa growls right back at me and flashes her hatchet at me again.

She's got some meat on her. And when she spins the hatchet in her hand, I get the distinct impression she could hit a bee on a tree trunk at forty paces.

Which doesn't bode well for my family jewels.

She uses her free hand to point to an old-fashioned landline phone on the kitchen counter.

Posturing.

The princess is posturing.

Nobody knows numbers by heart anymore.

Willow punches in a series of numbers, and after a few seconds, the distinct pulse of ringing on the other end drifts out of the phone. A man's voice answers.

"Björk stole the sheep at the clock tower," Willow says.

There's a pause, the man says something else, Ilsa glowers at me and spins the hatchet again, and Willow nods into the phone. "Yes, the queen, please."

No.

Fucking.

Way.

"Mom? Hey." A flurry of a tinny feminine voice sounds on the other end.

She's on the phone *with her mother*. Who's the *queen of an entire nation*.

I'm a fucking dead man.

I move to grab the phone, and Ilsa executes a kung-fu move that puts the hatchet half an inch from my nose.

"I know, I know, I'm sorry," Willow says. Her breath catches, and waterworks audibly cloud her voice. "I can't marry Martin. I just can't. I know I should've told you before I left, but then I ran into Dax Gallagher, and he had tickets for a boat ride to Scotland, and I'd had a little mead, and we—wait, *what*?"

And there's the final nail in my coffin.

They know who took her.

I thought I learned my lesson about drinking after my first marriage. Clearly, I was wrong.

Ilsa gestures with the hatchet. I lift my hands and take a slow step back. If she were armed with anything else, I'd have her subdued in under a minute. But *my* kind of ax—the guitar kind—is back in the

States, and I've never taken off anyone's body parts with it. Clothes, yes. Body parts, no.

"Easy," I say. "Not going to hurt anyone."

I'm not.

Kidnap?

Yes.

Rape and murder?

My gut twists. I love women. Married three of them, though I didn't get the better end of the deal on any of those. Also love sex. *Consensual* sex. Getting a woman off is a high I can only replicate on a stage.

Could.

Not can.

Not until this string of bad luck is over and I that fucking twat-noodle gives me my money back.

"No, I'm not with Martin. What do you mean he's missing?" Willow says.

I jerk my head to look at her. "What the fuck does she mean, he's missing?"

The hatchet comes within a hair's width of my left nostril. "Down," Ilsa orders me. Very clearly.

"No, I didn't see him. No, no, he's terrified of Zeus and Ares. *Please* tell them to go easy on him if they find him first, and Colden too—it's the sheep thing."

"Tell them to tear his fucking limbs off," I snarl.

"Would you *please* be quiet?" she hisses at me. "This is long distance and probably very expensive for Ilsa."

Ilsa scowls at me, and I feel the brush of her hatchet against my upper lip. Could probably shave my nose hairs with that thing.

But that pansy-ass fucknugget has my fucking money, and now he's fucking *running* for it.

"Where is he?" I say. As pleasantly as I can.

Willow rolls her eyes and turns her back to the two of us. "I hope he's not out looking for me…he left *what*? *Martin* did? But—but—but that's so—*mean*… I know, I know I left too, but I thought he *loved* me, and—I know, *I know*."

She's twirling the twisty phone cord. Her head drops, she squeezes her eyes shut, and she draws a shuddery breath that shoots a drop-ping sensation through my own chest and reminds me I have a heart.

I know that look.

Felt it on my own face the day I caught my first wife sleeping with my manager.

Ex-manager. Two weeks after our wedding. Our union was never supposed to be about love, but I still felt the betrayal to my bones.

But my fucking heart isn't going to get my money back, so I swallow the unwelcome sympathy away.

Ilsa's focusing so hard on me, I should have bruises from the force of her glare.

"Do his parents—" Willow starts. "Oh, right, of course not. I'm so sorry you have to deal with his mother. *Please* tell my friends to enjoy themselves. And eat all the bread for me. Yes, yes, of course, the cake too. Oh, take pictures of Viggo with the cake. He was so excited about the chocolate layer. And maybe Sia and Chase and Parker and Knox could take the carriage ride instead, they'd love that…"

I'm about to grab that phone from her and demand some damned answers, but the moment I shift, Ilsa shifts, and the distinct pain of a shaving nick sparks on my upper lip. I leap back, collide with a refrigerator, and Ilsa follows. "Jesus. *Fuck*. Back off."

I make a quick snatch for the hatchet, but Ilsa's fast.

Freaky fast.

I box. I run. I do tai chi.

But this woman has me pinned to the table, snapping my other wrist into a cuff, while the princess tells her mother she'll be waiting somewhere for a boat and hangs up.

"You should meet my friend Eloise," Willow says to Ilsa while she replaces the phone in the cradle. "I'm pretty sure she's as good with handcuffs as you are."

I shove away from the table, bang into a chair, and trip over my own two feet. My shoulder takes the brunt of the impact, sending shock waves through my skull, which was just starting to almost feel human again.

Little Miss Princess's fiancé better fucking pay up when I get hold of him.

But after that phone call, I'm one hundred percent positive I'm fucked.

Pretty much the story of my life the last few months.

5

Willow

ILSA MAKES us tea and toast while I try to ignore the hurt that came with having Mom tell me that Martin left me a Dear Jane letter. I focus instead on deciding what I should do with Dax. He quit flopping around like a beached, undernourished seal a few minutes ago, and now he's lying on his side, eyes closed, lips grim.

On the one hand, he kidnapped me, so I should toss him out to sea and be done with him. It's what my stepbrothers would do. Sia's brothers, Zeus and Ares, would probably take him into a hockey rink, and one of them would grab him by the ankles, the other would grab him by the wrists, and they'd spin him in circles while Chase, their best friend and Sia's boyfriend, threw peanuts at him until he barfed or something, and then they'd probably chase him with a Zamboni.

They're weird like that. But I like them anyway, because they're always doing crazy things I never have the courage to try, and usually people only get hurt on accident.

But Dax is such a terrible kidnapper that I'm not entirely certain snagging me was actually his plan. And he's definitely down on his luck. Rich, famous rock star or not, it's hard to see people suffering.

Whatever happened to him clearly has him in a bad place. He

reminds me of how I felt the first few months after Mom moved to Stölland with King Tor.

I told her to go—he was madly in love with her, she was madly in love with him, and who doesn't deserve to be loved by someone who worships the ground you walk on?

But I still missed her.

And I still felt like I'd been abandoned. Almost like I didn't know who I was anymore. But Martin was there through the whole thing, holding my hand, being a steady—if nervous—presence that was the sameness that I'd needed to feel normal.

A routine. Something to cling to.

Bits and pieces of running into Dax in the meadow just outside the palace last night are trickling back into my brain. I'm pretty sure I told him I was running away from my wedding. And that I recognized him.

And I asked if I could lick his tattoos.

I remember carrying around an extra bottle of mead after I barfed the first bottle's worth all over the sheep that usually sits under Colden's window, bleating for him all night long.

Did I give Dax that second bottle?

That part's still fuzzy.

I nudge his long, lean, denim-clad leg with my shoe. "What exactly is it you think Martin stole from you?"

This is probably a big misunderstanding that we can clear up with some help from Mom and the king as soon as we get to the ferry terminal. Because I'm taking him with me.

It wouldn't be fair to Ilsa to leave him.

Plus, you never know when having a rock star with you will come in handy.

"*Did* steal from me," Dax growls without opening his eyes.

He's no better than a preschooler. "Okay. *Did* steal from you. What was it?"

He snorts. "Like you're not in on it."

"My mother married a king six years ago. There's very little I could want in this world and not get. I don't need to steal anything from anyone." Not that I ever ask King Tor for anything. I don't need anything other than for him to take good care of my mom.

Okay, and buy me plane tickets to visit her now and again. I'll concede that he owes me that much for taking her away from me.

One hazel eye pops open. Dax studies me like he's trying to decide if I have a point. And I'm trying to ignore the way my belly drops when he focuses on me like he's *seeing* me.

Dax Gallagher.

Rock legend.

Seeing me. Little old *me*.

"Also, I could ask Ilsa to chop your liver out, but I haven't," I say. "So I think you owe me some answers."

"I'd chop it an' eat it, I would," Ilsa agrees while she slides a plate of toast onto the table. I think. I'm understanding more of her thick Scottish brogue, but it's mildly worrisome that I might've actually dragged myself and my kidnapper-slash-hostage into Scotland's own special gingerbread house, and the tea and toast are just to fatten us up.

"Thank you, Ilsa," I say.

"Aye," she answers. She kicks Dax in the boot. "Answer the lass's questions, aye?"

While Dax seems to be contemplating replying, I bite into thick brown toast slathered with butter, and a moan slips out. Holy moly, I'm *hungry*.

His eyes go dark. His whole expression goes dark.

And I don't know if it's because he wants the toast, or—

Oh.

Oh, my.

There's some squeezing going on in my nipple area.

I kick his leg too, because there's *no way* he's going to play the sexy beast card to get under my skin.

That's just not fair.

"Jesus titty-fuckers," he snarls. "He stole my money."

I stifle another moan on my second bite of toast. Once I swallow, I process the idea of Martin stealing Dax's money. "Why would he do that? He doesn't need money either. I mean, he's not as rich as *you*, but his family is very well-off. I think you have him confused with another Martin."

"How many Martin Sampson Vanderweilie the Fourths are there in the world?"

If sarcasm were bees, we'd all be swimming through a sea of honey right now.

"It must've been someone impersonating him." I take another

bite, but I don't taste the bread and butter so much, because the man is *intense*.

And he's vividly bringing back to life that dream I had when I was little. That squashed part of me that always wanted to do something wild.

Like run away with a boy band bad boy.

Except Dax is *way* more than a boy. And much harder than boy band quality.

I snap my gaze off his detailed dragon tattoos when he speaks again. "He has a picture of you at the otter exhibit at the Bronx Zoo on his desk. Your mouth is half-open like you weren't ready for the picture to be taken."

Well.

That's *very* specific.

And accurate. I hate that picture.

I take another bite of toast while I process that Dax might actually know Martin. And that Martin might have actually done some financial work for Dax.

And also *never told me he was working with a rock legend*.

That hurts almost as bad as hearing he left me a letter calling off the wedding. Which, yes, is completely contradictory of me, but I don't care.

At least I feel guilty for leaving him.

Mom wouldn't read me the letter, which leads me to believe it wasn't very complimentary *or* apologetic.

"I'm sure this is all a misunderstanding," I say to Dax, because I've spent seven years defending Martin, and I can't help myself. Plus, I really don't believe he has it in him to steal anything. He almost hyperventilated once when he realized after he got home that the cashier at the grocery store had missed scanning a half-gallon of milk. "Maybe he moved some of your holdings from a primary account into something safer, and you're looking in the wrong place?"

"Weilie-Johnson Traders *shut down*. There's no secondary account. No safe holdings. The accounts are fucking *gone*. He wiped out my drummer too."

I gasp. "Martin knows Danger Malone? And *he never told me*? That—that—*ugh*."

"Got a computer here?" he asks Ilsa. "Pull it up. Find the website. It's gone."

"Then obviously someone robbed Martin, because he wouldn't do this."

One of those muscles ticks in his jaw. "Then obviously you don't know your fiancé."

"E—ex-fiancé," I stutter. Wow. That was weird. I stick my chin out. "I know him better than you know any of your ex-wives." I don't want to talk about all the weird feelings welling inside me about having an *ex*-fiancé. Or about how maybe I *didn't* notice how much he was changing, or when, or exactly why mirrors freak him out when I didn't think they did before.

I thought it was wedding nerves. But maybe it was something more sinister?

If Martin *was* involved in Dax's money going missing, he definitely wouldn't have done it on his own.

The donkey brays at the window. Ilsa rises. "Och, och, coming, coming," she says to the donkey.

I rise too.

"Thank you so much for your hospitality," I tell her. "Is there some kind of transport we can get to ferry terminal? And may I please have your address? So I can write you a thank-you note and pay you for the long distance phone call?"

"Och, that's no' necessary." She looks at Dax. "I could feed him to the birds, I could."

He drops his head back on the floor with a defeated sigh, and my heart tugs. "I'll take him with me," I tell her. "He's famous in America. And he probably has his passport back in Stölland, just like I do."

That eyeball slides open again, and he studies me like he doesn't trust me.

"He might need some medicine too," I whisper to Ilsa.

She nods, goes to a cabinet, and pulls out a bottle of whisky.

"Oh, no, we couldn't," I tell her.

"Go on, go on. Me uncle will make more."

She pushes the bottle at me, then gathers the remaining toast into a cloth napkin. As though maybe she hosts strangers who wash up on her beach regularly enough to keep spare napkins and whisky bottles around, and I'll be insulting her kindness if I refuse.

I pull her into a hug when she shoves the toast at me. "Thank you, Ilsa."

"Aye, aye." She pats my back. "Come now. MacGregor up the road has a wagon that be leavin' without ye if ye don't hurry."

I don't know what wagon she's talking about, but I'm going to find out.

Hello, world.

Here I come.

At least until I'm on a boat back to Stölland in a few hours.

6

DAX

SHEEP SMELL LIKE ASS.

Or maybe that's me. Or this ancient truck where we're squished in back. Or this whole fucking situation.

Yeah, this whole situation smells like ass.

And I'm about to start believing in black magic.

If it had just been Edison's finger, or the pigeon incident, or any of the dozens of little things that have happened to the band in the last two months, I'd chalk it up to shit happening.

But together?

And now with the *sheep*?

Forget paying off the witch who cursed us. I'm fucking hiring myself a *better* witch.

Christ, I'm losing my mind.

Because this isn't about a witch.

It's about some bad decisions at a time when all five of us were feeling the pressure of having an undersold tour and stagnating album sales.

What we've always done isn't working anymore. And all the money I saved for the day this would come is fucking *gone*.

I shove at a sheep that's leaning on me in the drizzle that's rolled in as we make our way over a winding road that's supposedly taking us to a ferry where Willow will undoubtedly feed me to the wolves.

Princess Happy Pants is currently singing to the sheep.

Singing.

To the sheep.

In a voice that could make angels weep, because *holy fuck*. Despite everything, I'm getting a professional boner over here.

Of course she can sing.

Because that's just fucking perfect.

"Come on, Dax," she says. "You know this one."

"I'm not singing about Mary and her fucking lambs."

"Do you need more toast? It's getting soggy, so we should eat it soon. Before it gets any soggier. This is terrible toast to waste. It's almost as good as the bread in Stölland."

"You're fucking insane."

She's also covered with some kind of oilskin cape that her new best friend insisted she take to the ferry, huddled comfortably with her knees to her chest, cradling that bottle of whisky she won't share, whereas I'm cold, wet, and still handcuffed with my arms behind me, so I couldn't drink the fucking whisky even if she *would* open it, and she's been feeding me toast like I'm an infant. Also, one of the sheep broke wind in my face two minutes ago.

Willow grins. "The last time I had an adventure, I was five. I played hide-and-go-seek in the movie section of the library, and my mom almost called the cops."

"The last time *I* had an adventure, there were naked women, vodka, weed, and a fucking grizzly involved."

She blinks those big baby blues at me with that slow, hypnotic speed again. Her gaze drifts to my bare arms. She licks her lips and ends that show with her lower lip caught in her teeth. "I've never hung out with other naked women."

Blood surges to my cock, because of course it does. "Missing out, princess."

"That's what my friend Eloise says too." She twists—as much as she can with the sheep crowding around us—so she's facing me. "There's a lot of life I've missed out on. But now I can mark *get kidnapped* off my bucket list." A smile lights her face, and *fuck*, that innocent Snow White thing is working for her. Life's a bitch some-times. "And *be the kidnapper* too. I think I've been dreading today for so long, I didn't stop to consider it was something more than just

Martin's mother being a drama queen about the wedding, but I can honestly say that this is way better than a stuffy wedding. Although, I could go for some of the Stöllandic rolls that they always have at the palace. I don't know what the chef puts in them, but they're the most delicious bread I've ever eaten in my entire life. This toast is close though."

Hopping off this truck and sacrificing myself to the fates might be a better option.

At least my life insurance is paid up.

Maybe it could pay for the search for Danger.

If anyone here could identify my body so Edison or my pop could make the claim.

Christ.

Willow pats one of the sheep. It moves and steps on my foot. I pull my boot free, but *fuck*, wool weighs more than you'd think it might.

"Do you have a bucket list?" she asks me. "I don't know how much higher you can go beyond playing for the Queen of England and doing the Super Bowl Halftime Show, but do you?"

The guilt hits me square in the chest. I've had some amazing opportunities. Gotten to live the life of my dreams.

But I'm not sitting on top of the world today. My throne's been crumbling, and I can't afford to be friends with this woman. "Yeah. To get my fucking money back."

"You're seriously grumpy. Is that why all three of your wives left you?"

"They left me because I'm a heartless bastard." They left me because they got what they wanted out of me.

Same as everyone else. *He's a rock star. He can do blah blah blah for me.*

"If that were true, you wouldn't have tried to save me from Ilsa's donkey."

"I tried to save you because I can't get my money back if you're dead."

"Martin doesn't have your money." She frowns. "And he apparently doesn't want me either, so I guess this was a wasted trip for you."

I grunt, and two sheep turn and make crazy-eyes at me.

The worst part in all of this is that I'm starting to believe her. She doesn't have a clue what her fuckface *ex*-fiancé did with my money.

Danger, my drummer, was smart enough to not put everything he owned into one fucking basket. Not that it matters right now, because he's fucking *gone*.

Left six days ago. Took his wallet and his phone and that's it. No note. No mention he was taking off or when he'd be back, and he hasn't answered any messages.

Me?

I had other problems the day I turned all my cash over to the weasel. Like dealing with incessant phone calls from a one-night stand gone wrong and emergency meetings with the label's execs over falling sales.

"What's on your bucket list, princess?" I ask. With a sneer. In case she's uncertain as to where her little *bucket list* falls on my *priority list*.

"I don't know," she says.

"You don't know?"

"When I was thirteen, I wanted to run away and be a groupie for Bro Code, but I grew out of it. And once in college, I wanted to do a study abroad program in France, but I took Latin in high school, so that wouldn't have been too helpful for actually understanding what they said in school, and I also didn't want to leave Mom that long. Then Mom married a foreign king, and Martin always liked to play everything safe, so I joined a band and we play juice bars. And my friend Sia's brothers—you know, Zeus and Ares Berger, the NHL's twin tanks?—they sometimes crash our shows, which is fun. Ares knows words to New Kids on the Block songs that I don't even remember, and sometimes he brings his emotional support monkey along, which is also fun, because how often do you get to hang out with a monkey? Also, he talks sometimes. The monkey, I mean. Not Ares. Ares is pretty quiet. But I guess what I'm saying is, I've had some really neat opportunities and met some amazing people."

I can't decide if she's the most sheltered New Yorker I've ever met, or if she's yanking my chain. "You have issues."

"Probably," she agrees. "But I'm not the one handcuffed. I am sorry about that, by the way. But I haven't decided yet what I want to do with you, and I don't entirely trust you."

I smile. It's not a friendly smile. "As you shouldn't, princess."

"My mom marrying a king does *not* make me a princess."

"Maybe I should get what your fiancé owes me from your parents instead."

"Good luck with that. You'd show up at the drop site and probably find yourself face to face with six thousand angry Vikings, with my stepbrothers and their favorite guards in the lead. They're very possessive about what's theirs."

"And you're theirs?"

"They adore my mom. And I'm *hers*. So I guess, yeah, that makes me theirs." A sheep nuzzles her shoulder, and she reaches out to stroke its wool. "For all the trouble Martin's mother caused when we were planning the wedding, though, I wouldn't mind seeing what happened if you kidnapped *her* instead. That would be pretty epic. You know, a normal person would've just gone to the police if something was stolen."

"You think I didn't call the fucking *police*." Me and the cops, we're not friends. We're not enemies, but we're not friends either. Happens when you've been to too many cities with too much security and too many friends in need of the kind of inspiration that the law frowns on.

Might've partaken in that inspiration myself in my early years, but the look on my old man's face the one time I showed up at his house high—not going there again.

Man's supposed to outlive his children, he said to me. *You kill yourself with that shit, you're signing my death warrant too.*

My pop—he raised me solo. Sacrificed way too much for me to follow my love of music.

I owe him the fucking world.

He'd be shitting himself if he knew what I was doing here. Bad enough his hands are crippled and he can't do the work he loves anymore. Now I'm on a path to letting him down again too.

"If you did call the authorities, I'm sure they would've advised you that kidnapping wouldn't solve your problem," Willow says. "Unfortunately, because this has been fun. Do you know, I'm honestly feeling just crazy enough to offer to help you with a plan for Martin's mother. Because even though he probably wouldn't pay for her, it would be *so* much fun to watch her scream."

I called the cops. I called the fucking FBI. And they said the same thing. *Thanks for the report, we'll look into this and get back to you.*

My lawyer charged me two grand to explain that meant I was fucked. And that was before Danger disappeared, Edison sliced his finger, and our management insisted we pull the plug on the rest of this year's tour.

I'm hoping Danger's out hunting down Vanderweilie too.

That one of us gets somewhere, and we can get back into the studio, make new music, shake off this funk, and by this time next year, be back on top. The canceled tour will be forgotten, ticket sales will surge, and we'll all get back to doing what we love to do. My bandmates are fucking awesome. Best fucking musicians in the world. Best friends a guy could ever have, even if I don't deserve them.

The naïve little princess is squinting at me now. "Don't you have like eight thousand bank accounts? I mean, nobody puts all their money in one place. I'm a preschool teacher, and even I have three bank accounts. There's not a lot *in* them, but I have them."

"What is it they give out in preschools these days? Gold stars? Or do you get a whole damn trophy?"

"Hugs and lollipops for good behavior, but the crankypants get naps." She pats the sheep crowding closest to her. "And aren't we lucky? A whole bed of wool just exactly at naptime."

She launches into a lullaby, and I snarl.

Not because her voice isn't sin incarnate and prompting more blood flow to my dick, but because she's the absolute last woman in the world who should be turning me on.

"I don't need a fucking *nap*. I need my money back."

"You realize that if you'd ask politely, as soon as we're on the king's boat, I can call Martin and clear this all up for you. I mean, if he wants to talk to me. Which he might not. Given that we both ran away from the wedding and all. Oh my gosh. *I ran away from my wedding.*"

"I'm sure the twatwad appreciates it."

She slugs me in the chest. The sheep erupt in bleating, six of them crowd us, and I get a mouthful of wet wool. While I'm shouldering free from the sheep crush, she shoves a soggy piece of toast into her maw until her cheeks puff and eyes the whisky bottle between her knees like she'd rather be slamming that back. "You're a real pickle-head, you know that?" she says with her mouth full.

"A first-rate motherfucking bastard," I agree.

"Just because *you* can't stay married doesn't mean *Martin* and I couldn't have…oh my gosh, I'm going to throw up."

I lunge away while she does some heavy panting. Not that I can get far. The sheep freak out again. The truck heads into a curve, and my head once again reminds me that whatever the fuck was in that mead last night was vicious.

She heaves a few times, but nothing comes out.

Thank fuck.

"Maybe you should've stayed and married him," I say. "That is, if he would've stayed and wanted you."

I'm a dick like that.

She doesn't slap me.

No, she shoves buttered soggy toast all up in my stubble, over my face, and up my nose.

I've had beer poured all over my chest and down my pants while crowd-surfing. I've eaten slugs in foreign countries, and I kept a pet snake for eight years.

Buttered toast doesn't bother me.

This woman shoving buttered toast all over my face?

She'll fucking pay for that.

The truck brakes, four sheep lean on me, two more step on my feet, and Willow looks around. "Oh, good. We're in the city."

I look around too.

We're not in a city.

We're pulling up to three buildings between the water and more grassy hills.

I'm beginning to doubt this woman actually lives in New York.

The window for the cab of the truck opens, and the farmer shouts back at us. "Here's where you get off then. Safe travels to you, lassie."

"Thank you so much," Willow calls to him. "Oh! Before you go, could you please make sure Ilsa gets her cloak back? And please tell her thank you for me. Once I'm back with my mom, we'll send a formal thank you letter."

She stands in the truck and passes the cloak up through the window to the cab. Then she bends over and grips my bicep. Her fingers are warm—hot even, against my cold, wet skin, and an involuntary shudder slinks over my body.

"Come on, up we go. You can dry off in the terminal." She tugs my arm again, and this time a full-blown case of goosebumps erupts on my skin.

If I were her, I'd be dumping my ass in the river. Sea. Channel. Whatever the fuck it is.

But she's not.

She's pulling me out of the sheep truck.

"You realize we look like two deranged criminals," I say.

"You look like a deranged criminal. I look like a hero." She smiles. "And it doesn't matter, because the king's sending a boat for us. The crew won't care what we look like."

I put some distance between us when we're on the ground, which is a task I accomplish without face-planting onto the asphalt.

Mostly because Willow shielded me from falling when I leapt off the truck with my hands cuffed behind me.

People aren't *nice* to me unless they want something. This woman being nice to me? I don't trust her.

But I'm also not letting her out of my sight.

Not when she's the only leverage I have toward getting my life back.

7

WILLOW

IF YOU'D TOLD me yesterday that instead of walking down the aisle at the old abbey atop the fjords on the castle grounds in my lacy white wedding dress, I'd be hanging out with a broke rock star, battling rabid donkeys, meeting Scottish natives, and hitchhiking in the back of a sheep transport truck, I probably would've needed a paper bag.

Now, while we're sitting at the terminal, watching a gorgeous sailboat docked in the small port and waiting for the ship King Tor is sending, though this has been fun, I'm feeling weirdly unsettled.

And not because I'm not getting married.

I'm so relieved I'm not getting married, I can't believe how close I came to going through with it.

No, the panic settling in is more because my adventure will be over all too soon.

We're in two plastic chairs under a small overhang, where we're mostly shielded from the rain and getting fewer weird looks from the staff and other passengers than we did inside. Oh, we're still getting the weird looks.

And we deserve them.

I have handcuffs hanging off my belt loops, a bottle of homemade whisky in hand, and a tatted-up badass with a buttered face sitting beside me.

I'd be more worried if we *weren't* getting weird looks. It's just nice to be away from the majority of the people here.

I lean into Dax and nudge him, which makes his entire body go so tense the air itself seems to freeze and tighten. "Have you ever been on a sailboat?"

"I fucking own a sailboat."

Despite the f-bomb again, there's no heat in his words. He seems to be resigning himself to the fact that Martin's gone, and I'm useless for ransom.

If a caged animal *can* be resigned.

Every inch of him is coiled tight like a tiger ready to strike. He glanced once at his phone when I picked his handcuffs before we walked into the terminal—after making him promise he'd behave, of course—but other than that, he hasn't taken his eyes off me. Not to watch the main ferry depart for the next island over, not when I thought I saw a seal poke its head up out of the water, and not when a woman passing by sloshed coffee on him.

He's hardly blinking.

His attention should be disconcerting, but it's not.

No, it's more *exciting*.

Also?

The fact that he hasn't tried to overpower me and shove me into a bathroom or throw me in the water is a good sign.

I was briefly concerned.

Maybe my panicked ninja skills on the boat have him worried.

I glance at him again.

No, definitely no worry over the mad ninja skills.

"I've always wanted to go skydiving. Do you own a plane too?" I ask him.

It would give my mom a heart attack if she knew, but it's true. I want to freefall through the atmosphere, like a bird, watching the earth as far as I can see, without my view obstructed by dirty windows or poor angles.

And I've never pursued it, exactly because it would give my mom a heart attack.

Martin too.

It'll take some getting used to the idea that Martin is in the past.

Dax doesn't answer, but something ticks in his jaw.

I'm probably irritating him.

Understandable. I don't usually talk this much either, but last night, after the princes sparked the idea of not going through with the wedding, something dormant deep inside of me started to wake up, and now I can't stop.

"Did it hurt to get your tattoos?" I ask.

"It was like having my skin sliced off and then stitched back on, one millimeter at a time, with a rusty razor blade and metal slivers."

My belly drops. "Really?" I whisper.

"No, not really." He snorts. "Drink enough tequila, even having your nuts sliced off with a butter knife wouldn't hurt. Not me, anyway. You, though—you'd cry."

The sandpaper edges to his voice make me shiver, and not in a bad way. The insult itself rolls right off. I've been called a poopyhead too many times by people I care more about to worry about Dax thinking I'm a wimp.

If I were truly a wimp, I would've gone through with my wedding.

"I want a tattoo," I tell him. Mostly because he's my only audience. "A bird. On my shoulder. Martin never thought I should, but..." But Martin and I are through.

His opinion doesn't count.

And it probably shouldn't have ever counted over something like a small tattoo.

Also, every time I say Martin's name, Dax flinches and growls.

Just like he's doing now. "A bird," he repeats.

"Yes, a bird. A sparrow, or a bluejay, or...that's really lame, isn't it?"

He flexes his left forearm, drawing my attention to where two slender dragons have their necks intertwined in a funky geometric shape around a guitar. Their fiery breath licks at his wrist.

That flexing is clearly a silent *my tattoo will eat your tattoo for a midnight snack.*

I think about Dax, and midnight, and eating, and I suppress another shiver. In the last year, I've watched two of my very best friends in New York fall in love—plus Manning and both the Berger twins too, and there's always Eloise, who's never committed but always getting something freaky on the side—and some of the things Parker and Sia have told me about their sex lives have made me realize Martin and I aren't—*weren't*—all that exciting in the bedroom.

Okay, fine.

Boring is a good word.

Dax wouldn't be boring.

I'm almost positive.

I fan myself, because the gentle sea breeze in the cool northern summer afternoon is *not* enough once I start thinking about Dax naked and sweaty and hard and wondering if he's as talented in bed as he is on stage.

I fan harder, because suddenly I'm picturing Dax having sex on a stage, and *shew*, voyeuristic much, Willow?

He smirks.

It's one of those ugly *that's right, princess, I just made you think of me naked and you liked it* smirks.

I look at his arms again, at dragon tails slipping up under his T-shirt sleeve, and I wonder what else he has on his shoulder.

His chest.

His stomach.

Lower.

Yes, I am very much picturing him naked.

Naked and covered in ink and letting me trace every pattern, every design, while he licks all the places he thinks *I* should get a tattoo.

I shiver and scoot an inch away.

Then I remember I'm technically single now, and he *is* hot, even if he's a terrible kidnapper, and I scoot back.

An electric shiver rocks over my skin when our shoulders touch.

"Or I could get a kraken," I say. "My kraken could eat your dragons."

His lips twitch. "I only have one dragon, princess, and it's battled many a kraken in its days. Are you sure an innocent little kraken like yours would be up to the challenge of eating my dragon?"

My stomach dips, because he is *not* talking about mythological krakens and dragons. And the idea of sleeping with—no, *having sex* with Dax Gallagher is not at *all* repulsive.

No, definitely not repulsive.

The man's dragon probably knows its way around a kraken *very well*.

And I'm pretty sure my face is about to melt off, it's so hot. "Aaah —yuuu—buuu—*stop looking at me like that*."

"So I'm not on your bucket list? Too bad. And here we are, with nothing to do for hours and hours and hours…"

He's playing with me.

There's no way Dax wants to have sex with me, but his eyes have gone all dark and hooded, and he's touching his upper lip with the tip of his tongue like he's contemplating licking me.

My belly squeezes.

My kitty clenches.

And my panties go damp.

"Thinking about it now, aren't you?" he murmurs. "You're not just imagining me naked. You're thinking about me inside you. Wondering how big I am. If I care at all if you get off, or if I'd be in it just for me. If all I want is any pussy I can find, or if I want *yours*."

I should tell him to stop, but there's some not-unpleasant swelling and aching going on between my thighs.

Anticipation.

"What if I am?" I whisper.

"You're not imagining it well enough, because you can still talk."

Just the thought of him slipping his fingers between my thighs is enough to make a whimper slip through my lips. The hair on my arm where our bodies are casually touching is singeing. I imagine him spreading my thighs, bending over, licking—

I bolt upright and stand, pacing away. Martin isn't the only man I've ever slept with, but we were together for *seven years*, and my experiences before him hardly qualify me for sex champ status. "Whoa."

"And you can still walk," he says, his voice sex and whisky and gravel.

Whisky.

I could go for some of that sex.

Whisky. I could go for some of that *whisky*.

Since we're obviously not going to have sex to take this edge off, because—wait.

Why *couldn't* we have sex?

I turn and look at him.

That smirk.

Okay, yes, that's unattractive. But considering he honestly believes Martin stole his money, and until a few hours ago, I was supposed to be Mrs. Martin, of course he's going to smirk.

He has no plans to sleep with me.

But that doesn't mean I can't put *sleep with a rock star* on my bucket list.

I *am* a single woman now.

With the next two weeks off for my honeymoon in Bermuda.

Which I won't be going on.

Bermuda was Martin's idea. If *I* were planning a honeymoon, I'd go to Europe.

Climb the Eiffel Tower.

Go to the theater in London.

Catch a hot air balloon ride over the Alps.

Have a gondola ride in Venice.

And I'm *so close* to Europe. I'm already on this side of the Atlantic.

"Whoa, *what*? Oh. My. God. Ricky, look. *Look*. It's Dax Gallagher." A woman in white linen pants, a white sweater, and dock shoes draws to a stop right in front of us. A giant white straw hat hides all but a few blond flyaways, and the lenses in her sunglasses—yes, sunglasses in cloudy, rainy weather—are bigger than her cheeks. "You are, aren't you?" she says to Dax.

He gives her an eyebrow nod, then turns his attention back to me.

"Ricky! Ricky, get a picture. Oh. My. God. What are you *doing* here? Is it true Half Cocked Heroes are breaking up? We heard you disappeared on a ski trip in the Alps and that's why they had to cancel the tour. Can I touch your dragons?"

"I'm sorry, pictures are twenty dollars, and touching is off-limits," I say before I can process what's coming out of my mouth. "Mr. Gallagher likes his privacy."

She digs into her cute little pull-tie bag and thrusts a few hundred dollars at me. "Oh, honey, that's a bargain."

Before Dax can move, she sprawls on his lap, drapes her arms around his neck, and poses with her head tilted back and one leg in the air.

He spears me with a look that suggests this is *my* fault.

Which I guess it is, since I'm holding five hundred bucks in cash that basically means I'm not going to interfere.

Not because I want the money.

But because this opportunity must be worth a lot to the woman if she's willing to hand over that much for it.

It probably wouldn't be if she spent much time with him, but I'm not one to rob people of their fantasies.

Her companion, a dark-eyed, skinny man with a twirly mustache and a Panama Joe hat over a Hawaiian shirt and thermal undershirt, shakes his head. "Chrissy, you can't take a picture of him if everyone thinks he's dead. You'll tank his album sales."

She sticks her lower lip out. "I won't post it anywhere. I just want it for the hall of fame. You're okay with that, right, Dax?"

"Yeah, baby," he says. "Whatever you want."

My shoulders hitch.

She is *not* his *baby*.

And I can't decide if she's young enough to be his very much younger sister, or if she's old enough to be his mother, or somewhere in between. This would be easier if she wasn't wearing sunglasses.

"If your sister hears about this..." Ricky says ominously.

He's clearly in his late thirties or early forties, or possibly a little older. The silver threaded through his hair makes it hard to tell, but suggests he's not exactly a spring chicken. And he's also in sunglasses.

Maybe these two don't want to be recognized. Maybe they're famous.

Or maybe they're outlaws.

"Oh, poopoo to Missy." Chrissy pouts and flutters a hand that sparkles with a diamond about twice the size of the diamond I'm still wearing on my left hand.

I should take that off.

Immediately.

Except I feel like I shouldn't lose it before I give Martin a chance to take it back.

But then, he left me too, so what *is* the right protocol?

Dax shifts and gives me some kind of look. It's not a glare exactly, but it's not a smile either.

Chrissy's not grabbing him in the privates. Maybe he just doesn't like people sitting on him, which would be understandable. And I *did* say no touching. But if he wants her off him, he can say so himself.

I only take people's money.

I don't police his body.

Good gravy, *who am I*?

"Is that your boat?" I blurt, pointing at the sailboat bobbing in the mist. "It's beautiful."

"It's Ricky's baby," Chrissy tells me. "We're sailing around the world. And spotting celebrities." She smiles and wiggles in Dax's lap. "You want to come along?" she asks him. "Free rides. All you have to do is sing for us."

My heart pitter-patters.

A sailing tour around the world.

That would be so flipping amazing.

"I sing," I announce. "I'm in a band back in New York. We cover boy band songs, but I can sing pretty much anything."

Three sets of eyeballs swivel toward me.

I think. With Chrissy and Ricky in their dark sunglasses, it's hard to tell exactly where their eyeballs are pointed, but their heads are aimed at me.

Dax is clearly telegraphing *don't you firetrucking dare*.

So, naturally, I start singing.

And because I'm the biggest dork to ever live, I launch straight into "Walk Like An Egyptian."

I could be singing classic N*SYNC. I know some Garth Brooks. I can even do a dozen or so Half Cocked Heroes hits.

But I go for nineteen-eighties and The Bangles.

I love The Bangles. My mom and I used to dance like mad to The Bangles and Cyndi Lauper and Bananarama in our tiny kitchen when I was growing up, just her and me, singing our hearts out and striking poses to eighties girl band music. Actually, we rocked out to eighties hits just last Christmas at the castle.

But singing eighties girl band music for Dax Gallagher and his biggest fan is probably not the quickest way to get on that sailboat.

Chrissy slides her sunglasses down her nose. She has striking blue eyes with crow's feet in the corners, and she's plucked her brows to within a hair of their lives. "You know any Maroon 5?"

Requests! Yes!

I haven't warmed up at all, but I switch into "Moves Like Jagger," because I love to dance to that one, even if I'm also something of a dorky dancer.

Dax squeezes his eyes shut like he's in pain.

Chrissy's smiling.

Ricky's just gaping.

"Bruno Mars?" Chrissy asks.

"Oh, yeah. I can 'Uptown Funk' until the sheep come home." I launch into it, shaking my hips and emulating the moves from the video. Chrissy's clapping along with the beat, still sitting on Dax, who looks like he might want Ilsa's ax back to slit his own throat.

Well, fine. Just because I'm not some famous singer doesn't mean I can't enjoy the heck out of singing. I'm good enough to perform for juice bars, and that's good enough for me.

Forget him.

I'm having *fun*.

We rock out on the little patio, me singing, Chrissy clapping, Ricky holding up his phone, probably recording me. By the time I'm done Funking, Chrissy's on her feet, hip-bumping me like Sia's brothers do on stage while a few other tourists take pictures and videos, but since she probably doesn't even weigh a hundred pounds, I'm able to stay on my feet without much effort, unlike when Zeus gets carried away and sometimes knocks me off the stage.

"You wanna go see the world, pumpkin pie?" she says.

"Well, maybe just Europe. I only have two weeks before I have to be back at work."

Chrissy laughs. Ricky shakes his head. And Dax—

Dax folds his arms, crosses an ankle over a knee, and gives me another of those piercing looks that makes my breasts tighten. "What about your rescue boat, princess?"

Fairies suddenly take flight in my belly.

He's right.

Mom's sending a rescue already.

And I don't know Chrissy and Ricky, no matter how fun Chrissy seems or how resigned Ricky is.

But the funny thing is, I wasn't *actually* considering getting on the boat with these two.

Until now. When Dax reminded me that I can't.

"I'll call them off," I say with a shrug.

"Whoa, whoa, you're a princess?" Chrissy demands.

"No, I'm *not* a princess. I'm a runaway bride."

"High five, sister. Marriage is for the birds. Shacking up is where it's at."

I don't entirely agree, but maybe that's because I've never stopped to think about it. So I slap Chrissy's hand.

Yes, the one with the engagement ring on it. Apparently we all have issues.

"To shacking up!" I cheer.

"You want a ride to the continent?" she asks.

My belly dips. Going to Europe? On a boat? With strangers?

That's clearly a no-brainer. As in nobody with a brain would do that.

But going to *Europe*. On a *boat*. With new friends?

I hold up the five hundred dollars she handed me. "Lunch is on me. Let's go get some sandwiches and talk."

I get Dax by the ear in a move I've seen Sia do to her boyfriend and her brothers a few times. "Up you go, Mr. Rock Star. Because you're coming with us."

8

Dax

THE PRINCESS IS FUCKING INSANE.

Not that I can talk, because here I am, on a fucking sailboat in the North Sea with two complete strangers who have promised to take us to the Netherlands, because the princess decided she wanted to see windmills and try Dutch cheese before going on to the Louvre.

I don't know what was in the butter or toast she got at Hatchet Lady's house, but it was clearly psychedelic.

Or else the princess is finally hitting her rebellious teenage years.

Or possibly this is just the next phase in the witch's curse, and it has nothing to do with the princess and everything to do with keeping me off-guard.

A hex would explain why I went along with this entire plan. I've never had much belief in curses or hexes or magic, but karma might be catching up with me, and letting Willow go on her own with complete strangers seemed like a good way to tempt fate more.

And so here I am.

Not that I had a great deal of choice. *Get on the boat, Dax,* she said. *Get on the boat, or else I'm telling the authorities you kidnapped me.*

Apparently she likes the perks of having a famous rock star in her midst.

Join the club, sweetheart.

Everyone wants something.

My manager. My agent. Our record label. Old high school "friends." Ex-wives.

Her fiancé.

Oh, sorry. *Ex*-fiancé.

At least she's easier on the eyes. Even in grass stains, mud, and god only knows what else she has marring that outfit, I keep picturing myself peeling her out of it.

Have to keep reminding myself she's no better than the rest of them.

I have terrible taste in women.

"Do you think it's safe to BASE jump off the Eiffel Tower?" the princess asks. We're on day two of our sailboat adventure with Ricky and Chrissy, and Willow's sitting with her feet propped up on the rail at the edge of the sailboat, a notebook in hand, tapping her lips with a pencil while the pages flap in the breeze. The sun's come out, which means we're all above deck today and dry.

"Sure," I tell her. "If you want to die."

She gasps.

Which is exactly what I'd expect out of the woman who called her mother to tell her she was running away.

Yes.

She did.

She borrowed Chrissy's phone to call her mother to announce she was running away to have an adventure and see the world before she had to go back to being *stodgy, boring, rule-abiding Willow.*

I'm beyond grateful that Stölland doesn't have a military, because if they did, their entire navy would most likely be out here hunting for us right now. Have to wonder if the royal guards' boat is chasing us though.

I made a few calls of my own before we left the dock. The dick-stool didn't answer, so I left him a message letting him know I wanted my money back, and that I was holding his fiancée captive until I got it.

Doubtful I hear back from him.

Also called Edison. My bassist has been one of my best friends since kindergarten. Danger, Edison, and me. They're my brothers.

Edison reports no one's heard from Danger, we're being sued by at least four of the concert venues from our canceled tour and a stagehand from the pigeon show for *emotional trauma*, our tour insurance company dropped us, my pop's dealing with a new neighbor with a dog that barks all night long, and Cain's soon-to-be ex-wife told the press that we pulled the plug on the tour because I'd been checked into rehab.

After assuring Edison I *wasn't* on my way to, nor in need of, rehab and that I'd pitch in my fair share for the detectives he's hired to find Danger once I get my money back, I told him I'd be out of touch for a few days.

Looking for Vanderweilie.

Left out the part about kidnapping the princess.

He didn't need to know that.

Didn't need to know that she's suddenly more in charge than I am either.

"I don't think everyone dies who BASE jumps off the Eiffel Tower," Willow says. "I know I've heard of *someone* who survived."

"My cousin did it," Chrissy announces. She's behind us, on a tablet, and the hairs on the back of my neck are telling me I'm not going to like whatever it is she's doing.

Of course I won't.

She and Ricky are *lifestyle bloggers on a journey of self-discovery.* Which, in my world, is code for *heirs and heiresses to B-listers whose millions are drying up because they're not relevant anymore.*

One more couple capitalizing on a brush with my fame.

I'd make music with or without the fame. The songs, the rhythms, the melodies—they've always been part of me. Always will be.

But lately, my job isn't about the music. It's about doing favors and being seen and everything I can do for people.

Like the princess.

She wouldn't be on this boat if these two yahoos hadn't recognized me.

For now, I'm letting her think she has the upper hand. That I'm on the boat so she didn't turn me into the cops.

But I'm here because I wasn't about to let her walk away. Not when she's still my best bet for getting my money—and my life—back. And it's not like getting on a boat with complete strangers is the most insane thing I've ever done.

I dated fucking *Xandria* for an entire three months once. You want insane? Dating the pop diva who puts all other pop divas to shame is insane.

Could I have gotten us stuck in Scotland?

Fuck, yes. Neither one of us has passports. She's waltzing around with handcuffs strapped to her belt loops. And if being in the music business for well over fifteen years has taught me anything, it's how to make a menace of myself.

But if nothing else, watching the princess when she inevitably realizes she's trapped in the middle of the ocean with strangers who want nothing more than to exploit both of us will be entertaining as hell.

And eventually, she'll lead me back to the weasel.

Or to his money.

More specifically, *my* money.

I half expect she's on her way to meet him now. Like they planned this.

Also, if she's gotten herself tangled up with honest to god murderous criminals, someone has to be here to stop them.

Might as well be me.

Since it's my fault she left Stölland in the first place.

The music business hasn't entirely stolen my soul yet.

"Dax, you still haven't told us what you were doing in Scotland," Chrissy says.

"Soaking up the sun," I reply.

She titters. "You're so funny. Are you having a breakdown? It's natural to have a breakdown at least once or twice when you're as famous as you are. Is that why they canceled the rest of the tour? Because you had a breakdown?"

"Yep." I stretch back, close my eyes, and tilt my head to the cloudy sky while the boat crashes through the waves. It's not a dinky boat, but it's not a luxury yacht with a helipad either. "Total and complete breakdown. I've lost my marbles. They're so scattered I'll never get them back."

"Oh. My. God. You are *not* having a breakdown."

"He's having an ash-mole moment," Willow says.

"Ash…*oh*, you mean *asshole*?"

"I teach preschool. I can't use profanity."

"Honey, none of us are preschoolers."

"Once I start, I can't stop. I almost got fired from my first job because I said pi—the *p* word, and they only let me stay because I promised to never say even *dang it* again and then I pulled the step-daughter-of-a-king card."

I crack open one eyelid and peer at her. "Say *fuck*," I order.

"Fudge," she answers.

"Shit."

"Crap."

"Damn."

"Darn."

"Hell."

"Heck."

"Twat."

"Pfeffernuesse."

Chrissy cracks up.

Willow smiles, the sea animals launch into a fucking princess movie song, and rainbows sprout from every whale hole in a fifty-mile radius.

Fucking *smile*.

Fucking *pretty*.

Fuck me for noticing. She doesn't get to be funny. Or pretty. Or entertaining.

But she's all three.

And every time she pulls some random tidbit or word or nonsense out of her ass, she sucks me in.

For just a minute. A second.

Until I get my brain screwed back on right again. But the melody of her is starting to haunt me even when she's not talking.

"Ricky," Chrissy calls to her partner in crime, who's steering the boat from the small captain's deck, "we got us some real funny ones this time."

I reach over and snag Willow's notebook and pen. I'm going to write *say fuck* on this bucket list of hers, but before I can scratch the paper with the tip, she's tackling me.

"Give it back!"

"Hiding something, princess?"

"That's *not yours*."

I hold the notebook out of reach and try to read her clean, even handwriting while the boat's rocking and she's scrambling all over me. Fuck, she's soft. And though neither of us has had a real shower since we left Stölland two days ago, she somehow smells sweet.

"Ride a camel?" I read. "Scuba dive the Great Barrier Reef? Attend tea with the Queen of England?" Yeah, I'm being a prick.

But this woman's getting under my skin, and that's not acceptable.

She's the fucknoggin's woman.

She doesn't get to play sweet, innocent preschool teacher.

She probably shouldn't be playing wrestle the rock god either, because her skin's smooth and her hair's silky and she's so fucking *warm* when all I've felt for the last few weeks is *cold*.

I'm from Texas.

I don't do *cold*.

"And what's—*oof*—on your—*aaah*—list?" she demands while she sprawls and fidgets and lunges all over me. "Fornicate with a jelly-fish? Because that would—*argh*—serve you—*eeks!*—right."

Something whacks me on the head. "*Ow!*"

"Give her back her list, you twatosaurus dick." Chrissy's standing over us with a paddle.

She fucking hit me in the head with a *paddle*.

Willow snags her list, but not before I catch one last phrase.

Sleep with a rock star.

I get an image of her reclining on black satin sheets, slender legs spread, pussy glistening, nipples hard pebbles, those lush lips painted blood red and parted, her dark hair mussed, crooking a *come hither* finger at me, and my breath whooshes out of me and my mouth goes dry as burnt cotton.

Should dunk myself in the ocean.

Would help with that melody creeping into my head. It's dark. Dirty. Hot. Fast.

It's *her*. Not Miss Preschool Princess though. It's the wild side of her.

I scrub a hand over my face and push to my feet.

Need to get away from her. I don't trust the music right now.

I don't trust her either.

Except I'm starting to.

I leave them all laughing and head below deck. The galley below is stocked with fresh water, granola bars, apples, pears, nuts, cheese…but not a lick of alcohol.

What the fuck is *wrong* with these people?

I down two glasses of water and inhale an apple, then a second. Haven't eaten much since I boarded that plane to Stölland, and now, three days on, it's catching up with me. Not entirely happy about all the rocking of the boat either. Not down here. The waves are choppy. Like you'd expect of the ocean.

I slept fine in the bunk last night—for a few hours, at least—but I like being up above better.

I cool my jets alone for a while. Wander into the small sleeping quarters and debate grabbing another nap. Try to find that whisky Willow carried onboard, but come up empty.

Take some time to dig through Chrissy and Ricky's stuff too.

Not because I'm some vicarious weirdo.

Just want to make sure—again—that there's no evidence they're secretly world-traveling serial killers.

Usually my bodyguard would check that shit for me. But I can't afford bodyguards at the moment.

Christ. If anybody's bothering Pop while my bank account is empty—

I shake my head. Should've stayed home.

But I'm so fucking tired of not being a *person*. I'm a ticket into Michelin-starred restaurants without a reservation for an actress who thinks I don't know she's using me to get noticed by the right people. I'm a shortcut to millions for a dude looking for an endorsement on his magical sneakers. I'm one more record for a label that's had me and my band by the balls since my first agent dicked up our contract, and who keep pushing us further and further from the band we used to be.

Getting my money back was supposed to be the one thing I could control. The one thing I could *do*.

Because white collar crimes take for-fucking-*ever* to solve, and by the time the feds build their case, my money, everything I've busted my ass for the last fifteen years, is *gone*.

After a while, the rocking's getting to me, so I head back up to the deck and find Willow and Chrissy bent over her list at the edge of the boat, whispering like mad. They both glance up at me. Willow's gaze lingers on my arms. On my ink.

I flex.

She blushes and jerks her eyes away.

All I am to her is a walk on the wild side. I'm not feelings. I'm not talent. I'm not hard work.

I'm meat.

Her gaze focuses on something behind me, her eyes go wide, and that's when all hell breaks loose.

She bolts to her feet and points. "Oh my gosh, a whale!"

The boat crests a wave and dips, she flounders on her feet, arms flapping, body tilting at the edge. "*Aaggh!*"

Chrissy grabs for her.

I grab for her.

She latches onto my arm, still shrieking. The boat hits the crest of another wave, jerking us sideways. I stomp my foot to anchor it, yank her back to the center of the boat, trip over the railing, the hand gripping me slides off, and suddenly I'm floating through the air.

Floating.

Falling.

Crashing into the ice-cold ocean.

The water envelopes me, crisp and heavy and salty. I groan—okay, fine, I shriek like a fucking ninny—while the ocean swallows me. My throat aches out a protest, my nuts try to retreat into my body, and a shark glides past me.

A shark.

Swear to fucking god.

My life flashes before my eyes.

The drinking. The divorces. That electric feeling of standing on a stage in front of fifty thousand screaming fans, sweat dripping off my body, my band kickin' it, singing my fucking lungs out, feeding off the energy, soaking in the love, knowing I'm the luckiest son of a fucking bitch to ever live.

My pop.

Fuck. Who's going to fucking take care of my pop? He's slowing down. His bones are turning on him. And what should've been easy —affording the best medical care, anything he needs for comfort— the one thing I could've done for him, I can't do anymore.

I never told him *thank you*. I never told him *sorry*. I canceled trips home, because the band needed me, a gig came up, someone needed me to sit in as host for one of those late-night comedy shows, and the music was more important.

I scream again under the ocean, unleash my fury with myself at fucking Poseidon.

If this is the price of fame, of glory, of superstardom, I don't want it.

I don't fucking want it anymore.

9

Willow

MY HEART HAS STOPPED APPROXIMATELY six times in the last five minutes.

First, when I almost fell off the boat.

Second, when Dax _did_ fall off the boat.

Third, when he didn't surface right away.

Fourth, when it took us too long to toss him the life preserver.

Fifth, when he collapsed onto the bow of the boat, shaking and panting, once we'd pulled him up.

And sixth, just now, when he finally sits up, stares me straight in the eye with those hazel lasers like this is _my_ fault, grits his teeth while his chin wobbles and his muscles visibly spasm, and then shoves past all of us to head down to the quarters below deck.

"Did you get that on tape, babe?" Ricky asks Chrissy.

She slugs him in the arm. "_No, I didn't fucking get that on tape, you heartless bastard._"

"But I was a _hero_. I pulled him up like he weighed _nothing_."

"That's because salt water's buoyant. And he climbed up half the boat by himself. You couldn't even throw the ring to him right the first four times."

I leave them to their bickering and carefully make my way to the short steps behind the driver's cabin—is that what it's called on a boat?—and head down. I don't know where towels are, or if there's a washing machine on board—probably not—or what size Ricky wears and if we'll be able to get Dax fresh clothes while his dry out, but—

I turn the corner and duck into the sleeping area, and Dax is naked.

Completely, bare-bottom naked.

Oh.

My.

Holy.

Goats.

I squeak, and he glares at me over his shoulder.

I think he's glaring, anyway.

I'm not looking at his face, and I can't stop staring.

At the dragons warring on his back. The angels on his shoulders watching from their perch not on clouds, but guitars. The rolling hills made of musical staffs, the scales adding a decorative touch around the dragons.

Wait.

They're not fighting.

They're *playing*. Making music.

One has a guitar. The other a fiddle. The scales—some are drums.

"Oh, wow," I whisper.

I reach a finger out to touch, and he spins.

His chest is covered with tattoos as well, but that's not what draws my attention.

No, now my main focal point is that heavy dangle between his lean, sinewy legs.

I swallow.

Hard.

I should look away.

But as I'm watching, it's growing.

Thickening.

Lengthening.

Like he *likes* me watching him.

"I…" I swallow again, because I can't form words.

"What the fuck do you want, princess?"

That snaps me out of my trance. I jerk my attention back to his chiseled cheekbones and angry hazel eyes and drawn-down lips and try to not gape too much or let my gaze slide to the body of the dragon sloping over his chest and hard stomach.

"Are you okay?" I ask.

"What the fuck do you think?"

His voice is hoarse and shaky. It's subtle, but enough for me to notice he's still shivering.

While I'm standing here ogling him and wondering if I'm brave enough to ask if I can touch.

I have lost my ever-loving mind. And apparently all of my common sense.

"Oh, jeez. Right. You must be freezing. Here. Let me help." I fly to the small cabinet tucked by the door of the sleeping quarters and swing it open. There's a five-gallon water bottle for the dispenser in the galley, a first aid kit, and one small spare blanket.

I grab the blanket and shake it out, my hands wobbling when I approach him. The blanket blocks off most of my view as I wrap it around his body. "Here." My voice is barely a whisper. "Start with this. I'll see if I can find some towels."

Out of the corner of my eye, I see him shift the blanket around so it's draped over his back instead of his front. I hustle to the cubbyhole on the other side of the room and find a stash of nonperishable food, another water bottle, and some fishing and sailing supplies I can't identify. When I head out into the galley, Chrissy pokes her head down the short set of stairs. "You need anything, hon?"

"Dry clothes? Some towels? For Dax, I mean. Not for me. I'm fine."

She steps into the tiny space, and I move aside so she can lift the bench seat and dig in for a couple beach towels. "I don't know if Ricky's stuff will fit, but his clothes are in the drawer under the bottom bunk in there."

"Thanks. He'll appreciate this."

"You bet. Ricky needs a little help getting us back on course. Let us know if there's anything else you need."

Her wink suggests she could dig up anything from a fruit tray to condoms, and she won't think a thing of me asking for either.

Before I can stutter out a protest—she saw my insane bucket list too—she's headed back upstairs.

I slide open the pocket door to the sleeping quarters and find Dax hunched over at the edge of one of the two lower bunks, a death grip on the blanket wrapped around his shoulders and back, his head hanging low, his damp black hair plastered to his forehead.

"Hey," I say softly.

He grunts.

I step over the pile of his wet clothes and set the three towels on the bed beside him, then take the first one and rub it on his hair.

He jerks up, giving me another glimpse at his goods hanging between his legs. "I can dry my own fucking hair."

Like he hates me as much as he hates Martin. Whom I'm not yet convinced stole anything. Do I believe Dax's money is gone?

Yes.

But *Martin* stole it?

Then again, who would've guessed he would've gotten all the way to Stölland the night before our wedding before writing me a letter to dump me?

"Do you hate me because of Martin?" I ask.

He slowly lifts his head. His hazel eyes are flecked with green and ringed in dark gold, his lashes almost black, and the venom lurking in the depths makes something squeeze in my chest.

Maybe I'm not as safe with him as I thought.

"I don't hate you, princess," he says slowly, as though he's testing the weight of each word on his tongue. "You're just a pawn."

There's a bite to his words, but I don't care, because the intensity of that heavy-lidded gaze is making my belly do flips.

Being here is completely insane.

It's also liberating. Exhilarating.

I lick my lips. His eyes track the movement, and his pupils dilate.

"Do you know the quickest way to get warm?" I whisper. I don't want to be *boring*. I want to be brave. And bold. I want to have stories to tell my grandchildren someday. Okay, maybe not *this* story, but a girl has to start somewhere.

He visibly swallows. "Careful, princess. You're playing with fire."

"Maybe I like fire."

"You don't have a fucking clue what you like. You're a sheltered baby doll."

"Then maybe it's time I find out what I like."

"By fucking a rock star?"

I flinch. "I didn't say I wanted to ffffu—to have ssssse—to s-sleep with *you*. Maybe I just want to touch your dragons."

"My dragons? Or my *dragon*?"

"B-both."

The old Willow has fled the planet.

But I do. I want to touch Dax's tattoos. I want to know if his skin is rough or smooth. I want to get right up on him and study the artistry. To watch the dragons move when I rub at them. To feel the hard muscle underneath.

I've never felt hard muscle.

Martin was always in okay shape. Never heavy, but never solid either.

Dax though—I doubt his ink is hiding any fluff.

And I don't want to stop at his arms. His back. His chest.

My kitty's getting tight again. Intrigued.

Probably because he's not trying to shield me from the view of his rigid length, completely erect now. Thick. Veiny. With a bulging head. Bobbing.

"Go on, princess. Touch me."

He doesn't think I'll do it.

I bite my lip and trace my fingers over the dragon wing cresting his shoulder.

His breath catches. Goosebumps erupt on his already prickled flesh.

My breath catches, and a shiver races from my neck, over my breasts, and beelines straight between my legs.

"Not warming up yet," he says through clenched teeth.

Because he's cold?

Or because my touch is repulsive?

I've never been repulsive to anyone. I'm too *nice* to be repulsive.

Maybe I'm tired of *nice*.

My fingers drift over his collarbones. There's no ink there, but they're sharp and fascinating.

He grips my wrist, pulls me between his legs, and *holy sheep*, my panties just went damp.

"Lower, princess."

"I'm *not* a princess."

He smiles.

It's a raw, dirty, *I like making you mad* kind of smile, and my panties go damper.

I stroke lower on his chest, dropping to my knees, tracing the body of the dragon. His skin is wet, and while it was chilly at first, it's heating now. The remnants of my pink manicure stand out against the dark ink.

I'm watching my hands. That blasted ring that I should throw in the sea.

He's watching me.

"I should touch you too," he says.

"I'm not your payment."

"He owes me more than you're worth."

He makes me sound moderately filthy, and possibly cheap, and I *like* it.

Willow Honeycutt, *dirty girl*.

My hands drift to his abs. He leans back to give me better access. His hard length strains higher while he continues to watch my face.

And my brain short-circuits.

I shouldn't be—*no*.

No. I'm done with *I shouldn't be*s. I'm done with *I can't*s.

"Lower, princess," he commands. "Go on. Touch me."

Martin never would've ordered me to touch him.

But Martin never wanted to do anything with the lights on, and didn't even like it if I saw him naked in the shower.

Dax doesn't seem to have any hang-ups about his body.

He's *proud* of it.

As he should be.

He's a walking work of art. Painted by a master. Sculpted by a god. And he clearly takes good care of the gifts he's been given.

My hand stalls at his belly button.

"Chicken?" he breathes.

Am I? "You don't have any tattoos there."

I swear it shrinks half an inch.

"Would you tattoo your pussy, princess?"

My nipples pucker, but the pulse growing heavier between my thighs isn't subsiding. Not in fear.

No, it's...intrigued.

"Maybe," I whisper.

"*Christ*." His voice is hoarse and his eyes go impossibly dark.

The boat dips, and two things strike me at once.

One, we could be interrupted at any moment.

And two, I've wasted *seven years* of my life with a man who was just barely good enough, who I thought was everything I *should* want instead of everything I *do* want. I've wasted too much time being *good* for everyone else.

I love my mom, and I know how much she sacrificed to give me a better shot at life, but I don't want to spend one more second being afraid to live.

I stroke my hands down his lower abdomen and grip his shaft. It's thick, hot, solid as platinum, and silky smooth. A drop of moisture glistens at the tip, and I can feel my heart beating in my clit, surging my arousal higher and higher. I stroke up, my hands overlapping, and he drops his head back, a low groan coming from the back of his throat while his eyes clench shut.

When I brush my thumb over his engorged tip, he hisses out a breath. "You're not nearly as innocent as you pretend to be, are you, princess?"

I don't answer, because I don't *know* the answer.

Am I innocent? I'm not a virgin, but until, well, *now*, I wouldn't have called myself the kind to be stroking a practical stranger's privates on a boat in the middle of the North Sea either.

Not that I'm planning on stopping.

There's something taboo and wild and thrilling about watching Dax thrust into my grip.

Like maybe I'm *good* at this.

I never knew if I was good at sex with Martin.

He climaxed most times. Sometimes I did too.

I'm about to climax right here, just watching Dax's inked chest rise and fall, stroking his thick length while he grunts incoherent noises and surrenders his body to me.

The room suddenly tilts hard. I drop his penis and flail, pitching forward onto his body.

His erection nestles inside my barely-there cleavage, and my face collides with the tail of the dragon on his hard stomach.

"Need to aim lower, princess," he says.

He smells like sea water and something else I can't identify, but it reminds me of New York.

Complex.

Layered.

Gritty and beautiful and wild.

And I might be feeling bold, but I'm not a sucker. "You first."

I'd thought his eyes couldn't go darker.

I was wrong.

In one swift motion, he has me lying prone on the bunk, his body covering mine, my legs spread to cradle his hips. It's like being trapped by a feral cat.

My heart's sprinting. My lungs are burning. And all I can think is that I'm in bed.

With a rock star.

Who's completely naked.

This is probably one of those things my mother would worry about.

But she's not here. And I am. And Dax is.

And this is thrilling.

"You want me to eat your sweet pussy, princess?" he growls.

My belly drops like I'm on a roller coaster, and a hot glow swells in my core. "Maybe," I whisper.

He slips his hand between my legs and strokes me at the juncture of my thighs. I gasp and arch into his touch, not at all embarrassed or shy about wondering if he can feel how wet I am. My skin is buzzing. My kitty aching. Desperate.

Needy.

"Right here?" He's looming over me, the angles in his face hard, his eyes black as night, his nostrils flaring. He palms my clit through my pants. "You want me to lick you right here?"

"*Yes*," I moan.

"Too bad."

I gasp as he shoves off me, turns, and grabs a towel. My body's an over-tightened guitar string, everything suspended in disbelief and an aching need for release.

"B-buu," I stammer.

"Go find another plaything, princess."

He wraps a towel around his slim hips, grabs another and covers his shoulder, and stalks out of the bunkroom.

While I try to process what the *hello* just happened.

10

DAX

THE SKY'S black ink tonight. No stars. No moon. No fans waving with their cell phones lit up like lighters while my band rocks on a stage lit with so many spotlights and screens and fireworks that we're all sweating before we're into the first chorus in Miami, where Half Cocked Heroes were supposed to be playing tonight.

Black sky.

Black sea.

Black mood.

I'm stretched out at the bow of the boat, looking for elusive peace while sea spray mists over my face, a single headlight illuminates the ghostly waves ahead, with the only sounds the boat slicing through water, the gentle hum of the boat's motor, and the tinny melody of some country music coming from Chrissy's headphones.

In fifteen years in the business, I've never been an asshole.

When we're touring, I'm picky about the food catering brings in. I like my bus temperature set at sixty-eight degrees, I don't like to write songs before noon, and I don't tolerate sloppiness or laziness in my crew.

I play pranks. Sometimes I get in fights. I told Cain not to marry the chick who's putting him through the ringer in this divorce. I still give Edison shit about not asking out Cherry Wickers in high school. I'm not always nice, but I'm not an asshole.

Until two days ago.

I've been a total, complete asshole to Willow.

She spent dinner chatting with Chrissy about her preschool kids. Telling stories about The Great Finger Paint Incident and losing Beatrix Clara Clementine when she tried to climb a pine tree at the zoo and the pictures her kids have drawn of her that make her look like she has boobs sprouting out her ears while she spins around stripper poles that are actually brooms, because she's always sweeping up something or other in the classroom.

After the food was put away, she told stories about her friends' romance book club and their band and the time her friend Parker got locked in a men's restroom with a sexy librarian.

She didn't drop names about being related to royalty. She didn't mention her pro hockey friends again. She laughed at the stories Chrissy and Ricky told.

She asked me if I wanted more to eat.

Either she's an exceptional actress, or she really is a sheltered preschool teacher with good intentions at heart who got sucked in to almost marrying a fuckhead.

And I don't think my regret is only about the fact that she has the most fan-fucking-tastic touch on the planet. When she was yanking on my cock—*Christ*, I saw stars.

I've gotten off plenty in my lifetime.

Can't tell you the last time I saw stars just for having a woman's hands wrapped around my dick.

I don't want to be an asshole.

But I don't know how else to keep my distance from her. And if I don't keep my distance, I'm going to touch her again.

Kiss her.

Help her mark *fucking a rock star* off her bucket list.

It's a damn good thing the night air's cool and the sea water even cooler.

I need the cold shower.

But more, I need to actually do something my pop would be proud of. Because the last few months—hell, the last few *years*—I haven't always been the model son.

Willow's stories about her kids today are reminding me of being a kid. And of all the time I spent with my pop.

He never held me back from going for my dreams. Got me guitar lessons. Bartered a kitchen table set for singing lessons. Drove me and Edison and Danger to bars before we were legal to be there. But he had standards for himself, and he set standards for me.

I pull myself up and hold the grips while I make my way aft.

When I pass Chrissy, she gives me a wink and two thumbs up. And that's when I notice Willow sitting at the back of the boat.

Knees up, balancing a notebook that she's writing in with the aid of a flashlight tucked under her chin.

The notebook with her bucket list, I'm almost positive.

I clear my throat, and her head—and the flashlight—jerk my way, momentarily blinding me.

I wince, and the light disappears. "Oh," she stammers. "I was just —I didn't think—I'm heading to bed."

"Wait." For the record, crow tastes like shit, but I've earned this bite. I put a hand out to stop her from packing up while I settle beside her in the little nook over the engines that are powering us tonight.

She tenses, and I realize it doesn't matter what I feel like I need to say.

Forcing an apology on her when she doesn't want to hear it is just as bad as everything else I've done the last three days.

It makes everything all about *me*. "I'm sorry," I say. "I'll go."

I start to move, but her light voice stops me. "Not off the side of the boat this time, I hope."

I bite back a sarcastic *hardy har har*, because I've been enough of an ass. Also, the teasing note makes something loosen in my chest. "You're kinder than I'd be in your shoes."

"Everyone has bad days."

"Still. I'm sorry. For everything."

Her gaze is unnerving in the eerie glow off her flashlight. "Thank you." She flips the flashlight off, and the world plunges into darker shades of black for a moment while my eyes readjust. "Thank you for saving me from going overboard earlier too. Most kidnappers probably wouldn't have done that."

I snort.

She giggles.

And more of the pressure in my chest eases. "I'm a fucking terrible kidnapper."

"You should probably keep your day job," she agrees.

I don't answer.

Because my *day job* is crumbling. It's not just everything since the pigeons ran us offstage at our last tour stop. It's the bickering that was building over which songs should go on our next album. The increasing pressure with sales wobbling like they might break. The unspoken fears that Half Cocked Heroes are about to become has-beens.

I'll always love music.

I just don't know that I love where the band is headed.

"You get extra points for saving me from the donkey and trying to talk me out of getting on this boat," she adds. "That was very gentlemanly of you."

I answer with a vague, "Hm."

"Is this really just about Martin and your money?" she asks softly.

I cut a glance at her in the darkness, because while I owe her an apology, I'm not ready to offer explanations.

"Sorry. Never mind. I know. Total stranger here. It's just—when Mom married the king, it took my stepbrothers almost two years before they'd talk about family stuff in front of me. The first time Colden came to New York, maybe five years ago, we went to see *The Lion King* together on Broadway, and the next thing I knew, there were stories floating around that we were in love and I was carrying his baby. Martin's mother nearly had a heart attack, and we almost broke up over it."

I growl, and she sighs. "Sorry. That's not my point," she says. "My point is, I get it. Or at least I think I might get some small part of it. I can't imagine living my life in the limelight. The few weeks I've been followed for whatever reason—like after the wedding, and when people thought Colden and I were dating—were just awful, and I hated it. You don't have to tell me anything. I'm basically nobody to you. But I just wanted you to know you can trust me. Even though you should never trust people who say you can trust them, because it's usually a lie, but I really am trustworthy. Even—I'm making this worse, aren't I?"

"Way worse," I agree gravely.

She squeaks, much like she did on the first boat, and then I'm being shoved sideways. "You are *such* a jerk."

I rub my arm, realizing I haven't smiled like this in I can't remember when. "You're freakishly strong."

"I've been lifting weights with my friend Knox so I could punch Martin if he tried any anal action on our honeymoon."

I choke on sea air, and her laughter rings through the night.

"Oh man, my mom would *die* if she heard me say something like that," she says through giggles. "And you should see your face. Wait. *Oh my gosh*. You're picturing me having anal sex, aren't you?"

"No shame in exploring new heights with that bucket list, princess."

I get another shove to the shoulder.

We lapse into silence, me trying to get my dick under control while thinking about her ass and how tight it would be, her thinking about—who knows, honestly.

Maybe the same.

Maybe not.

I'm about to leave her in peace when she speaks again.

"Did you know you'd end up divorced when you got married?"

I glance at her sharply. She's staring straight out at the sea, and I can just make out her profile. "Regrets, princess?"

"No. Sheer nosiness. I always thought Erica Schmidt was such a phony. I was really disappointed when I found out you got married. Not that it was any of my business, obviously, but—"

"We're all phonies," I interrupt. Because it's the truth. After a while, you start to believe in your public reputation, even if you sometimes wish you could be just a simple Texas kid who loves music a little too much.

"So you married her for the three minutes of attention?"

"No, that was Chandra." The truth slips out unintentionally, and I suspect there's nothing I could say or do to convince her I'm joking.

And I don't actually care.

Tomorrow I will. But I don't tonight.

"You knew your *very first* marriage wouldn't last?" she asks.

"That's public life. You think your mom's marriage will last?" Not trying to be an asshole.

Just being realistic.

"I do," she says, so firmly I almost believe her.

When I don't say anything—trying not to be that asshole here— she straightens. I can almost feel her spine stiffen. "You don't know my mom."

"I don't," I agree.

The boat hits a wave, and I instinctively brace myself and reach across Willow to keep her from falling off the boat. Not that we're near the edge, but still.

Can't be too careful.

She slides a look at me, and heat creeps over my forehead.

But instead of calling me out on doing something nice, she asks, "Did you love any of them?"

I pull my hand back and put more distance between our shoulders. "There's no such thing as love in the music business."

Not entirely true.

Some people make it. I don't have a fucking clue how, but they do.

She pulls her knees to her chin and stares back out at the sea. "That's really sad."

"But the pay's good."

There's no hiding the sarcasm.

She doesn't reply.

She doesn't have to. I can *feel* the sympathy radiating out of her.

I don't deserve her sympathy. I've had a good life. Might not have the love of a good woman, or however it is that the thousands of songs about love go, but I've definitely had a good life.

"Was it worth it?" she asks softly.

This time, I don't answer.

And I can tell myself it's because the answer's none of her damn business all I want, except I know the truth.

And the truth is that I can't answer the question, because I don't know.

11

DAX

WE PULL into Amsterdam early the next afternoon. Willow's been singing or chatting most of the day, and while I could tell you she's been annoying, I'd be lying.

What's been annoying is how much I want to touch her.

I fucking *kidnapped* her. I don't get to *touch* her.

Even if we did clear the air last night.

Mostly.

Once we're docked, Chrissy and Ricky sneak us off the boat and around Customs as though they've done this before, and Chrissy insists Willow take a few hundred euros they just happened to have stashed in the boat.

Willow has two new best friends.

I have a headache.

Probably because I'm not looking forward to informing the princess that we're going to find a police station, ask for a ride to the American embassy, and head home.

I don't expect the conversation to go well.

And I half expect her to somehow leave me chained to a light post while she disappears to explore Europe on her own.

Which is completely unacceptable. If she'd stroke my dick just because it was there, what the fuck would she do with the next asshole to proposition her?

This has nothing at all to do with that insane desire creeping at the edges of my brain, demanding that I find out what her pussy tastes like.

It's all responsibility.

Yeah.

We'll go with that.

"We could take him back with us and dump him overboard and *not* rescue him," I hear Chrissy whisper to her while they say their goodbyes behind a building not far from a bus stop.

"Oh, stop," Willow whispers back. "He's not that bad."

"Are you sure there's nothing else you need before we pack up and go? We're headed up to Norway before we swing south to Spain, but we could stall a day or two."

"Oh, no, I don't—wait. Could I call my mom one more time? Do you mind?"

That simple request pulls so hard at something in my heart, it's dislodged itself.

She has people who worry about her. People who love her.

And she's walking that line between finding herself and assuring them they don't have to worry.

I should call my pop. But he's probably so disappointed in me right now, I can't bring myself to dial the number. My pop—he knows me.

I hate letting him down.

But that doesn't mean I can't make other phone calls.

While the princess dials her palace, I put some distance between us and call Vanderweilie. It rolls straight to voicemail, so I leave him another very explicit message about what I'm going to do to his fiancée if he doesn't call me back, even though I'm almost positive the rat bastard doesn't have even the half-drop of courage it would take to call me back and save her.

Or if he even cares enough to want to.

And he doesn't know me well enough to know it's all a lie.

I'm fucking glad she didn't marry the twatosaurus.

While Willow rambles and promises her mom she's fine, I call Edison. Glad my phone finally works here. Damn well should, for what I pay for the international plan every month.

No telling how long until my credit card company cuts me off though.

"Fuck, man, where *are* you?" Edison says without preamble.

"Vacation."

"Fucker."

"Cool your titties. I'm alive. Trying to get my money back and my head on straight. How you hanging?"

"You fucking disappear for two fucking days, your phone going straight to voicemail, nobody knows where you are, rumors are swirling about drugs and breakdowns and accidents, while Danger's still missing too, and all I get is *how's it hanging*? I'm gonna beat the ever-loving shit out of you, you dumbass."

As he probably should. "Cops catch Vanderweilie yet?"

"You're fucking insane."

Yeah. Sounded about right. "Did they?"

There's a heavy sigh on the other end. "Heard he skipped out on his wedding and his family doesn't know where he is. That's about it."

"No news on Danger?"

There's a heavy silence.

"Edison?"

"Talked to the cops last night. They say every day that goes by…"

"No. *Fuck*. Shut the fuck up. Can't they trace his cell? His credit cards? *Something*?"

"I know. I know, man. When you getting home? Me and Oliver have some new stuff you need to hear. And I think your pop knows something's off. Call him. He needs to know you're okay too."

I don't like that Edison didn't answer about Danger's cell and credit cards.

"I'll be home soon," I lie. "Just tracking down a few more things to try to get my money back. Danger's money too."

Two days on a boat, listening to Willow chatter on about her preschool kids and her mom and her friends, watching her smile while she basked in the sea air, listening to her sing to herself like she didn't even know she was doing it—going home *soon* would be good.

She's getting to me.

Especially with the way my skin vibrates every time she gets within a foot of me.

I'm forgetting that she's supposed to be a bargaining chip whenever Vanderweilie answers his phone.

But she's not a bargaining chip, and I know it.

She's a woman breaking free who deserves to fly high without any of my shit or his shit or anyone else's shit bringing her down.

"You staying clean?" Edison demands.

It's been a decade since I touched anything stronger than weed, and at least five years since I downgraded to just booze. The question should be insulting.

But I'm wasn't *me* when I left the States. I'm still not *me* today, though I'm feeling closer. And none of us know why Danger disappeared, or if he got into something he shouldn't have too, so it's a legit concern. "I'm good."

He pauses for a minute, like he's deciding if he wants to believe me. "Don't you dare go fucking dark on me again."

"I'll be on text. Call me when Danger surfaces or when they catch the asswipe. I gotta go."

I disconnect to a slew of words Willow won't say. Takes some strength of character not to kick at the rocks in the crusty pavement.

I want my friend back home safe.

Want to be out on tour, getting our sales back up. Want to be cutting new music. Want us as a band to be the way we used to be, back when we were struggling but knew who we were, playing for the love and the dreams and the high that came just from being on a stage.

Any stage.

For any audience.

Willow's hanging up, so I mosey on back.

Like I have all the time in the world.

Like I'm not worried she's going to take off without me.

I reach the group again as she's throwing herself at Chrissy. "Oh my gosh, that's too sweet of you. I need to get a camera. My friends Sia and Eloise are going to pop a gasket when they see."

Pop a gasket.

Who talks like that?

No one. That's who.

A month ago, she would've amused the hell out of me.

A month ago, I probably would've invited her into the studio to goof around. Try a duet. See how high that sweet voice could go. Introduce her to a few people.

Talent like hers shouldn't be wasted.

But a month ago, I still had my money, my pop's respect, my band, and we were only dealing with a small handful of little annoyances. Edison hadn't tried to chop his finger off yet. Cain was reconciling with his wife. The stalker calls from that one-night stand gone wrong were just annoying.

Not creeping me out yet.

Not until she found my second new number and started sending pictures of voodoo dolls and charred remains of paper, roses, and incense, along with hints that if I didn't call her back, my life would only get worse.

Thank fuck the restraining order worked.

But she's not my problem.

I'm my problem.

"Yes, of course. I'll text you. And let me know when you get somewhere permanently. I'll pay you back. For everything." Willow's hugging Chrissy and Ricky again like they're long-lost cousins. She's still clutching Chrissy's phone.

Ricky claps me on the shoulder. "Don't know what's eating you, man, but I hope you figure it all out. And if you don't treat our Willow right, we'll come hunt you down and slice out your spleen and make you watch while we feed it to a sperm whale. *Capisce?*"

"Might want to work on your Italian before you head down the coast."

"He'll be fine," Willow interrupts before Ricky decides to slug me. "He just needs to find his land legs. Dax, say thank you to Chrissy and Ricky for the ride."

That's exactly what's getting to me. *Mind your manners, boy, I ain't raisin' no hellion.* Pop would like her. "I'm not one of your little brats." I add a halfhearted smirk, just to get her hackles up.

She doesn't take the bait. Not really. "But you act like one." She smiles, my heart goes lightheaded, and *fuck me*, she's right.

I need to find my fucking land legs.

And my brain.

Because the brain currently running my head is demanding we get to know this woman better.

Much, *much* better.

"Text me," Chrissy orders while she and Ricky turn back toward the road that leads to the dock.

"I'm going to text you so much, you'll wish you'd never given me your number." Willow blows them a kiss. "And thank you again."

They walk away, she turns to me, and her smile is equal parts devious and innocent, and it's such a fucking turn-on that I can't breathe for a minute.

"I've come to a conclusion," she announces.

My eyes narrow, because they know they're supposed to be suspicious even when my dick doesn't. "Why do I get the feeling I'm not going to like this?"

"Because you're apparently a smart man. Sometimes."

"Whatever you're up to—"

"You're coming with me," she announces. "You need it as much as I do. Since you don't have a bucket list, I wrote one for you." She pulls a notebook page from the drawstring shoulder bag Chrissy gave her and dangles it so I can read part of it.

Help Willow get a tattoo.

Show Willow the Eiffel Tower.

Take Willow on a hot air balloon ride.

I'm starting to grin at the theme developing here when I skip to the very end, and my smile dies.

Trust Willow with the truth.

"Are you fucking serious?" I don't have to agree to any of this, and she knows it.

She shrugs. "It'll do both of us some good. And since you kidnapped me, this is your penance."

"Playing that card, princess?"

"The other option is that I let you walk away, and goodness only knows what kind of trouble you'll get into on your own."

Fuck.

What kind of trouble would *she* get into on her own?

I reach for the list and let my fingers linger against hers longer than I probably should. She's so fucking soft. Everywhere. "What if I don't agree with your list?"

"Then I head to the nearest police station, tell them the entire story, and probably get us both thrown in jail."

She's bluffing.

I'm almost certain that was a wobble of uncertainty in her voice, and her pupils are too wide, and her delicate little pixie nose is flaring too quickly.

But three days ago, I would've bet every dime I had against us standing here in an alley in Amsterdam even having this conversation.

Also, she told me a story about her friend Sia going to jail, and she seemed to honest-to-god *admire* her for it.

"Besides," she adds, "you can't let me go yet. Because you haven't talked to Martin yet. I could still be a bargaining chip."

"You're not a fucking bargaining chip."

She smiles so brightly the blue in her eyes puts the sky to shame. "But you're coming with me regardless. I told my mom you'd watch out for me. And you do *not* want to disappoint a queen. Trust me. It doesn't end well for anyone."

I'm going with her. No question.

If I don't, fuck only knows who she'll find to hitch a ride with—and in what kind of transportation—next time. Because I have a very strong suspicion she's planning a hitchhiking trip through Europe to check off this bucket list of hers, which is probably identical to the one she wrote for me. But longer.

The lady has more balls than I gave her credit for.

Or possibly, she's finally figuring out what to do with her balls.

"Where the fuck exactly are we going?" Seems smart to let her think she has the upper hand, so I can snatch it away when I need to.

"First, shopping for a few new clothes and a bag. And then to get a tattoo."

Christ on a cracker. My blood pressure shoots so high my eyeballs pulse. Apparently *now* is when I need to prove to her who's going to be in charge on this little adventure. "Where the fuck are you getting this tattoo?"

"On my hip. You were right about the bird though. That's lame. I'm going for a tiger."

"Not on your *body*," I grit out, ignoring the way I'm suddenly sweating at the idea of tracing a tiger tattoo on her hip with my tongue. "Who's doing it? Where are you going to get it done?"

She shrugs. "I'm sure I can find a tattoo parlor. I'll just ask directions when I get my clothes."

And here I thought my blood pressure couldn't go any higher. She's going to end up in an addict's backroom letting some Joe-Bob whoever stick needles in her skin. "When's the last time you had a tetanus shot?"

She blinks.

Slow. Dark-lashed. Like she's trying to seduce me with her fucking eyelids.

I should let her walk away, because this woman suddenly has *trouble* flashing in a giant neon sign over her head.

Fuck.

I do love some trouble.

Edison's going to kill me. My pop will probably help.

"Where did you get yours done?" she asks. Coyly. She's being fucking *coy*.

"Not here."

"I'm not an idiot, you know," she says. "My friend Eloise has tattoos. I went with her to get another one this spring. She tried to talk me into getting one too, but I'm really not the pirate-flag-on-my-bottom type, and that's all she was willing to pay for. But I think I can tell the difference between a back-alley shyster and a legit, licensed tattoo parlor."

A *back-alley shyster*.

She's fucking with me now, I'm almost certain. Because no one says *back-alley shyster*.

"Clothes," I growl. "Where are you getting clothes?"

She brightens, and her blue eyes sparkle.

They fucking *sparkle*. Again. "Chrissy says there's a really cute second-hand boutique just a couple blocks over. And the best part? It's in the red light district. How cool is that?"

My gut tightens, my nuts ache, and I can't decide if I want to toss her over my shoulder and turn us both into the authorities, or if I want to see just how far she's willing to take this charade.

But there's one thing I'm not uncertain about at all.

I need a fucking drink.

Just one. Two's how I got into this mess in the first place. And also how I got my third ex-wife.

"Have you ever been to the red light district?" Willow asks. "Oh, wait. That's where you met your third ex-wife, isn't it?" She grins. "Come on, Dax. Let's go. Before I decide to get those handcuffs out again."

The handcuffs.

God help me, I'm putting *Strap Willow into the handcuffs* on my bucket list.

12

I NEVER HAD a puppy growing up, because we lived in a one-bedroom apartment in the Bronx that barely had enough room for Mom and me, much less a pet. Though I did have a pet frog for about three months. He lived under the sink in the bathroom and Mom didn't know about him until the end, when it was time to let him go to froggy heaven.

But today, I have a pet Dax.

And I can't decide how I feel about it.

The man took me to the brink of what promised to be the most amazing orgasm of my life and then left me high and dry. Then he apologized for *everything*, which I assume covers the kidnapping through leaving me without that orgasm. And now he's following orders while I make him escort me all over Amsterdam, which is prompting some inner guilt.

Even if I do have good intentions.

He looks like he needs a vacation. Plus, I'm starting to get an idea about how I can help him with his lost money, but I need him around to do it, because there will be questions I can't answer when I put out a call for the favor I'm going to need.

Every time he cuts those hazel eyes at me, I get goosebumps. And I wish the thrift shop earlier had had padded bras, because this satin one isn't doing anything to mask the way my nipples keep getting hard either. Although I'm digging the vintage Rolling Stones tee I found there, along with the ripped jeans and the biker boots.

I'm also digging his new jeans and the too-tight black T-shirt that I made him get. Not that I'll tell him that.

"Is it weird to *not* be recognized?" I ask him as we leave the tattoo studio he insisted I use. Apparently he has friends in the area who could vouch for the safety of this one, and they gave me a really steep discount when Dax agreed to pose for a picture that they could hang on their wall.

Which basically means I could actually afford the tattoo.

He was going to pay for it outright—sure, *now* he mentions he's had his wallet on him the whole time—but his credit card was declined for a fraud alert, and when he called his bank, they said it would be twenty-four hours—at least—to get everything straightened out.

Definitely a smart move on my part to trick him into coming along, even if I *am* annoyed at how he's acting like I'm a total dumbdumbhead likely to get herself killed on any given corner. Trusting Chrissy and Ricky was a leap, yes.

But I'm still aware of who's around me, the vibe on the street, which streets and alleyways seem less-trafficked, and I'm not going to randomly stop in the middle of the street to make Dax pose for tourist pictures.

"It's nice to have some privacy," he says. Begrudgingly. Like he doesn't want to admit anything to me.

"People all over Stölland recognize me now when I go visit Mom. It's weird. I'm just *me*, but because I'm their queen's daughter, they think I don't spend my days wiping snot and finger paints and macaroni and cheese off a roomful of kids."

He makes a noncommittal noise.

I suck in a grin.

He's rather adorable when he's pretending to be grumpy. There's always a chance he *is* actually grumpy, and this isn't just an act, but I keep catching him glancing at me.

And sometimes, it reminds me of the way Sia's boyfriend, Chase, looks at her. Or the way Parker's boyfriend, Knox, looks at her. Or the way Manning looks at Gracie.

Like he's picturing me naked.

I suppress a shiver and ignore the pleasure pinging between my thighs, because while I still have *sleep with a rock star* on my bucket list, that star is *not* going to be Dax Gallagher.

It's too complicated and messy.

Plus, it's entirely possible he's playing with me.

But all that aside, I'm enjoying wandering through Amsterdam with Dax.

We're strolling down the street with no real direction in part of the red light district, along with other tourists and some locals. We pass a pub, and lively music spills out on the street. My belly rumbles, and I stop myself from asking him if he's hungry.

"I'm going to get something to eat," I say instead.

Not asking permission is new.

I could get used to this.

There's definitely enough money left from the cash Chrissy gave me so that I can afford a hamburger.

No, not a hamburger. Something Dutch. And a beer.

Dinner is a must, but I'm not sure how I'm going to afford a hotel tonight. Maybe they'll take PayPal? After the training with King Tor's guards, there are a few numbers and passwords I've committed so deeply to memory that they'll probably find them etched inside my brain when I die. My PayPal account is one.

Or I'll just have another adventure in Amsterdam before I figure out how I'm going to get to France tomorrow. Or the next day. I'm flexible.

Flexible is so amazing.

Dax follows me into the dim pub off the main drag. We take seats at the bar, because that's where I want to sit. Everything's dark wood and red leather, with stained glass light fixtures dotting the room. The bartender speaks English, and he suggests a Witbier and bitterballen.

I can picture Zeus and Ares—and probably my stepbrothers too, let's be honest here—giggling over something called *bitterballen*, so I go with the bartender's recommendation. Dax orders a gin and tonic and fries.

"Do you have any ideas of a place to stay tonight?" I ask him.

He rubs at his temples like the motion could massage away the gray hairs I'm probably giving him.

"Do you?" he counters.

"Not yet, but I will."

He doesn't answer.

"Am I annoying you?" I ask him.

This earns me full-on eye contact for the first time since our stare-down over whether he would accompany me *inside* the tattoo studio.

I lost that one.

Clearly.

But then, I meant to. I'm a very quick study in how to annoy Dax Gallagher, and to get him to do what I want without him realizing it.

"No, you're not annoying me," he says.

Quite distinctly.

"I'm obviously not *pleasing* you either, and your attitude is killing my buzz."

"You haven't had anything to drink, so you don't have a buzz."

"It's a high-on-life buzz."

His eyebrow twitches.

"Do you get that kind of high? When you're on stage?" I ask. "Or do you secretly have stage fright and have to medicate yourself to make it through a performance?"

He scrubs a hand over his face. His eyes seem more deep-set tonight than they were earlier. Like maybe stress or a lack of sleep are getting to him.

"Do you always talk this much?"

"No." Maybe? I don't actually know.

But I do know I'm beginning to suspect there's way more to his story than just that his money's missing. Because while Dax is rough around the edges, with all the tattoos and the divorces and the hot, heavy songs about sex, drugs, and rock 'n' roll, he's also been way more protective than he should be.

With the donkey. With watching Chrissy and Ricky to make sure they didn't pull anything. With keeping me from falling out of the boat. With being ridiculously picky about where I got my tattoo.

This is not normal behavior for a man who's only in my life because his plan was to use me as ransom. I think. First kidnapping and all. For both of us.

His eyes pinch shut.

"Sometimes I sing this much though," I say, because I've been singing along to every song we hear that I know the words to, and we've passed enough shops with open doors and music pumped in that I've sung half the early evening away. "Do you not sing when you're not at a concert? Or recording an album? I'm not asking for a show or anything, but I sing all the time. I can't imagine having your voice and not using it, but I haven't heard you sing at all in the last three days."

Sometimes I get rotated into the toddler room at my preschool, and I can't understand half the things any of them are saying for the first two hours of the day.

Dax is staring at me like I'm speaking toddler jibberish.

Except I know he understood every word.

Which means he's faking not understanding.

Or else he's having a stroke or something, or possibly he's narcoleptic and just fell asleep with his eyes open, but I don't think that's the case.

I poke him in the arm. "Why don't you sing? Do you not love it anymore?"

The bartender slides our drinks across the bar. Dax grabs his, takes a deep gulp, shudders, and starts to signal for a refill, but stops himself.

I could ask how he's going to pay, but I'm more interested in why Dax doesn't sing.

I can't imagine going a day without singing *something*. And honestly, being a preschool teacher rocks, because I do get to sing every day.

Not always boy band or rock songs, but singing is singing.

"If you don't tell me, I'm going to pass the bartender a note telling him I'm being held captive against my will, and you'll be thrown in a Dutch prison and never see the light of day again."

I'm *so* not going to do that.

But watching his pupils dilate while he studies me to decide if I'm telling the truth tells me he's not entirely certain I'm bluffing.

"I don't sing on vacation," he finally says.

"You're not on vacation."

His lips twitch. "Close enough."

"I really don't think traveling halfway around the world to kidnap the fiancée of the man you think robbed you of all of your money counts as anything *close* to vacation."

The man on Dax's other side turns and looks at me.

I smile. "We're writing a screenplay," I tell him.

Dax finishes his gin and tonic, and I swear he does it to hide a smile.

Which gives me another longing pull deep, deep in my core.

Dax Gallagher is a dangerous man with a dangerous smile.

I sip my beer. It came with a lemon, which is adorable. Before I forget, I pull out the small digital camera I snagged at a convenience store and snap a picture.

"You write film?" the man says in a heavy accent. He's Italian, maybe. Definitely not Dutch. He's around thirty, with dark hair buzzed short and a suit coat that's just a smidge too big, like maybe he's lost weight recently.

"It's a hobby," I lie.

"I write film," he tells me. "Grand love story film. The story of the woman who never loved me back. She left me in a pond of crocodiles. Ran off with my brother."

I gasp. "How terrible."

"Never been a love story written like it," he declares.

"I sincerely doubt that," Dax mutters.

"Crocodiles!" the man shouts. "My own brother!"

"You poor thing," I say.

"My wife ran off with my cousin," says a man on my other side. He sounds more Dutch to me. "Stole all my chickens and peed on my cheese too."

Dax coughs.

I clap a hand over my mouth, because I shouldn't giggle at *peed on my cheese*.

Not until I'm alone, anyway. Sia will think that's hilarious. And then probably make me promise to never give her brothers that kind of idea.

"*My* brother re-used the ring *I* bought her."

"My cousin fathered all of my children."

They both rise.

"My brother also stole my business!"

"My cousin also has four children with my children's schoolteachers!"

"Oh my gosh, you guys." I jump up and put myself between them. "Why don't you combine it all and write a script together? And add a camel. Every tragic love story is better with a camel."

They both look at me.

"And if camels can't unite the world, then I don't know what can," I finish.

Yeah, I definitely spend too much time making sense of preschoolers.

The two men look at each other.

"Drinks for the lady!" the Italian cries.

"Your dinner is on the house, *schatje*," the Dutchman says.

I smile back at Dax.

He's watching me with his mouth half-open.

"Preschool 101," I say.

His gaze dips to my mouth, and for the briefest of moments, I wonder how differently our adventure together could've been if it hadn't started because he thought Martin had stolen all of his money.

I suppress a shiver.

Because Dax is oddly likable even when he hates me.

I don't want to know what I'd think if there was any chance he might actually secretly *like* me.

13

WILLOW

FOUR HOURS LATER, I'm once again on the tipsy side, but this time my belly is full of fried meatballs and four kinds of Dutch cheese that I can't pronounce, much less spell, and puffy pancake dessert thingies. I've heard more about Luuk—the pub owner—and Antonio—the Italian—and their lives than I'll ever be able to remember, and we even got a few stories out of Dax about things like the time his stage was overrun with goats and once when his bus broke down somewhere in Arizona and he and his band hitched a ride to a show with a guy who had a cactus in a hat, sunglasses, and shawl in the front passenger seat of his VW van.

Luuk—*Luuk*, how cool of a name is that?—insists that I sleep in the apartments above the pub, and because Dax has played the mildly charming bodyguard, Luuk insists he, too, stay in the guest quarters.

"You take care of our *schatje*," he orders Dax before closing us into a guest room together.

The bed—it can't be larger than a double—is draped in a textured white blanket that features the outline of a windmill, if you look at it right. Brown curtains blow softly in the breeze coming in from the paned window overlooking the streetlamps below. The single nightstand in the room is simple, with a drawer and a ceramic water pitcher and cup on top. Family photos hang on the walls.

There's also an attached bathroom with black and white tile walls. It's so small I can't spread my arms all the way.

But that doesn't matter.

"Oh my gosh, we're in *heaven*," I say as I plop face-down on the bed. I should shower. I really should. I haven't showered in *days*, and I think I have sea spray in my hair. I know I dropped a fried meatball down my shirt, and I could really stand to brush my teeth.

But *bed*.

Not a bunk on a rocking ship. A solid, soft, warm, sweet-smelling *bed*.

My skill prickles, and I look back to find Dax staring at me.

No, not at *me*.

At my *butt*.

I give it a wiggle.

He turns sharply away, strides into the bathroom, and slams the door.

I flop onto my back.

Dax is a mystery, and I'm getting more interested with each passing minute.

The beer probably helped.

He's world-famous. A few people in the pub recognized him after they heard me say his name a few times—with the overgrown stubble, he's harder to recognize, because he's almost always clean-shaven in public—but he played everything low-key and down to earth.

Friendly too.

Like he maybe *likes* people.

Except me.

But he's still *here*.

And I don't think it's because he's expecting to ransom me, and I don't know if it's because he actually believes I'm capable of holding *him* captive to be my tour guide.

I did add a few things to his bucket list tonight. Things like *bawk like a chicken in a pub* and *spend an entire day pretending to be a mime*.

And he didn't argue.

He didn't bawk like a chicken in tonight's pub, but I have hope for a new pub tomorrow. And while he texted a few people over the course of the night, he didn't ignore me and stay on his phone all night either.

Not like Martin did the last time we went out for dinner before we left for Stölland.

I contemplate starting a group text with my best friends—my mom sent me their numbers for this pre-paid phone Chrissy insisted I take—but my fingers are too weary to even contemplate pulling my phone out of my pocket.

So I close my eyes.

Just for a minute.

Except the next thing I know, the world is pitch black, someone's breathing heavily somewhere nearby, and something else is making the distinct noise of a phone vibrating on wood. I sit up with a gasp.

My whole body gives one of those groans that comes with heavy slumber after a day of non-stop activity—my muscles have hardened like Play-Doh left out too many hours—and it takes me longer than it should to slap at the phone on the nightstand near the heavy breathing.

Which is on the floor.

Not in the bed with me.

A number I instantly recognize dances on the screen. I answer on instinct, half-asleep. "Hello?"

"Willow. You're safe."

The wobbly voice on the other end has me fully awake now, the last three days tumbling back to the front of my brain, along with the realization that I'm not on *my* phone. "*Martin*? Where are you? Why do you have this number? *You left me at the altar.*"

"Willow. I saw pictures of you with Gallagher. How did you—never mind. You have to get away from him. He's dangerous."

"Is that the fuckwit?" Dax growls. The light flicks on, a lightning bolt spears my brain, and my eyes squint shut.

"Ow. *Ow!* Some warning next time," I say.

Martin's hyperventilating breathing comes through the phone. "Willow. You *have* to get away from him."

I bat at Dax and get him with a foot to the gut when he approaches. "He says you stole his money," I say to Martin. "But that's ridiculous. Please tell him you didn't steal his money."

Silence.

Dax makes a jab for the phone again, my eyes finally open fully, and—

"Where are your pants?"

He's naked. Buck naked. With the lean muscle and taut, inked skin, and thick bulge growing between his legs while I stare.

"Willow, you're in serious danger," Martin squeaks.

And suddenly my phone is gone, the naked rock star is standing inches from my face, and he's growling into the speaker while his dangly parts dangle halfway between relaxed and ready to roll, but getting closer to full mast with each passing second. "Where. The fuck. Is. My money?"

I struggle to tear my gaze off his growing erection and concentrate on the conversation.

"I...Let Willow go." Martin's voice is distant and shaky, but I can make out his words.

"Where's my money, Vanderweilie?"

"I don't have it!"

I straighten. Martin shouldn't be saying he *doesn't have it*. He should be saying it's *right where Dax left it*. That it's safe.

"Who does?" I ask.

"Who does?" Dax repeats.

Martin's labored breathing comes over the phone. "Let Willow go and I'll...try to find out."

I gape at the phone.

I know that tone.

He's *lying*.

"You have twenty-four hours," Dax growls. "Starting *right now*."

"She's not my fiancée—"

I flinch, even though Dax hangs up before Martin can finish his sentence.

She's not my fiancée anymore. She's not anything to me anymore.

My new reality slugs me in the gut once again, but I push it away.

I don't think I'm mourning the opportunity to be Mrs. Martin Sampson Vanderweilie the Fourth.

I think I'm mourning the seven years I lost thinking that Mrs. Martin Sampson Vanderweilie the Fourth was what I wanted to be.

But with Dax prowling the room, glaring at his phone, stark naked, now isn't the time to ponder my life choices.

"Martin said you're dangerous," I tell him.

He rolls his eyes. "Of course he did."

"Why? What did you do?"

I wait for him to tell he sacrificed a chicken in Martin's office, or that Martin once had to transfer money to cover paying off a fan he poked in the eyeball with his guitar or something.

Instead, he collapses at the edge of the bed, his back to me so that I can see all the musical dragon artwork on his skin, and drops his head into his hands. "I told him I'd pluck your toenails out one by one, eat them, and then slowly take off all your body parts an inch at a time, unless he gave me my money back."

My breasts physically contract into my body and I draw my knees up to my chest while I struggle to scoot as far away as I can.

"I'm not going to hurt you," he says on a sigh. "I don't fucking hurt people. Not on purpose."

"Then why did you say that?"

"I didn't say I was a good guy. I said I wasn't going to hurt you."

The overhead light buzzes softly, and someone outside the window on the street below shouts to a friend. A series of shivers slink over my body.

"I want my fucking money back," he mutters. "I just want my fucking money back and my fucking *life* back."

There's no edge now.

It's all defeat.

Part of me wants to squeeze him in a hug, to tell him everything looks bleak now, but it'll be okay. The other part of me is remembering the threats that just came out of his mouth.

"Martin's mother might be able to help," I say.

Would she? I have no idea. But for as long as I've known Gwendolyn Vanderweilie, the one constant in her life has been that Martin is her world. She might not have fully approved of me—though she definitely approved of my connections—but in her world, Martin can do very little wrong.

Okay, maybe I'd just enjoy watching her melt down at the idea of having the FBI and the CIA and probably some Navy SEALs and maybe even other secret government groups hounding her about Martin.

Bonus if they sent in the clowns too.

That would be like the best government takedown *ever*.

She'd have to be medicated.

Possibly sedated.

And the family dog, who doesn't like strangers, would probably pee all over her prized Turkish rugs.

I'm beginning to enjoy this fantasy.

"Go on. Laugh." He's turned so he's looking at me, and there's no mistaking the resignation sharpening his cheekbones and killing the life in his textured hazel eyes. "You think it was easy to work all the way to the top? You don't know what *sacrifice* is, princess. To have it all taken away by a fucking shit of a human being who's never earned a fucking thing in his life? I'm getting my fucking money back."

I hadn't realized I was smiling, but I'm not anymore, and not just because his voice cracks and all his conviction is gone. "Sorry," I whisper. "Do you need to get home? I can call my mom. She and the king can—"

"I don't want your fucking charity either." He leans over, snags his pants, and shoves his legs in. The view of his hard cheeks disappears as he yanks them up.

"He knows where your money is."

Every muscle in his back clenches, and my mouth tingles dry.

He turns slowly, so slowly I'm not certain he's actually moving. "Do *you* know where my money is?"

I gulp. Twice. Because having Dax's full and complete attention focused on me with a laser-like intensity is enough to make my heart forget how to beat. "N-no. But I know when he's lying."

"How do I know you're not lying?"

I spread my hands, because there's no right answer to that question. "I guess the same way I just have to trust that you're not going to murder me in my sleep."

His hazel eyes flick to my hands, then back to my face. It's like being watched by a caged animal, except I don't know if I'm dealing with a tiger or a dolphin.

Either way, excitement is sizzling in my veins again.

And that's before his gaze dips to my lips, and his pupils widen.

My belly dips like I'm on a roller coaster, and my kitty pulses.

"Don't even think about it, princess," he growls.

"Why not?" I whisper. I haven't exactly been in the dating game for a while, but I think I recognize the signs of interest.

Dilated pupils? Check. Checking out my butt? Check. That bulge in his unsnapped jeans that seems to be getting bulgier?

There's some throbbing and extra blood flow going on between my legs too.

"Because I don't fuck women after I kidnap them."

I suck in a breath.

Not because of his blunt statement, but because I expected his refusal to be about *Martin*. "I went willingly on that boat. And I don't regret it. *And* now *I'm* in control. So you can tell yourself you kidnapped me all you want, but I wouldn't be here if I didn't want to be."

"I'm also not a tool to make something off your bucket list."

"Oh, so *now* you're going to be picky?"

He flinches. My immediate instinct is to apologize, but I squash it —barely.

Because he *does* have a reputation. I read *Rolling Stone* and *People*. And Chrissy flat-out asked him if he'd do a three-way with her and Ricky too.

He declined, but the wicked grin when he shook his head—that man has done things I can't even imagine.

Maybe I shouldn't be so blunt though.

But then, why should *I* always have to be the polite one?

"Or are you having performance issues?" I ask.

"Do I *look* like I'm having performance issues?" He grabs his crotch.

"Just because it *looks* operational doesn't mean it *is*." I'm blushing and I know it, but I keep going. I can't help myself. I *want* to goad him. I'm also starting to see why my friend Sia likes to bicker so much with *her* boyfriend.

"Oh, it works," he says. Smugly.

"If you say so."

"I could prove it."

"Could you?"

"I could. And just because you doubt me, I'd make you watch."

My kitty clenches, my nipples go so hard my belly dips, and my lips part.

He'd make me watch him have sex with another woman. To prove to me that his equipment works.

The idea isn't entirely despicable, and now my breasts are tingling and my kitty's throbbing and I'm picturing Dax, his muscles tense beneath his dragons, a woman who looks remarkably like me writhing in pleasure beneath him, legs spread, neck arched, moaning his name, while he thrusts into her and orders *come for me, princess, come now.*

"That's—you're—" I stammer.

He winks.

He *winks*. And smiles.

Oh dear sweet sprinkles, he *smiles*. "Don't try to out-game a master, princess. You'll lose every time."

This game is doing more for me in the last five minutes than Martin did in the last *year*, so what does he know? I have to swallow hard, but I find my words. "Oh, I don't want *you*. I'm just practicing."

His gaze flickers down my body again. "Good. I don't want you either."

I'd be lying if I said that didn't hurt. And I'm lying about a lot right now, but I can't deny the dagger to the heart on that one.

No, not to the heart.

Maybe to my spleen. Or gallbladder. No, to my appendix.

Yeah. His insult is a useless dagger to a useless organ.

I flop back on the bed. "Glad we agree. Shut the lights off. I'm going back to sleep."

"I sleep better with the lights on."

"Monsters aren't real, Dax. You don't have to be afraid of them."

"Once again, princess, how little you know."

I peek one eye open and glance at him. Because that wasn't his *I'm a rock god and I will verbally eviscerate you* tone.

It was softer.

Darker.

Laced with regrets.

And now I'm both horny and curious what he'd do if I were to hug him.

Which has to be the oddest combination of feelings I've ever had, and in the last three days, I've had a *lot* of oddly mixed feelings.

He glances back at me.

I slam my lids shut.

He sighs.

Defeat? Frustration?

Exhaustion?

I fake a snore.

He coughs like he's trying to cover a laugh, and even though I'm lying here half-turned on, knowing I'm not on the verge of breaking free and having crazy monkey sex with Dax, I silently chalk up a victory point for myself.

The lights are still on. There's that sunset glow behind my eyelids that says he hasn't turned them off yet.

Maybe he's watching me.

Anticipation tingles over my skin.

Game over?

We'll see about that.

14

DAX

MY BLOOD PRESSURE is almost back to normal after the phone call with the fuckweasel, and arguing with the princess has actually helped. I turn to shut the lights off, but the sight of her stops me cold.

She's rubbing her nipple through her T-shirt.

Not a casual _it itches_ scratch.

Oh, no.

She's going full-circle, arching into her own touch, eyelashes touching her cheeks, lips parted, pleasuring her nipples with her fingers.

My dick hardens so fast I feel it in my spine.

Walk away.

I need to walk away. Leave this room. Leave this building. Leave this fucking town.

But instead, I stand there, balls aching, mouth dry, adrenaline pumping, contemplating adding _watch Willow touch herself_ to that bucket list while she shifts to part her legs and runs her other hand over her hip.

Like her fingers are looking for her pussy.

She's still fully clothed.

In jeans.

Her pink fingertips are snaggle-toothed, and the diamond ring still lists on her finger on the hand now pinching her nipple.

Her breath is ragged.

Fuck, *my* breath is ragged.

I've watched women get off before. I've brought women to climax more times than I can count.

But watching *this* woman touch herself—fully clothed, dark hair a mess, her whole fucking *life* a mess—is about to make me come undone.

Her fingers dip between her legs. Her head arches back, and a soft whimper slips out her lips.

I'm sweating. My cock is straining harder than it has in months. Maybe years.

Sex is something I do. I eat, I sleep, I play, I sing, I screw.

Usually without a lot of thought, because I'm not sure a woman has ever wanted me for anything more than being able to say she screwed Dax Gallagher, and I enjoy getting off just enough to not much care.

I'm thinking now.

I'm thinking about how the asswipe who stole my money was probably the last man to touch her bare skin. About the sound of her nails on the denim covering her pussy. About how much I want to peel those ripped jeans off her and bury my face between her thighs.

She's winning.

She is *definitely* winning this game.

Her fingers quicken.

"That'd feel better on your bare pussy, princess," I say.

Or croak, more accurately.

"Would you—" her breath catches "—like to see—*oh*—that?"

Fuck.

"No," I lie.

Again with the croaking.

Her fingers flick faster over the denim. She's rolling her nipple tight between her thumb and forefingers. "G-good," she gasps. "Because I—*whoa*—wouldn't show you—*ahhh*—anyway."

I reach into my pants and grip my cock, because *Christ*, it needs to be touched too.

By those slender fingers.

Her firm grip.

Her thumb circling my crown.

Like she did yesterday.

On the boat.

With her pupils so wide, all I could see was the ring of navy around her irises. That lip caught between her teeth while she concentrated on my dick. The way she tugged like she wanted to hurt me, but wanted to pleasure me more.

She's panting faster now. Squirming. Thrashing. Legs wide, knees angling toward her chest, as though she can get a better angle by pulling her thighs up.

I jerk at my dick.

I want her to come.

I want to watch her get herself off.

I'm a fucking douchebag, but I want to see her lose her mind.

And then I want to show her how much better I can do it for her.

"*Ohmygosh*," she gasps. She gives one low, keening wail, her legs go straight, her toes curl back, her shoulders lift off the mattress, and *fuck me*, she's coming.

Her hips gyrate.

She cups her pussy and grinds her palm to her center while she jerks on the bed.

My cock pulses as though her pussy's wrapped around it instead of my fist, and suddenly I'm coming too, my release jetting to freedom before I can stop myself.

Holy *fuck*.

Just holy fuck.

She collapses back on the bed, panting, eyes still closed, cheeks stained pink, lips rosy and parted and half-turned up in a smile.

My wobbly legs get the memo to move, and once more, I retreat to the bathroom.

Slam the door.

And drop to my knees.

Because if I don't, I'm going to have to touch her.

And I can't afford to touch her.

I can't afford to touch anyone.

Not while my life is this much of a fucking mess.

15

WILLOW

SLEEP IS ELUSIVE. Even with the post-orgasm high and the bold pride that comes with seizing my sexuality enough to pleasure myself while someone watched, I can't get back to sleep. I shut the lights off myself while Dax hogs the bathroom—either he fell asleep in there, or he pried off a vent and escaped through the ductwork or something—and I try, but dreamland won't come.

So I do what I normally do when I can't sleep, and I text Eloise.

She's the drummer in our band. If Steven Tyler and a pixie had a love child, I'm convinced Eloise would be the result. She's short, she's horny, she's pierced and tatted, and she has no idea that Sia, Parker, and I have finally figured out who she is.

Thanks to Parker's boyfriend, Knox, of course. He's a librarian. Which is more or less the same as being a CIA officer, except without the guns and covert assignments, because there's pretty much no puzzle Knox can't solve through his mad research skills.

And two weeks ago, he broke Eloise's code.

And now that I know who she is and what she can do, I'm even more interested in talking to her.

Willow: Hey. It's Willow. Don't call me—I don't want to disturb my neighbors by talking out loud. Are you up?

Eloise: Fuck, Willow. Not wanting to wake your neighbors means you're not getting laid tonight, doesn't it? YOU'RE FREE. GET LAID.

Willow: I need a favor.

Eloise: Only if you promise to have hot raunchy sex with someone and tell me all about it.

Willow: I'm hanging out with Dax Gallagher.

Eloise: Duh. Why do you think I want to hear about you having sex?

Willow: He's a eunuch. That last divorce didn't go so well.

Eloise: That's not funny.

Willow: He says Martin stole all his money, and I actually think he's not wrong. Can you sort of dig around and see if you can find out anything?

There's silence.

And because I'm on a prepaid phone, there aren't any bubbles indicating she's texting me back.

I hope this doesn't mean she's going to abandon our band. Parker, Sia, and I had a silent pact to not let her know we knew, because we weren't sure if she'd be comfortable with us knowing, or if she'd disappear into the night, dye her hair blond, invest in plat-form shoes, get a fake ID, and move to her own private island where she could secretly rule the world in comfortable anonymity again.

Not that she rules the world.

We don't think.

Knox's research only turned up so much.

The phone vibrates, and I blow out a breath I hadn't realized I was holding.

Eloise: Assuming I could do such a thing, or find someone who could, it'll cost you.

Willow: I'm sure we can arrange something.

Eloise: I want to sleep with your stepbrothers. All three. At one time.

First, *gross*. No matter how many times she asks, I still almost throw up in my mouth.

Second, she knows Manning would refuse, both because he's already told her so and because he's not ever going to sleep with anyone but Gracie for the rest of his life. Also, as crown prince, Gunnar can't have random flings with women who may do border-line illegal things. And as the sheep-lover in the crowd, Colden might not even be able to perform with a woman.

And third, I'm almost positive she only asks to sleep with all our brothers because she likes our reactions. She continues to torment the heck out of Sia about her twin brothers too, even though both of them are also in committed relationships.

Willow: Never mind. I'll call Parker's brother. He's a SEAL. He can do it if you can't.

Eloise: That's low. Really, really low. Especially coming from you.

Willow: Nice Willow is dead. Deal with it.

Eloise: I'm so fucking proud of you right now. Take a picture of yourself holding up your middle fingers. I need to confirm this is Willow, or else I'm going to fucking go apeshit and kill whoever's messing with me and pretending to be you.

Willow: I'm not going to hold up my middle fingers.

Eloise: Is this the new and improved Willow who's going to prove to me that she's alive and I'm not talking to a murderous fiend trying to trick me into giving away all my secrets so she can destroy me, or do I need to fucking disappear?

Willow: Okay, drama queen. Hold on.

I snap a picture of myself—yes, fine, holding up a middle finger —and then duplicate the effort with the second hand since I can't hold up two middle fingers while I'm taking a picture.

It takes two full minutes, but she finally replies.

Eloise: I'm showing that to your mom.

I gasp. Out loud.

Eloise: Heh. Kidding. But if you don't enjoy the fuck out of your adventure, I WILL show it to your stepbrothers. I mean, the ones who haven't filed restraining orders against me. What's up with the sheep dude? He's touchy.

Willow: Who needs a European adventure when she's friends with you? And leave Colden alone.

Eloise: You have much to learn, my child. Much to learn. Now tell me about Dax Gallagher. I want a picture of his penis piercing. And then I want to know how much money Martin stole, and how he got his hands on it.

I ignore the penis piercing request—though it does make me curious to look closer if I get another chance to see Dax naked, because I didn't see a piercing, but I'm never completely certain if Eloise is serious or not—and I give her the basic details I know about Dax, Martin, and the money.

Then I tell her lies about my stepbrothers and the diseases they haven't actually contracted over the years, along with sending her fake names of their previous girlfriends, before I remember that I'm using up all the data on this prepaid plan and tell Eloise I need my beauty sleep before the next round of adventuring tomorrow.

But after I've set the phone aside to charge, I still can't sleep, so I sneak over to the bathroom and peek in.

Dax is curled up on the tile floor, a towel under his head, shirtless, pants unbuttoned, snoring softly.

Asleep, he looks ten years younger. Still tense, but not as much so. I reach up and flip the bathroom lights off. His breathing doesn't change, and the soft light filtering in from the bedroom would make him almost boyish if it wasn't for the tattoos and thick stubble.

I wonder what more there is to his story. His tour was canceled, but I don't know why. Obviously the reports that it was because he checked into rehab were wrong. He stopped after two gin and tonics at the bar, he hasn't lit so much as a cigarette, and there's nowhere he could've been hiding drugs the last few days. If he has a gambling addiction, he wasn't getting the shakes while we were at sea for being unable to log into the internet, and he hasn't even been on his phone that much.

It doesn't make sense that an otherwise reasonably sane rock star would travel all the way across the Atlantic to kidnap the bride of the man who robbed him.

Unless he snapped.

Like I did, when I ran away from my wedding and hopped on a boat to Amsterdam with strangers.

But for all the opportunities he's had, he's right.

He hasn't hurt me. He's been rude a few times, yes, but vicious and dangerous?

If anything, I think he's been tagging along to make sure I *don't* get hurt. Like I'm his responsibility.

But I think he's right.

I think Martin stole his money.

Which means more than ever, Dax is now *my* responsibility too.

I didn't steal his money. But I lived with the man who did. And I assumed that when Martin got jumpier and jumpier the last few months to the point that his own reflection startled him, it was because he had wedding nerves.

And that I could fix him. That all he needed was for me to be steady and calm and reassuring. That I could love him enough to make him whole.

When possibly, none of his life was really about me.

Except for the part where dating a preschool teacher who was the stepdaughter of a king made him look good.

I didn't love him enough to marry him. But I didn't expect the sucker punch that keeps creeping up on me when I realize he didn't love me enough to even let me all the way into his life.

At least Dax is honest.

All he wants is to use me.

And he has lines he won't cross to that end.

Scary when the kidnapper has more morals than the man I was supposed to marry.

16

Day four of this adventure has begun, and it's clear where I'm headed.

All I need is the handbasket.

Which won't be a problem for long, because I'm almost positive the nun two rows up is weaving it right now.

"Did you ski?" Willow's asking Sister Mary Basketweaver and Sister Mary Pruneface. "I've never skied, but I would love to learn."

"Oh, you should learn from Fabio," Sister Mary Pruneface says. "He was a very good instructor."

"A very cute instructor," Sister Mary Basketweaver replies.

The entire nun brigade breaks into giggles.

We're in a fourteen-passenger van, driving through the Netherlands, in transport arranged by our dear friend Luuk after he heard that Willow wanted to see the Eiffel Tower.

Apparently Luuk has an American aunt traveling with her nun pack on a European vacation. I think the aunt is Sister Mary Leadfoot at the wheel, but I'm not entirely certain.

I haven't asked many questions since I woke up this morning handcuffed with my face smashed against the toilet.

Partly because I've been trying to get my boner under control at the idea of letting this woman do whatever the hell she wants to do to me while I'm cuffed. Again.

When she ordered me to get in the van, I got in the van.

And I'm still handcuffed.

With my hands in front of me this time, so I can get to my pocket and check my phone—or that bucket list that she wrote me—but still with a nun on either side of me.

One's wielding knitting needles. The other has thick, massive arms that suggest her daily prayer routine takes place with dumbbells. Or maybe with small farm animals that need lifting.

And all of them are in jeans, tourist T-shirts, and habits.

And I swear to holy fuck, Willow better have plans for me and these handcuffs once we get to Paris.

I'm getting my own ideas about what needs to go on this bucket list.

The woman has me thinking of *bucket lists*.

It's the handcuffs.

Has to be the handcuffs.

"Have you been to Rome before?" Willow's full of questions, and she's firing them off almost faster than the nuns can answer. "I want to see the Colosseum. And the catacombs. Are they spooky? In high school, I took Latin, and we studied all kinds of Roman culture, and I always thought the catacombs sounded so creepy."

"You studied Latin?" Sister Mary Knits-a-lot asks.

Willow turns from her perch in front of us, where her dark hair has been swaying gently with every curve of the van. "Semper ubi sub ubi," she says.

All of the nuns crack up.

Including the driver, who swerves while she cackles.

Willow turns to me with a bright smile that makes her eyes dance and her teeth shine. "It's a really bad translation for *always wear underwear*."

I saw her in her underwear this morning. Stumbled out of the bathroom while she was pulling on her pants. She looks like she didn't eat for the last six weeks, but her ass still had some curve to it, and those legs go on for miles, and her fresh tattoo—a tiger, mouth open in a roar—was hot as fuck.

And that white satin bra.

Dear god in heaven, that white satin bra.

Her gaze holds mine, and her eyes darken as though she knows I'm thinking about her naked.

Thinking about her naked is all I seem to be able to do.

I shake my head and think of Sister Mary Biceps naked, because I've done a lot of crazy shit in my life that I should probably regret, but popping a nonstop, raging boner in a van full of nuns isn't something I want added to that bucket list just so Willow can check it off.

Even I have some limits.

Although I'm seriously contemplating asking them if they can pray away bad karma or black magic or whatever the fuck's going on, because Edison texted this morning that a storm blew through Corpus Christi last night, where Cain is from, and tore off his roof.

Dude's in the middle of a divorce, worried as much as we all are about Danger missing, and now his roof's gone.

It's probably a miracle I'm in a van with this many nuns, because surely God won't strike them all dead or make us tumble over a cliff or get sliced to bits by one of those windmills dotting the landscape.

I never gave *luck* or *fate* much thought until all the shit started hitting fans a few months ago, but it's getting harder and harder to be logical about this.

And revitalizing the band and getting back on top is seeming farther and farther away.

"Did you take a foreign language in high school?" Willow asks me.

I smile at her, because I know it throws her off her game, and I need to be in charge of *something*. "I studied the language of love."

Three nuns *tsk* me. Sister Mary Knits-a-lot goes pink. Sister Mary Leadfoot eyeballs me in the rearview mirror, and Sister Mary Biceps slides me a look. "You were in seminary in high school?"

My jaw slips. Oh, *fuck*. She thinks I've been making whoopee with Jesus.

Her brows slant down, a stern frown growing on her beefy lips.

Sister Mary Freckles, who's sitting beside Willow, stifles a giggle, and the next thing I know, every last one of the dozen nuns in this van is laughing hysterically.

Sister Mary Knits-a-lot laughs so hard she pokes me in the thigh with one of her needles. Sister Mary Biceps has to wipe tears. And Sister Mary Leadfoot actually pulls over to the side of the road.

"I wish I had a picture of your face," Willow tells me. She's not laughing, but she is smiling. "Nuns are people too, you know. They have senses of humor."

"I laugh at fart jokes," Sister Mary Pruneface announces.

No, I don't know any of their names. Yes, I should probably learn them. But if I'm going to hell, I might as well earn the trip.

"Oh, my nephew tells the best fart jokes," Sister Mary Elephant Ears tells us.

"The older nephew, or the younger nephew?" Sister Mary Sudoku tucks a pen back behind her ear.

"The younger one. He's four now."

A chorus of *aaw*s fills the van.

"I teach four-year-olds," Willow says. "But we're supposed to redirect them to talking about vegetables or animals if conversations veer toward farts."

Now everyone's *tsk*ing again.

"Flatulence is a normal bodily function," Sister Mary Biceps informs us all.

"Like breathing," Sister Mary Knits-a-lot agrees.

Sister Mary Leadfoot puts the van back in gear and pulls onto the two-lane road again. I miss my own bus driver. Biscuit's a driving machine—raised in the South, grew up plowing cotton fields on his daddy's tractor, doesn't take shit from anybody.

Except me.

And then he gives it right back.

Fuck, I miss home.

I miss *normal*. Shooting the shit with my band and crew. Busting out our instruments on the road and jamming for the hell of it. Dropping in to visit my pop on a random Tuesday. What is today? Is today Tuesday? I think it is.

If we hadn't canceled the tour, we'd be headed to Chicago. To play for twenty thousand at Wrigley.

Should've been thirty. But ticket sales are down.

Everything's down.

Sister Mary Freckles glances back at me and goes pink. "Dax, speaking of farts, may I ask you something?"

More giggles.

"Sure." I'm handcuffed and trapped in a van with twelve nuns and trying to distract myself from imagining Willow sitting where Sister Mary Biceps is, so that she's close enough to touch. Not like I'm going to say no.

"I really love 'All Yours,' but I've never been able to figure out why you say you've got your fart all over her."

More giggles.

Sister Mary Biceps nods. "Me neither."

Willow's the only one not laughing.

She's bent forward, shoulders shaking as she hacks a lung out.

Two points for the princess for trying to hold it in.

"I've got my *heart* all over you," I correct.

A collective *Oooh* rolls through the van.

Sister Mary Freckles's cheeks turn into beets. "It…really does sound like *fart*."

"It does," Sister Mary Knits-a-lot agrees.

Willow's sitting straight again, wiping her eyes. "My friend Parker thought it was *shart*," she announces, which prompts even more giggles. "That was totally awkward the one time we tried playing it in rehearsals."

"Princess, you just said *shart*," I point out.

"That's what she thought you said."

"You know what *shart* stands for?"

"*Hush*. Have some respect. You shouldn't cuss around nuns."

"It's okay to say shit, damn, and hell," Sister Mary Biceps tells her. Several of the nuns nod. Sister Mary Freckles crosses herself.

"They're just words," Sister Mary Leadfoot agrees. "And a loud *damn it* feels good when you stub your toe."

More nodding.

Sister Mary Freckles crosses herself again.

"She's taken a vow of no profanity," Sister Mary Knits-a-Lot murmurs to me.

"Dax, do you ever smile?" Sister Mary Pruneface asks me.

"Usually for reasons that would make you ladies blush," I reply.

Much to my delight, Willow blushes. "You're incorrigible," she tells me.

I wink at her.

She blushes harder.

And once again, it strikes me that if she were anyone other than Vanderweilie's long-time girlfriend and almost wife, and if we'd been thrown together for any other reason, I'd probably be talking her out of her panties right now.

With or without the nuns around.

But definitely still with the handcuffs involved.

Her eyes go dark again and her breath catches. She turns back to face the front of the van again.

"Do you ladies like to sing?" she asks. "Because I think we should play a game. How many Half Cocked Heroes songs can we corrupt with the wrong words?"

Turns out, a dozen or two.

Some of the nuns can carry a tune.

Some can't.

Willow can belt it.

She's fucking phenomenal. Plays juice bars, she says.

She should be playing stadiums.

She would've fucking outsold us at Wrigley.

We stop for a potty break—yes, a *potty break*, the nuns say so—about ten miles from the Belgian border. Willow studies me too closely before springing me from the handcuffs so we don't draw attention at the gas station. "You're going to disappear, aren't you?"

Can't deny I'm considering it. I should get back to the States. Help Edison and Cain and Oliver. Go sing on a street corner for cash so I can afford to help pay for the search for Danger. "Would you miss me, princess?"

"I would," she replies. "You're a pain in the tush, but I think that's just because you're stressed. You're probably a nice guy when you're not dealing with someone stealing all your money."

Christ.

I've long given up hating her on principle of who she almost married.

But the further I get from my normal reality, the more I can't resist liking her.

And I'm starting to like her entirely too much.

WILLOW

MUCH TO MY SURPRISE, Dax is waiting in the van when I get back with Sisters Veronica and Glenda. He's stretched out in the front passenger seat, checking his phone.

And frowning.

Frowning *big*.

"Problems in the potty?" I ask him.

When he doesn't even growl in response, I take a closer look. The lines at the corners of his eyes are deeper, and I swear his beard is graying.

I settle into the front row of seats since Sisters Violetta, Ruth, and Honey are still picking out snacks inside. "Is there something else going on? Besides Martin stealing all your money?"

Now his attention shifts to me.

It's different.

The first day we were together, he was condescending, mocking, and spiteful.

By the time we got off Ricky and Chrissy's boat, he seemed almost resigned.

Today, he's been guarded, but agreeable.

I get the feeling he's not going to tell me anything.

So much for *Trust Willow with the Truth* on that bucket list of his. Not that I expect him to trust me.

But he's still here, isn't he?

"You know what happens after you work with four-year-olds for a few years?" I ask him.

"You get immune to the smell of shit?"

"Well, that too. But I was going more for the *you know when someone's lying* angle. And you should *not* lie to nuns."

"Though God will forgive you if you're penitent about it," Sister Veronica says. "And we also know you're lying about why you put him in handcuffs."

The back of my neck gets hot. I told the nuns he got handsy, which is why they put him between Sister Francie with her knitting needles and Sister Heather, who's a recreational body builder in her spare time.

"Willow didn't want to embarrass you," Dax says smoothly. "She's secretly kinky."

My neck goes hotter. "I am *not*." Yet. But I'm wondering if I could be. "And you're trying to change the subject. Maybe I should call Eloise back and tell her to quit looking for your money."

He blinks twice before his face evens out into a lazy, mocking smile. "So now you're trying to help me."

"I could tell the sisters why we're together in the first place," I offer.

He looks past my shoulder. I turn too.

Sister Heather and her massive arms are headed our way. I'm almost positive she could hold her own arm-wrestling against Zeus or Ares for at least ten seconds. Maybe eleven.

"What makes you think your friend—your friend?—could help find my money?" he asks.

"Eloise? She's the drummer in our band. We just found out she's actually JDC's granddaughter, and she hacks computers for fun in her spare time."

His lips part and his eyes narrow. "JDC?"

"Yeah. *That* JDC."

"I have…no idea who JDC is."

The sisters gasp. "You don't know JDC?" Sister Veronica says.

Dax pinches his lips together like he's keeping from guessing Jesus "Diddy" Christ.

I slug him in the arm on principle. "Jimmy Dossel-Cleave? The bellbottom hero?"

"We wouldn't have had the seventies without him," Sister Glenda says.

Dax squeezes his eyes shut and snorts a short breath through his nose.

"JDC," I repeat. "He led the fashion pack in introducing bellbottoms. He sold his JDC brand and made a fortune, then died, supposedly without any heirs. Except he had a secret love child."

"Your friend."

"No, my friend's dad. But the point is, if anyone can track Martin down and find your money, it's Eloise. Well, okay, there are probably also government hackers and spy agencies who could find him, but I doubt they're putting the same resources and manpower into the search as Eloise will. She's ruthless when she has a goal."

I have no idea how much of that's true—the part about Eloise dedicating her life to this, I mean—but it sounds good, and Dax doesn't seem to catch that I'm making it all up as I go.

"So," I finish, "you can just sit back and relax and enjoy the rest of the trip to Paris, because I have all your problems squared away."

"Fucking insane," he mutters, but his lips are twitching like he's amused, and possibly like he wants to smile at the idea of someone *helping* him instead of stealing all his money.

"Oh, now, that one's going to cost you three Hail Marys," Sister Veronica chides.

I kinda doubt Dax is going to get down on his knees and launch into prayer. But he surprises me when he doesn't sneer his refusal to Sister Veronica.

Instead, he nods to her. "You'll have to say it for me, Sister."

Then he surrenders the front seat—the seat with the most legroom—to Sister Hazel and climbs back to take his place between Sisters Francie and Heather.

I go back to my seat too. And I hope that Luuk was right—that we'll be able to cross country borders without anyone realizing Dax and I don't have passports, because no one questions a van full of nuns.

Once we're in Belgium, though, I have more questions for Dax.

Because I'm becoming more and more positive that his money isn't his only problem.

Dax

Willow holds her breath while we cross the border into Belgium, like she thinks a van full of nuns will randomly be pulled over for a passport search despite the open borders in Europe.

I can't resist leaning forward. "You know your life doesn't end if you get arrested."

"Maybe not for you," she replies. "It's like a badge of honor in your line of work. But I make a living teaching *preschoolers*. I could get fired."

"All my best preschool teachers caused international incidents at some point in their lives."

"You can name your preschool teachers."

I smother a grin at the sarcasm creeping back into her voice. She's getting riled. "Only the hot ones."

Half the nuns sigh, the other half cast their eyes heavenward as though they're praying for my soul.

"Quit teasing the poor girl," Sister Mary Biceps orders.

"Even if you did look at someone wrong, we'd vouch for you," Sister Mary Pruneface tells Willow.

She starts breathing normally again and pulls out her notebook with her bucket list.

I barely resist reaching into my pocket to check the list she made for me again.

Because it's starting to amuse me.

A while later, we're past Antwerp, and the nuns have made our first detour.

To see a church.

Naturally.

"Are you going in?" Willow asks when I climb out of the van to let Sister Mary Biceps pass. The princess is in ripped jeans again today, with a Rolling Stones T-shirt, her biker boots, and a black backpack dotted with skulls slung over her shoulder. Not exactly church attire.

And though I got a shower last night, I'm not looking much better.

"Banned for life," I reply. "They didn't like it when I pissed in their holy water on our *Sounds Good* tour."

Her eyes almost bulge out before she catches on that I'm pulling her leg.

"The Lord forgives that which you're truly sorry for," Sister Mary Knits-a-lot reminds me as she strides past on the cobblestone road to catch up with the rest of the nun brigade.

None of them insist we have to go in.

But I probably should've followed them. Because two seconds after they disappear around the corner of the Gothic cathedral, Willow's phone beeps, she looks at the read-out, and once again, I'm on the receiving end of being shoved.

"What the h-e-double hockey sticks?!" she shrieks. "*Danger's missing*?"

"Tourists without passports shouldn't make scenes in public squares," I remind her. Softly. Though the square isn't large—it's more a patch of grass and shrubs and trees across the street from rows of decorative shops labeled with foreign words—we *are* drawing attention both from the people taking pictures of the monster church and a few people passing between shops.

And I'd rather distract her than discuss my missing drummer.

She tucks her phone back in her pocket. "Is *that* why you need your money so bad?" she whispers. "So you can go find him? Or is he secretly in some really expensive rehab facility?"

"Do you like it when tabloids make up fake stories about your friends and brothers?"

"I can't stop myself from creating crazy stories because I think something broke in my brain when I left Stölland. Also, it's not a tabloid speculating that Danger's missing. It's Eloise. And she *knows* things."

A shiver slinks down my spine.

"And what's this about a witch?" she whispers.

"Holy fuck, *shut up.*" I grab her by the elbow and pull her closer to the van, which is parked between a compact European delivery truck and an even more compact silver coupe in a small parking lot across from the church. "Who's this friend? Let me see her picture."

She yanks her arm out of my grasp. "Eloise. She's *my* drummer. You can't have her just because *your* drummer's missing."

"Her *picture.*" Am I mad to think that maybe this all-knowing *Eloise* is yet one more complication?

Maybe.

Or maybe not.

Willow rolls her eyes. "Give me your phone. This burner only has data for texts."

Later, I'll think about how easily I trust her with my phone. But right now, I want to see a picture of her friend.

She doesn't snoop, just pulls up a browser window, types something, and soon, she's flashing me a picture of a pixie of a woman with spiked dark hair and a nose ring, tongue hanging out, drumsticks in hand, posing between the hulking Berger twins.

My one-night stand gone wrong was tall, with an oval face, long chestnut hair, and she hadn't even had her ears pierced.

I'm one hundred percent positive I've never met this Eloise chick in my life.

I sag with relief.

But only temporarily.

"How the fuck does your friend know anything about my business?"

"I told you. She's good. And possibly not operating within the confines of the law, but desperate times, and I'm pretty sure I have plausible deniability. You want your money back, right? You can't be picky. When's the last time you saw Danger? And your money? And what's this about…a llama? Or was it an alpaca?"

Fuck, she hacked my text messages. Me and the band—we agreed to *never* speak of the alpaca incident. And we don't.

Ever. "Why's your friend investigating *me* instead of your dick-weasel fiancé?"

"*Ex*-fiancé, and maybe she's doing both to make sure you deserve the help. Also, I don't want to tell you what she knows about Martin and your money because *you're* being a doodoohead."

My molars crack together. "I am *not* being a doodoohead."

"Yeah, but I just got you to say *doodoohead*," she says triumphantly. She grins, the sun shines brighter, a choir erupts into song, and six dozen angels get their wings.

Dammit, she's pretty.

"Didn't that feel good?" she prods. "Freeing? Like maybe there are a million other creative ways of expressing—*mmph!*"

I push her against the van and silence her with my mouth.

Because she's fucking with me, and because I *like* her fucking with me, and those lush lips are temptation incarnate, and I haven't so much as kissed a woman in weeks, and I swear on all that's holy, the moment my lips crash against hers, everything shifts into place.

For the first time in months, I'm grounded.

Solid.

Where I'm supposed to be.

Doing what I'm supposed to be doing.

Which is fucking insanity, because this woman is *not* what I need in my life.

But her lips—plump pillows.

Her mouth—hot bliss.

Her tongue—sweet Christ, she's grabbing me by the neck and licking my lower lip, and I suddenly have no blood left in my brain because it's all surging to my cock.

There are reasons I shouldn't do this.

I can't remember what they are, and even if I could, I suspect I wouldn't care.

There's exactly one thing I care about right now.

More.

More of her mouth. More of her hands. More of her scent. More of her body. She angles her head, pulls me closer, deeper, and I grip her waist, my thumbs inching up.

I want to touch those sweet buds that I watched her tease last night.

I want to pull her shirt up and suck on them.

I want to make her moan like she made herself moan last night.

Except I won't stop at one. I'll make her moan all day long. All night long. All fucking *week* long.

She hooks her arm around my neck and slides her free hand down my chest. Lightning sparks everywhere she touches, even through the cotton of my shirt.

And that deep, dark, desperate hole in the pit of my gut suddenly doesn't seem so deep or dark or desperate.

"Hey. *Hey.*" Something pokey shoves my side. I lift my head to growl at whatever fuckwit is interrupting me, and I have to look up.

And up.

And up some more.

"Oh my gosh, you're as tall as the Berger twins," Willow says.

A tall dude, thankfully not as beefy as one of the legendary Berger twins, is crowding in between the cars, glaring down at us from…stilts?

"*Ne vous embrassez pas,*" he says. I have no idea what his words are, though his tone clearly says *no fucking*. He's in red-and-white striped pants and a puffy blue shirt with sleeves that would give an 80's prom queen's shoulders a run for her money, balancing on two-by-fours painted to match his shirt. Without the stilts, he's probably five-ten or so. With the stilts, he's probably seven feet.

"Sorry," Willow says. "We didn't know this was a no-touching zone. Or whatever it is you just said. And I didn't mean to kiss him anyway. It was an accident. We fell on each other's faces. Wow, you have amazing balance."

"We fell on each other's faces?" I echo.

"Do you have a better explanation?"

I clench my fingers into fists to keep from shoving them through my hair in frustration. "I had to kiss you because you're a fucking vixen."

"Oh, sure, blame the woman." She pokes me in the chest. "Well, you want to know what you do to me? You make me *crazy*. I don't go on road trips with nuns. I don't sail across the North Sea with strangers. I don't—no, wait, I do karaoke when I've had too much to drink, but I also karaoke when I'm sober, so that's not your fault, and I'm actually glad I'm here. But I *never* kiss men like that. *Ever.* And that *is* your fault."

"Oh, princess, you have been missing out."

"*Ne vous embrassez pas ,*" Stilt Guy says again.

"Gaston! Gaston, *laissez-vous les tourtereaux seuls*. Leave zee love-birds alone."

A second man on stilts, this one in blue striped pants and a yellow fluffy shirt, stops behind the van. "My apologies, mademoiselle." He bows, on the stilts, and Willow gasps as I picture the guy toppling over onto his head. But he stays on his feet and rises back to his full height. "Gaston has had his heart broken, and now he...how you say...has zee insecurities."

"Why do so many people's hearts have to break?" Willow says. "I'm sorry, Gaston. I hope you know you deserve better."

"He perhaps does not, as you say, deserve better." The second man flashes a grin that makes Gaston glower at him. "But perhaps *thees* will teach him to have hope."

I glance around and notice eight or so other men approaching on stilts. We're being surrounded by the stilt people.

And I'm relieved none of them are in kilts.

Because kilted stilt people would make for one hell of a different kind of show.

Good *god*, that sounded like something the princess would say. What the fuck is she doing to me?

"Oh my gosh, is there a circus nearby?" Willow claps her hands. "You are all so amazing. How do you stay up there? I'd fall on my bottom."

"Mademoiselle. We are *not* zee circus. We are zee Stilt Warriors, and we have protected our god and our country from zee outsiders for four hundred years. Come, come, we will show you."

She starts to move, but I grab her wrist. "Your friend," I remind her quietly. "What did she say?"

"Nothing that can't wait." She grins. "You know your nostrils flare when you get frustrated? It's adorable."

Adorable?

Christ. I'm not *adorable*.

She looks at my nose and giggles.

And I realize she's baiting me.

"Come on, Dax. How often do you get to watch men on stilts?"

"More often than I'd like, apparently. Does your friend have a lead on Danger?"

She brushes past me to follow the stilt men down the cobblestone road. "She just found out he was missing. What do you think?"

I think she's not the only one who's losing her mind. "I want to talk to her."

"She might not want to talk to you."

"I can—" I stop, because I *can't* fucking make it worth her while.

Willow's smile fades into something between sympathy and—no, that's just all sympathy. She reaches back and grabs my hand. "Come on, Dax. Trust me."

Trust me.

I can count on one hand the people I trust, and I've known most of them all my life.

"What brings you to our city, mademoiselle?" Stilty McFlirterson asks Willow.

"We're on an adventure," she replies.

He puts a hand to his heart. "Zee woman wants an adventure. We shall give you an adventure, and zee winner of our duel shall win your hand."

She giggles.

I don't.

First, because I'm not a giggler, and second, because the jackass is turning on all his French or Belgian or *whatever* charm to flirt with her.

It's a fucking good thing I got in that van with her this morning. Because I have a feeling she's just met the next guy who'd try to feel her up, and I don't like it.

I might actually like it even less than I like that Danger's missing.

Which means I'm sinking into some pretty serious trouble.

19

WILLOW

BAPTISTE, the leader of the stilt fighters, introduces us to all the stilt fighters and leads us down the street and around to the other side of the cathedral, where there's a larger park area. A small crowd bursts into applause as the dozen men in their uniforms—half blue shirts, half yellow shirts—step onto the battlefield.

He instructs the crowd to part and makes me stand at the very edge of the roped-off field. "You shall go to the victor," he declares.

The men cheer.

The crowd cheers.

Dax snorts like a bull. He and Ilsa's donkey are beginning to resemble each other more by the day.

Except when he's kissing me.

Then, just—*wow*.

Baptiste bends low and takes my hand, pressing a kiss to my knuckles. "I play for your honor, mademoiselle."

I smile through a blush. I've never been hit on by a Frenchman—Dutchman?—before. "Good luck, Baptiste."

"Fall on your head and die," Dax mutters.

I elbow him in the gut. "Be nice," I hiss. "It's all just a show."

"The way he's looking at you is *not* a show."

"You're not any better." Hello, bold Willow.

"Yeah, but I trust me. I don't trust him."

"Do you trust me yet?"

"No."

Huh. Was that hesitation, or my imagination? Probably my imagination. He should've told me Danger was missing. Eloise would've started looking *hours* ago. She has a soft spot for drummers. "Maybe I don't trust any of you."

"Then you might be smarter than you look."

I elbow him in the gut again, because I can. And he takes it stoically, probably because he knows he deserves it.

Or possibly because he doesn't want the stilt fighters to see him get taken down by an elbow if he's planning on going caveman if any of them try to claim me for real.

Men are so juvenile sometimes.

Dax crowds closer to me while the show starts. His scent—clean soap, leather, and sweat—tickles my nose, and every time our arms brush, sparks erupt from my arm hairs and make my skin pebble into goosebumps.

The two teams are doing a complicated dance on stilts while trying to knock each other down, and it's fascinating. "Have you ever tried walking on stilts?" I ask Dax.

He doesn't answer right away, so I glance up at him and catch him watching me.

Not the show.

He looks away.

I poke him.

Not hard.

Just enough to be annoying. My friend Sia has taught me a *lot* about how to be annoying since she finally introduced us to her brothers a year ago. "Have you?" I press.

"Once." His voice is grittier today. More gravel, more sex.

I have to make myself concentrate on interrogating him about stilts, because Wild, Wanton Willow is not yet ready to jump a man in public. "Oh my gosh, for real? Were you on stage? Or was it a dare? Did you fall down?"

"I was six. Made them with scraps out of my pop's wood shop. And I faceplanted in dog poop."

I laugh. He must've been adorable as a boy. It's hard to picture now, with all the sharp angles to his face, the tattoos all over his body, and the general hard-ass attitude he's perfected, but for a brief moment, everything about him softens.

"Go on and laugh, princess. You wouldn't do any better."

I'm starting to like when he calls me *princess*. "Maybe, but I wouldn't be picking dog poop out of my nose hairs for weeks afterward."

He ducks his head, but not before I see a wry grin. "Oh, shove it."

Huh. We might actually be growing on each other.

Baptiste and Gaston are in the center of the battlefield, dancing with their stilts, slicing sticks at each other. The rest of the crew are in sync, choreographed perfectly to keep gasps rolling through the crowd every time it looks like one might fall. After ten minutes or so, the battle comes to a head with the blue team victoriously knocking down all six members of the yellow team.

The crowd cheers, the blue team helps the yellow team back to their feet—back to their stilts?—and all of them take a bow.

Then Baptiste gestures to me. He says something in French that I don't understand, but then he translates. "Gaston. Your team's prize awaits."

Gaston the Broken Hearted eyes me as he approaches the sidelines.

My belly flops.

I know he's not *actually* going to take me away, but there's something odd about being stalked by a man on stilts who didn't like catching me kissing Dax, especially when he doesn't know either of us.

I giggle, but I'm nervous. The crowd is growing uneasy around us, and murmurs are starting up, though I can't make out any particular words.

Dax crowds closer. "He's not fucking taking you anywhere," he mutters.

"He can if I want him to," I say for argument's sake.

"I'm picking better next time I kidnap a woman."

I laugh an honest laugh. I really was bluffing when I told him I was trouble, except…apparently I wasn't.

Gaston stops at the rope.

I smile. Nervously.

It's just a show. I know it's just a show. I'm not going to be kidnapped, again, this time by a band of stilted Dutchmen.

Gaston's ankles touch the rope, since his stilts make his ankles sit about a foot and a half above the ground. His hooded brown gaze lingers on me, sneer forming on his lips, sweat glistening on his high forehead.

The crowd is rumbling more, and I don't like the currents making the air crackle around us.

I'm not entirely in favor of this idea of being the prize.

It's the first thing that's given me pause since I racked Dax in the coconuts on the fish ship.

I gulp.

Gaston shifts his attention to Dax.

And before I can blink, he bends, snags Dax, and throws him over his shoulder.

I gasp.

Dax grunts and struggles, but Gaston grips him tight. When he wobbles, Dax freezes.

"Oh my god, it really is Dax Gallagher!" someone cries.

"Half Cocked Heroes!" someone else shrieks.

The middle-aged woman who was on Dax's other side looks at me, eyes round as her mouth. Her silver-streaked hair is piled in a messy bun. "Well, blow me silly, was I standing beside Dax Gallagher this whole time?" she asks in an adorable British accent. "He's my fucking hero."

I don't waste breath telling her she could probably pick a better hero, because I'm stumbling over the rope. There's something about the way these guys are manhandling Dax that I don't like. "Hey! *Hey!*"

"The spoils of war go to zee victor, mademoiselle," Baptiste calls. His team cries out something I don't understand, because my French is terrible.

Non-existent, actually.

I should work on that. I'd love to be able to curse in French. Cursing in French would be so classy.

Dax is twisting and struggling. The stilt fighters are almost running, which should be impossible, but it's not. A familiar voice rings out behind me while I hustle down the field. "Sister Hazel, get the van. He's gone and gotten himself tied up with more miscreants," Sister Heather calls.

"Stop," I call to the men. I'm running, and I'm falling behind. "*Wait*. He's my—"

My what?

My escort? My prisoner?

"My baby daddy!" I yell.

At least a dozen women gasp behind me.

Sister Heather jogs up beside me. "Dear child, I hope that's not true. And may the Lord forgive us for what we're about to do."

"Do you think he'll sign autographs?" the British tourist asks me. She's jogging alongside us too now.

"I, um, kinda doubt it," I say to her.

And I can't say much more, because Sister Heather can book it, and apparently I need to catch up.

Before we lose Dax to kidnapping Belgian stilt fighters.

Or maybe to the people behind us who are starting to bust through the rope too, all calling Dax's name.

I could've been on a beach for my honeymoon this week.

This is way more fun.

20

DAX

YOU KNOW the only thing worse than being dragged away by a guy on stilts?

That would be being rescued by a nun.

"Put him down and the Lord doesn't have to get involved," Sister Mary Biceps says.

Willow's tripping along behind her. "Hey, Dax," she calls, and despite being held so tight by four of the stilted guys that I'm wearing myself out thrashing, that breathless quality in her voice makes my gut stir.

In the *I want to make her breathless* kind of way.

"Madam," the stilt leader says to Sister Mary Biceps, "we're merely removing him from danger."

"What kind of danger?" Willow asks.

Because she apparently hasn't noticed the masses breaking past the rope back on the field.

Or else she doesn't have a clue what a crowd that size can do.

Which is equally possible.

"Oh, fuck," I mutter.

"It's Dax Gallagher!" a woman shrieks. "Dax! Dax! Sign my breast!"

"Sign my pussy!"

"Can I have your love child too?"

"Oh," Willow says. "*That* kind of danger."

The nun van screeches to a halt on the cobblestone just past a giant oak. Sister Mary Leadfoot cranks the window down and waves a hand. "Get in! Quick!"

"Is *thees* your car?" the stilt leader asks.

"It is," I confirm.

"You shall come fight with us next time you plan in advance," he says. He snaps his fingers, and the four men holding me set me down.

Okay, they drop me. And they snicker.

But they also line up and form a wall, blocking our view of the stampeding women and pulling their stick-swords out of their belt loops.

"Come on, rocker man." Willow snags my hand and helps me up.

I let her, not because I need the help, but because her hand is soft, and she's being nice, and that smile—just *fuck*.

With her chest still heaving from running and her cheeks blushing with the exertion, those dark lashes framing her ocean blue eyes, she's radiant.

She's the sun.

And I'm getting sucked into her orbit.

Sister Mary Biceps hustles us into the van. The door slams, and we all topple all over each other while Sister Mary Leadfoot peels away from the church.

I end up with my face smushed into Willow's ass.

Which is not at all a bad place to be.

She gasps, wiggles, and if she bends forward just a bit more, I could get my nose right up—

A hand grabs me and hauls me over one seat and into the next, where I suddenly have a face full of nun crotch.

Sister Mary Freckles shrieks. I roll and flail about and finally get up, only to be pitched back onto her, my chest colliding with her knees, when Sister Mary Leadfoot takes a curve too fast.

"Slow down, Sister Hazel," Sister Mary Basketweaver chides. "You're going to get us all arrested."

"The Lord forgives the penitent," Sister Mary Freckles reminds everyone.

"Well, damn," Sister Mary Knits-a-lot says. "We didn't get to stay for mass."

"Next time, you're coming with us," Sister Mary Biceps informs me.

"Are you sure the church won't catch on fire if he does?" Willow asks.

The nuns all titter.

And for the first time in days, I find myself laughing.

This entire trip is fucking nuts.

And it's fucking fantastic.

Wherever Danger is, I hope he's having half as much fun as I am.

Fucking Willow.

She's a witch in her own right. Except her kind of witchcraft is slowly cleansing my soul.

Reminding me of the simple joys in life.

And the glory of making new friends.

21

WILLOW

THERE'S SO much traffic in Brussels that we get through two rounds of "Ninety-Nine Bottles of Beer" before we're south of the city. Sister Hazel pulls the van over to fill up with gas.

Or petrol.

I like calling it petrol. So fancy.

Dax looks like he could use a nap. He moves to let Sister Heather out, and then stretches out on the back seat with his knees up so he'll fit. Once we're the only two left in the van, I turn sideways to talk to him. "Eloise texted," I say.

He pops one lazy eye. "To ask if her eye shadow makes her eyes look fat, or to weigh in on your new tattoo?"

My tattoo is a little sore today, but I *adore* it and am honestly looking forward to getting to a…someplace…tonight so I can look at it again in something other than low bathroom lighting in a gas station bathroom. "You won't find out if you can't be nice."

"That *was* nice."

"No, that was passive-aggressive and condescending. *Nice* would be, 'Oh, thank you so much, Willow, for helping me *even though* I tried to kidnap you and blamed you for something your ex-fiancé did and for my own stupidity for putting every last dime I have into a single account."

"I could pop out the distributor cap on this van and leave you and the Sister Marys stranded while I hitch a ride with the first person who recognizes me."

"Eloise says the lights and the air conditioning at your house in Texas are all hard-wired through the home security system, and it would basically take her fifteen seconds to activate the emergency locks, shut off all electricity to your house, and then change your password. How hot is Texas in June? I can't remember."

"Jesus fu—"

"You're *traveling with nuns*. Have some respect."

"You're talking about piercing your nipples with Sister Mary Sudoku. That's not disrespectful?"

"*Sister Mary Sudoku?*"

He pinches his lips together and his sculpted cheeks take on a ruddy hue.

I burst out laughing.

He closes his eyes.

But his lips curve up in a smile. "Out of curiosity, would you have them pierced at the same time, or would you do one, and then the other, regardless of how much the first one hurt?"

"Is that how you pierced both of your boy bits?"

His body stills. His chest stops moving up and down, his smile freezes half-formed, and his thumbs, which have been twirling casually around each other on his linked hands, freeze. "Angling for another private performance, your highness?"

"Shy Willow is dead. If I wanted to see your balls and chain, I'd ask. This is research to decide if I want to try something crazier." If he opens his eyes now, I am so busted. I don't actually know how I got through that sentence without stammering.

"You've been texting your friend about my love spuds."

"*Love spuds?*" I'm picturing him with potatoes between his legs— red potatoes, with sprouting eyes, and I almost choke on a hysterical laugh.

"Since we clearly can't say *testicles*, Princess Preschool Teacher."

"You're ruining all of my good memories of you naked."

Those eyelids part, and he gives me a lazy, hooded once-over, which is impressive, since there's a van bench seat in the way of most of my body. The space in the van is shrinking, thanks to sticky humidity combined with heat magnified by the windows.

And possibly also caused by the sensation that his hazel eyes are seeing through my clothes and remembering what *I* looked like half-naked this morning too.

"We could make more memories," he says.

"I thought you didn't sleep with women you kidnap."

"You took me hostage and threw me in a van with a dozen sisters of the immaculate road trip this morning. We're even."

"It was for your own good."

"Was it now?" He doesn't seem put out. If anything, that lazy smile says he's having fun. And I heard paper crinkling earlier.

I'm pretty sure he's been studying that bucket list I gave him.

"You clearly needed emotional support. I gave you twelve trained emotional and spiritual guides. Plus I had a feeling you needed Belgian chocolate."

His lips are twitching as though he's ready to call my bluff. "I think you want to draw all over my body with Belgian chocolate, and then lick it off."

Hello, hot flash in the nipples. "And what if I did?"

"You'd have to tell me what your friend found out."

I remind myself this is a weird situation, and eventually we'll part ways regardless of how much fun I'm having disappearing into the world for a while, and that his reaction isn't personal, but I still feel my shoulders droop. "She hasn't found anything on Danger, but she did discover that Martin's uncle's company doesn't exist."

"You drag me halfway through Belgium, still no chocolate, and no new information. Princess, you're asking for a spanking."

My lips part. "Would you...do that?" I've never been spanked. Not during sexytimes. And I don't know if I'd like it, but I don't know that I wouldn't either.

His eyes go dark. Before he can answer, the van door slides open, and Sisters Veronica and Ruth climb in. "Do you need to pee before we leave?" Sister Ruth asks.

"Or get some chocolates." Sister Veronica triumphantly waves a foil bag.

Dax shoves up. "Chocolates sound delicious, Sister."

I picture myself rubbing a truffle all over his chest, feeding the dragon band tattooed there, and I probably go six shades of red.

But I won't let the blush win.

I'm on an adventure. With a rock star who's becoming more intriguing by the hour. And *that*'s the important part.

22

*D*AX

W*E* SHOULD'*VE* BEEN in Paris by now, but we're not. I'm not sure we're even in France yet.

My cell phone went dead an hour ago, not long after a message from Edison that Vanderweilie's family had filed a missing persons report on him and were suggesting the fucking king of Stölland had something to do with his disappearance. No word from Danger.

No word from Willow's friend either.

Still not sure how I feel about the friend. Seems odd that a straightlaced preschool teacher would be friends with a hacking heiress, but then, I'm not the small-town Texas kid I once was either, and some of my classmates have gone on to do more questionable things than starting a rock band.

Maybe being friends with this Eloise character is Willow's way of staying in touch with her crazy, since she's stifled her wild side on her way to becoming the stepdaughter of a king and the almost-Mrs. Martin Sampson Vanderweilie the Fourth.

It's dark now, and the road is lit only by our headlights and the occasional semi-populated area. After our dinner stop two hours ago, where Willow used her last euros to pay for waffles and chocolate for both of us at a diner somewhere, everyone switched seats in the van. Sister Mary Biceps is driving now—and insisting her internal GPS is better than the satellite device on the dash—and Sister Mary Lead-foot took Willow's spot, which means Willow's now her leaning on my shoulder, snoring softly. She has been for almost as long as my phone's been dead.

Half the nuns are asleep too, which means now would be an excellent time to cop a feel if Willow were awake and willing, but she's not.

Sister Mary Knits-a-lot, however, remains fully awake.

She's becoming Sister Mary Talks-a-lot.

Not that I mind. Talking, I've realized, is a great distraction. And since every time I suggest that I take over driving, half the nuns immediately cross themselves and Sister Mary Biceps herself tells me to shut up, sit down, and strap in if I want to make it to Paris, there's nothing else I can do to make the trip go any faster.

"Did you steal her from her wedding?" Sister Mary Talks-a-lot whispers. I can still feel her arms shifting beside me. She's been knitting all day. Should have a blanket big enough to cover the whole van by now, but in reality, I think she has six socks, three fingerless gloves, and a few dozen washcloths to show for it.

"She ran away from her wedding," I answer quietly.

"Because she loves you?"

I snort softly. *Love* is a four-letter word tossed around by women more interested in alimony payments and ten minutes of fame than commitment and family.

At least, in my experience.

"She'd never considered anything besides marrying her fiancé," I tell Sister Mary Talks-a-lot. I don't know if I'm right or not, but I do recognize a breakdown when I see one.

Even if I didn't *want* to see it the first day or two.

But the tattoo, the wild hair to hop on a boat with strangers, the carefree exuberance at dragging me into a van full of nuns to go to Paris—she's tasting freedom.

And it makes me hate Vanderweilie for stifling her for so long.

"Why *did* she have you in handcuffs?"

I scrub a hand over my face and accidentally bump her with my elbow. "Sorry."

"Accidents happen, dear. Now. The handcuffs."

Willow sighs in her sleep and nuzzles my neck, tickling my jaw with her hair. Wrapping an arm around her would be so easy, but I shouldn't get attached to anyone right now.

Least of all Vanderweilie's new ex.

"She knew I was in a bad spot and didn't want me to hurt myself."

"You're alone in Europe?"

I wave my phone at her, a useless gesture in the dark. "No. But I…"

"Lost something dear to you," she finishes.

Willow bolts straight up. "Grab the sheep!" she cries.

So maybe we're watching out for each other. "No sheep, princess."

"Damn stepbrothers," she mutters. She claps a hand to her mouth. "Oh, shit."

"Let it out, my child," Sister Knits-a-lot says. "We're not preschoolers."

Willow leans forward and drops her head against the back of the next seat. "Dammit, dammit, dammit."

"You want to try *hell* next?" I suggest.

"You're perhaps not the best influence," Sister Mary Knits-a-lot says.

"I didn't suggest *fuck*."

Four nuns snort, sit up, cross themselves, and then nod back off.

Willow doesn't poke or elbow me for saying *fuck* in front of the nuns. And now I'm worried. "Bad dream?" I ask her.

"Colden's sheep were eating Martin's…penis…and every time, it would grow back like a banana with half the peel hanging off."

Sister Mary Knits-a-lot stops knitting. Even I'm not sure what to say about the dream.

"At least his penis isn't your concern anymore," I offer.

Sister Mary Knits-a-lot sighs.

Willow shudders.

I pat her back, because I forget that every time I touch her, shivers race over my skin and this time, I realize just how very small she is.

She's not frail—she's too full of life to be frail—but she's slender, and I can feel the bumps of her ribs under the thin cotton of her shirt. "Have you been eating?"

I expect her to shove away. Instead, she arches her back into my touch. "Did you not see the three waffles tonight and all the fried meatballs last night?"

"Before your wedding?"

She shudders. "I don't want to fucking talk about it, okay?"

I suppress a smile while Sister Mary Knits-a-lot clucks her tongue.

"Sorry, Sister," Willow grumbles. "He's making me crazy."

"He worries," the nun replies. "It's often the people who make us craziest who care the most."

She twists her head on the seat. In the low light, all I can see is her profile, and not very clearly at that. "Martin's mother made me crazier than he did. But I drove *him* crazy. Eloise sent me a picture of the letter. He says I was stifling him."

I almost choke.

"I thought I was protecting him from his mother. She's very... insecure. And I don't think she's realized how it's impacted Martin that she always wants him to look good for her. But I guess I wasn't any better."

Now I'm stifling a growl. Because the princess might not be easy, but if she put half the effort into her relationship that she's putting into *living*, then Vanderweilie is an even bigger fuck-putz than I thought he was.

"Not your fault he's a dickwad," I tell her.

"But it's my fault I didn't recognize it."

I'm stroking her back harder without even realizing it. I loosen up, and she whimpers. "Don't stop. That feels nice."

And now I'm instantly sporting a boner in a van full of nuns.

Thank fuck it's dark in here.

Pretty sure I've just finalized payment on that ticket to hell though.

"Do you have a motorcycle?" Willow asks me.

"For now."

She makes a funny grunt. "Eloise will get your money back. You're not going to have to pawn your Harley. But when she does, so you know, I want a ride."

An image of her straddling my Ducati, her hands gripping me low on my stomach while the wind whips around us, flying up the California coast, takes hold in my brain, and I'm not hard anymore.

No, now I'm fucking iron.

The van swerves, Sister Mary Biceps slams on the brakes, Sister Mary Basketweaver shrieks, and a cow stands in the middle of the road, staring into the headlights, chewing its cud, getting closer by the second.

Someone screams. Half the nuns launch into prayers. I grip Willow's knee, and my arm ends up around her back. By the time the van stops, sideways in the middle of the narrow road, she's holding onto my leg and huddling into me.

The van sputters and dies.

The cow moos loud enough for us to hear it inside the van.

And Sister Mary Biceps mutters something that sounds suspiciously like *whoops*.

"Sister Heather," Sister Mary Basketweaver says suspiciously, "did we just run out of gas again?"

Sister Mary Biceps—fine, *Sister Heather*—cranks the engine.

No dice.

The nuns collectively groan.

"We were almost there," Sister Mary Biceps says.

"I *knew* we should've stopped for directions an hour ago," Sister Mary Freckles mutters.

"How many times do we have to run out of gas before you learn?" Sister Mary Knits-a-lot demands.

"We've always come through just fine, haven't we?" Sister Mary Biceps retorts.

"It's nearly eleven. We can't go knocking on people's doors at this hour of the night," Sister Mary Sudoku declares.

"And what about the cow?" Sister Mary Basketweaver chimes in.

"Oh, the cow's fine. We just need to push the van off the side of the road."

Willow's shaking.

I tighten my grip around her before I realize she's not scared.

She's *laughing*.

I feel a smile creeping on.

Should I be home? Or out looking for Danger? Or banging on the FBI's door every day to get them to look harder for Vanderweilie?

Probably.

But I've been around the world. I've played sold-out stadiums. I've had records go platinum.

I've had pranks pulled on me on *Ellen*. I've done *Carpool Karaoke*. Danger once filled my tour bus with pygmy goats in unicorn horns, and I retaliated by swapping out all his toothpaste for diaper rash cream.

And running out of gas with a bunch of nuns on this backcountry road somewhere in Europe has just topped them all.

Not because it's epic.

But because there's nothing I can do except join in laughing with Willow.

And laughing with her is making something loosen in my chest. That knot that's been holding my every breath hostage is fraying and collapsing and unwinding itself.

In this moment, I finally have something I've been missing for days.

Weeks.

Months, probably.

I have belief.

Belief that everything is going to be just fine.

23

WILLOW

TEN MINUTES AGO, I would've said my favorite part of the trip so far was when Dax softly clucked like a chicken while we were eating dinner tonight. Checking that insane item off the bucket list I made for him.

But it's been replaced now with watching Dax take off his shirt and wipe his face after helping Sister Heather push the van to the side of the road.

And I don't think I'm alone.

Sisters Hazel, Honey, and Violetta are all fanning themselves too.

And I think the cow might've also been impressed. It's hard to tell in the dark. But with all the sisters' cell phones lit up and shining on the road to help Dax and Sister Heather see the way, there was no need for imagination to watch the bunch and flex of his muscles under his ink.

"I think the Lord sent the devil to tempt us," Sister Violetta whispers while we all trudge up the long walk that we're almost certain leads to a farmhouse. Sister Francie was able to get a cell signal by sitting on Sister Heather's shoulders and angling her arm just right, and when the map finally loaded, we realized we're pretty stuck. The nearest town is at least five miles away.

So, we're once again relying on the kindness of strangers.

I walk beside Dax at the back of the group while the twelve nuns climb onto the porch of the adorable farmhouse just down the road. Sister Heather knocks softly, and a minute later, lights flip on, and an astonished middle-aged couple gapes at all of us.

I stifle a giggle. *Twelve nuns, a rock star, and a runaway bride break down in the middle of nowhere* is the start of a joke.

Except it's also our reality right now.

Dax is clearing his throat like he's also stifling some snickers.

He's still shirtless, and he smells faintly like leather and sweat. Our eyes meet, his smile hits the pause button, his gaze dips to my lips, and *holy ducks*, he's going to kiss me.

Again.

On purpose.

That weird jumpy feeling in my belly that started when he was massaging my back in the van returns in full force, only this time, the jumping is more like twenty toddlers hopped up on triple chocolate espresso brownies. The cool night air makes my lungs shudder, but my heart's working overtime to heat up everything.

Everything.

When I put *sleep with a rock star* on my bucket list, I didn't mean Dax.

I intentionally meant for that to *not* be Dax.

But sleeping with him would be one memory I'd be happy to make before our trip here is over.

We could sneak off tonight. Find a pasture. Try some more of that kissing thing from this morning.

I'm a single woman.

I can kiss a single man.

Move on. Start fresh. The post-Martin years are going to be fabulous, and this entire trip has been unexpected and crazy and I wouldn't trade a minute.

And I don't want to waste any opportunities that I might not ever get again.

"Are you two coming?" Sister Veronica asks.

We both jump. Looking away hurts like an electric shock in winter. It's a sharp prick of electricity, but it's not going to keep me from looking again.

"We're coming," I answer. The rest of the nuns are filing into the farmhouse. I missed the conversation, and only partly because I don't speak whichever language they were using. Mostly because I was paying attention to Dax watching me like he's seeing me as something more than the woman who was supposed to marry the man who stole his fortune.

Like maybe he's glad he's here with me.

Like maybe he wants to get to know me a little better too.

"Actually," I hear myself say, "I've never slept under the stars in Europe, and that's on my bucket list."

Half the sisters turn and look at me. "By yourself?" Sister Ruth asks.

"I'm a chigger magnet," Sister Heather says with a shudder.

"Do they have chiggers in Europe?" Sister Glenda asks.

"If they do, they'll find me."

"Willow will be fine," Dax says.

"I will," I agree. "The cows aren't secretly alien spies sent to beam me up to the mothership or anything. And who else is going to be sneaking out around random country farms this late? I mean, besides a bus full of nuns?"

Everyone gets a good chuckle, and Sister Hazel says something to the farm couple.

Ten minutes later, I'm spread out on a thick wool blanket under the stars, with nothing but fresh dairy air and a cool evening breeze flowing around me. I've found a spot not far from the house, but without the old leafy trees blocking my view of the galaxy.

And this far out in the middle of nowhere, I can see the entire Milky Way. It's a hazy, thick cluster of stars, almost purplish in the black night, along a cragged line that I mistake for a cloud when I notice it.

I've *never* seen the Milky Way before. There are too many lights in the city. I've seen the northern lights in Stölland once or twice, but I've never gone far enough into the countryside to see this kind of night sky.

We should've been able to see it from the boat the other night, but I guess the two nights with Chrissy and Ricky were too cloudy.

This would be amazing to share with my mom.

But since it's late, and I don't want to disturb her, but I don't want to be entirely alone either, I text Eloise.

She'll be up.

Willow: Any news?

Eloise: The Yankees beat the White Sox yesterday.

Willow: That's great! But I meant about Dax and his money and Danger.

Eloise: Have you slept with him yet?

Willow: Would you work faster or slower if I said yes?

Eloise: That depends on if he was any good. I'm not busting my ass for some dickhead who can't at least give you two orgasms in one go.

Willow: He gave me sixteen orgasms while we were riding in a van full of nuns.

Okay, fine, that's not true.

But there were a few moments in that hour or so after dinner, when I was sleeping on his shoulder, that I had some very vivid dreams. And while a stronger woman probably could've appreciated that light back rub as nothing more than a light back rub, there were parts of me he wasn't touching that were living vicariously through my back.

Is that a thing? Body parts living vicariously through each other?

If it's not a thing, it should be a thing. Because my panties are still damp from that back rub.

After a few minutes of waiting for Eloise to answer, I pull out the notebook that Chrissy gave me, update my and Dax's bucket lists to add—and then cross off—*travel with nuns, get kidnapped by Dutchmen on stilts,* and *sleep under the stars.* After I'm done, I flip to a clean page.

I never know exactly what it means when Eloise goes silent. Maybe she's getting some sleep, or she got the answer she wanted from me and has now buried herself in her computer.

Or possibly she's cheating on our band and drumming for someone else for the night.

You never know with Eloise.

There's a flash of headlights and the chug of a motor, which I assume means the farmer is headed out to look for the escaped cow.

Escaped cow-vict?

Ha. I'm funny tonight.

But I'm also feeling poetic. And free. And *happy.*

I scrawl phrases onto the notebook, bits and pieces of my day, some of my feelings, and pause to glance at the Milky Way every now and again.

I know I can't hitchhike across the world the rest of my life. But I don't think I'll be the same jumpy, overanalyzing, afraid-to-step-on-toes Willow when I get back to New York that I've been the last few years either.

On impulse, I send my mom a text message too, even though she's probably asleep. We've texted back and forth a few times today —mostly me assuring her I'm in very good hands, because you can't get much better than a bunch of nuns, even if Sister Heather's internal GPS system doesn't work in Europe—and part of me wishes she could be here with me.

When I was thirteen, she surprised me with tickets to a Bro Code concert, and she went with me, and we had the best time dancing and singing along, and I never knew how she afforded the tickets, but she did.

This trip?

She'd be laughing and having fun too, and I'd be loving the extra time with her.

But another part of me knows I need this journey to be solo. With no expectations or limitations—either from the people who love me, or from what I *think* everyone expects of me—and as much as I know my mom loves me and wants me to be happy, this wouldn't be the same trip if she were here.

For one, she would've brought passports and cash. We would've been staying in hotels instead of sleeping in farmers' yards and on strangers' boats.

I know this trip isn't *normal*.

But it's showing me that the world won't stop turning if I step outside my comfort zone and do some of those things I never thought I should do.

A shiver of anticipation rolls up my back, and I realize I'm no longer alone.

"How'd you get past Sister Heather?" I ask the tall, lean figure approaching in the dark.

Dax drops to his rear and sits beside me, close enough that our shoulders and thighs are touching. I have to restrain myself from reaching out to touch his shirtless back.

"I waited until it was her turn in the bathroom and then I dove out the window," he tells me.

"Making sure I don't run away?"

"Making sure you take me with you if you do."

"Because you want your money back?"

He doesn't answer.

But his focus narrows to laser intensity while he studies me in the dark. I don't know how clearly he can see me, but I can feel his gaze and I know he's watching.

"I'd understand if that's all you want," I tell him. Because I do understand. My mom barely made ends meet for us when I was little. I don't know anything about Dax's childhood, but I do know that if I worked my ass off for years to build some comfort for myself, and suddenly all of my cash was gone—

I shiver, because I've always had love, but I haven't always had financial stability. No matter how much Mom tried to hide it from me, I knew we were moving because rent got too high when I was fourteen. And I knew why we moved in with friends between apartments.

Because she needed to save money for a deposit and look for someplace cheaper. Again.

It didn't happen often, but kids remember things.

"I don't deserve to want anything from you," he says quietly. "I shouldn't have used you. You're not a pawn. You're a human being. A better human being than I'll ever be."

"That's true," I say.

His head jerks up, and I fall back laughing.

"Sorry," I sputter, even though I'm not. "It was so easy, and you were there, and—"

"And you're not the sweet princess you let the world think you are," he finishes dryly.

"Or you bring out the worst in me."

"Also entirely likely."

"I'm glad you do," I tell him. "I feel like...like I've been sleep-walking through life. Doing what I'm *supposed* to do instead of ever stopping to ask myself what I *want* to do. But now, I'm just *free*. For this week, anyway."

He peers down at me but doesn't say anything.

His silence speaks for him. *You could be free every week, Willow. You don't have to go back to being boring when you get home.*

I shiver.

He might be learning a few things about me.

"You probably do what you want all the time, huh?"

"All the fucking time," he agrees.

I don't believe him. There's something too dark, too biting in his words.

Manning almost had to marry a woman he didn't love because of duty and family responsibility. Dax wasn't born into royalty like my stepbrother was, but he's self-made rock royalty, and I imagine that comes with its own set of obligations and rules and complications.

Like not even being able to watch stilt fighters outside a cathedral in a small Belgian town without people wanting him to sign their boobs.

"What do you do for Christmas?" I ask him suddenly, because I want to know. I want to know who the man is underneath the rock god façade.

"Sometimes Jenny," he says, "but more often Monique."

I gasp, and he tips his head back and laughs.

"That was terrible," I tell him. Primly. Like Old Frumpy Willow. "If you're going to go for shock factor, at least say you do them both together."

There.

That's better.

Curtains move in one of the windows of the farmhouse, and Sister Honey peeks out. I poke Dax. "You need to be more quiet. You're keeping the Sisters up."

"They're just making sure I'm not destroying your virtue."

That was probably accurate. "You know my virtue is already gone."

He makes a strangled noise, like he's thinking unflattering things about my sex life. Which is probably unfortunately fair, all things considered.

"Christmas, hm?" he says.

"Unless you'd rather talk about my virtue."

"I hang with my pop back home near Corpus Christi. Edison and Danger usually come with their families. We all grew up together."

"None of your ex-wives join you?"

"Never been married over Christmas, don't have anything to do with them now."

"Why'd you marry them?"

"Alcohol, blackmail, and bad career advice."

I don't think he's lying, and my heart squeezes.

He leans back on the blanket next to me. Our arms are still touching. Our thighs still touching. "What do you do for Christmas?" he asks me.

"I don't know."

He twists his head away from the spectacular view of the Milky Way to peer at me. "Are you sure you've never been married? Because two of mine were because I didn't remember how I spent a weekend."

"I *remember*," I clarify. "I just don't have anything I *always* do. Not since I was a kid when Mom would give me Christmas pajamas on Christmas Eve, and then Santa would bring something small Christmas morning. Since she married the king, sometimes I'll go to Stölland and sometimes Martin would go with me, or sometimes I'd stay in the States and go to his family's dinner."

"Is the dickwad's family Christmas as horrific as I'm picturing it?"

"Worse, probably. One year we spent the whole day searching the house for some crystal piece his mother was convinced the maid had stolen. Dinner was cold, Mr. Vanderweilie abandoned us all and went to the office, the dog was so worked up that he peed all over the Christmas tree, and when we finally found the vase, it was under Mrs. Vanderweilie's bathroom sink, holding a toilet brush, where she'd staged it so the maid *wouldn't* steal it, but so she'd know who to blame because no one else in the house would dare to touch a toilet brush."

I can't make out his expression in the dark, but I don't think it's complimentary. "You voluntarily almost married into that."

Not a question. No, more a statement judging my mental stability.

"At least I would've gotten his name right when I said my vows."

Dax laughs again, a lighthearted, no-offense-taken laugh. Because the tabloids were all over the video of his second wedding, when he drunkenly called his new bride *Chandra* even though her name was *Joy*. "Touché, princess."

I sigh and study the stars. They're endless. Glitter spilled over a black canvas. I never see the stars like this in the city. "You know what I regret the most?"

"The day you met him?"

"That I never fucked with his mother." I slap a hand over my mouth while Dax laughs softly. This is *not* going to be a fun habit to break when I go back to work. Also, I wish Sia and Parker and Eloise were here, because they'd be laughing their asses off.

Yes, their *asses*.

I enjoy a good round of profanity, and after stifling it for so long, I'm never entirely certain how long the words will slip out.

Or how often.

"You could fuck with her now," he says. "Didn't you say your friend could hack any home security system?"

"Oh my gosh, Eloise would *die*. With sheer happiness, I mean. I didn't know until a few weeks ago about the hacking, but I kinda suspected she was dangerous, so I threatened to tell my stepbrothers she has crabs if she ever intentionally attacked Martin's family. Not that that would be the only reason the princes would all refuse to sleep with her, but she doesn't need to know that."

He's laughing again.

"I really do love Eloise," I say quickly. "I hope it doesn't sound like I don't. But she's so…so…"

"Wild and free?"

"*Yes*. She's my hero. She's so fucking fearless and she just says what she wants and I want that. I want to be able to say things and not lose my job or the respect of my friends and family."

"Princess, if anyone doesn't appreciate your true opinions and desires, fuck 'em."

"I've done that for the last seven years. I'd rather fuck someone who *does* appreciate me."

An electric charge ripples between us. He rolls to face me. "I'm starting to appreciate you."

I have to swallow hard before I can answer, because my mouth has gone dry and my lungs are getting tight. "You're only saying that because you know the nuns won't sleep with you."

"Sister Mary Knits-a-lot *is* hot."

I laugh so hard I accidentally snort. A cow moos somewhere in the distance, which prompts more mooing, like it's a midnight moo fest.

His fingers brush my lips, and my laughter catches in my throat.

"You're hot when you laugh," he murmurs.

I've never been *hot*. I wrinkle my nose and push his fingers away, even though they're making my lips tingle in a delicious kind of way, just like his backrub did for me in the van. "Honesty will get you farther than flattery."

"That *was* honesty."

If it weren't for the hint of offense in his voice, I'd scoff again. "Seriously."

"These lips? That laugh? Your voice? Yeah. You're fucking lava."

"M-my voice? You hate my voice."

"Who the fuck told you that?"

"*You* did. Every time I sing, you—you—"

"Get fucking pissed because there's no way I could talk you into a studio with me."

I suck in a surprised breath.

"I get so hard I want to rip your clothes off, lick you from head to toe, and make you hit notes so high you shatter glass."

Arousal surges hard and heavy between my legs. "Is that why you won't sing with me?" Talking has never been so strained, and I don't know where the sexy, husky kitten voice is coming from, but he's stroking my hip now, and even though there's a layer of denim between his fingers and my skin, I don't want him to stop.

Ever.

"I don't sing because you'd put me to fucking shame, and I'd never be able to get on stage again without feeling like a fraud. Because I don't deserve to sing with you. Because I'm fucking *lost* and my band's falling apart and my best friend is missing and I haven't had anything to sing *about*."

I touch hesitant fingers to his chest.

The last time we were here, he left me panting and desperate for more.

But he's different tonight. Something changed today. And he didn't mention his money.

Which is probably the only thing he thought he could control.

I would've gone after Martin too if I were in his shoes, because he knew where Martin would be, he knew Martin had what he wanted, and because Martin's a push-over.

"You're not lost," I whisper. "You're on a farm."

He freezes for a split second before he snorts. "You're insane."

The accusation has no heat or scorn. If anything, it's admiration. "No one else would believe you if you told them I was crazy. I have a pristine reputation."

"Maybe so, but you have terrible taste in songs. 'Ninety-Nine Bottles of Beer?'"

I'm laughing now too while our noses inch closer together. "I didn't hear you suggesting anything better."

"I was trying to get a high off Sister Mary Biceps's perfume."

"Was it working?"

"No, dammit. She wasn't wearing any."

I'm still giggling when his lips touch mine, but the laughter fades into desperate whimpers when he strokes his tongue past my lips and into my mouth.

I'm going to do this.

I'm going to sleep with Dax Gallagher. And I'm not going to worry about if I'm not very good, or if he's only doing this because I'm here and convenient. I'm going to do this because I don't want to be afraid to *live* anymore.

His stubble scratches the delicate skin around my mouth, his fingers dig into my hip, and his tongue gives no mercy. He kisses me like he intends to ruin me, to put all other kisses to shame, to set a new standard for every man I ever meet for the rest of my life.

He's already recalibrating everything between my legs. I've never been so wet so fast in my life, and I've never felt so thrilled and so empty and so excited for sex *ever*.

I pull him down, on top of me, and when he shifts his body over my other hip, I gasp.

My tattoo. It's still tender.

"Spread your legs, baby," he says. "I'll make it all better."

He doesn't have to ask twice.

I part my legs, and he moves off my tattoo and settles between my thighs, his hard length nestling between us. My clit swells hot and needy, and my pulse is pounding deep in my core.

He grinds his pelvis against mine, and my eyes cross.

"Oh my gosh, are the nuns watching?"

"No," he lies.

"*Dax!*"

"We'll be quiet. And they can't really see us in the dark anyway." He punctuates his statement by grazing my earlobe with his teeth. His stubble scratches my neck, and pinpricks rocket over my skin. My nipples tighten, my center throbs, and I lift my head and nip at his shoulder.

"*Fuck*, that's good," he gasps in my ear.

"Is it?" I whisper.

He answers by pulling at the collar of my shirt, exposing my shoulder, and nipping at my skin beside my bra strap. He licks away the sting, and the mix of sensations makes me arch my back off the ground.

"Okay, yeah, that's good," I pant.

"I want to rip your shirt off and suck on your titties until you can't remember your name."

Is it possible to orgasm because of words alone? "You talk so dirty."

"Wait until I tell you I want to fuck your pussy with my mouth."

I gasp.

Not because his words are scandalously shocking—my day job might be squeaky clean, but my friends are *not*—but because the idea of him going down on me is such a turn-on. A hardcore jolt of desperate desire arrows straight to my *pussy*.

"And then I'm going to fuck you with my fingers until you come so hard you can't talk, can't breathe, can't think."

I wrap my legs around his hips and jerk against his hard length. "P-prove it."

His hand cups my breast, and he rubs a circle around my nipple. "And then I'm going to feed you a cheeseburger," he growls.

I laugh, and the tightening of my abs pulls at my core.

"Are you wet?" he asks.

"Y-yes."

"And hungry?"

I'm suddenly picturing myself sucking on his cock, and the idea of sucking him deep in my throat makes everything squeeze and clench inside me. "Yes."

"What do you want, Willow?"

"I want—you—to f-fuck me." A surge of power flows through my body. "I want you to fuck me until I can't walk," I whisper.

"*Fuck*, princess," he growls against my neck. "That mouth was made to talk dirty."

I squirm under him, because I have too many clothes on. "Take my shirt off," I order. "*Now*."

His teeth flash in the darkness.

He's amused.

"Yes, ma'am," he says, and a hint at a slow Southern drawl makes my panties melt harder. He shimmies down my body, pushes my shirt up, and he nips and sucks and licks my stomach as he inches the fabric up past my breasts. I'm gasping and twisting into his hands, his mouth, because my nerve endings are lit up like the 4th of July, and I don't want him to stop.

Ever.

He traces the edges of my B-cups, and I strain up into his touch.

When his lips pull at my nipple through the thin cotton, I grip his hair, and I offer him more.

I can't believe I missed out on sex like this for *seven years*.

And I'm still mostly dressed. "Oh my gosh, don't stop, don't ever stop."

"Quiet, princess." He pushes my shirt up to cover my mouth, and I giggle.

Until he sucks on my breast again, and then I'm back to moaning.

He rolls my other nipple between his fingers, and I try to hump his stomach. "If you leave me hanging again I'm going to fucking kill you," I grit out.

He chuckles.

It's a devious, terrible chuckle, and it makes the party between my thighs rage harder. My hips are jerking, but they're not finding satisfaction, no matter the bolts of pleasure radiating from my breasts to my very center.

My ankles are hooked behind his back, and I'm not close enough to his body. I yank my shirt over my head and toss it away, and when I lift my shoulders, he pulls a slick move, sliding his hand around my bra and releasing the clasp.

He stops me before I can yank the straps down. "Mine," he says.

His fingertips are rough, but his touch is gentle while he pushes the straps off my shoulders. He glides them down my arms, the pads of his fingers leaving a trail of goosebumps and eager flesh.

I'm a desperate, horny, needy ball of lust.

And I'm completely okay with this.

Unless he leaves me moments before orgasm again. Then I might see if I can get those mooing cows to stomp the ever-loving shit out of him.

But he doesn't leave. He presses kisses to my fingertips when he pulls my bra strap off, and then repeats the erotic touch on my other arm. "Your skin is fucking delicious," he growls. My nipples harden when the cool air touches them, but then Dax's mouth is back, covering me, his tongue flicking expertly to spiral me to new, desperate heights.

"More, yes, *there*," I chant, my voice a breathy whisper, high and uneven.

I don't recognize myself.

And it's glorious. "Dax...touch me. Touch my pussy."

He shifts to slide his hand between my legs, pops my button one-handed, and snakes his fingers inside my panties.

"Oh yes, *oh yes*," I whisper. I arch into his touch, his fingers brush my clit, over my seam, dip inside me, and that's all it takes.

My inner walls clench, I squeeze my thighs together, holding his hand hostage while waves of pleasure clamp around his fingers. He thrusts them deeper. "More, princess. Give me more," he orders.

I shudder. He crooks a finger, and *ohmydearheavens.*

Stars explode behind my eyelids. The skies part, and a boy band launches into a jazzed up version of "I Wanna Sex You Up." With trumpets. And saxophones.

And Dax's hard body. His dragon tattoos roaring.

And I'm coming hard and deep, my toes curling, my breasts tingling, my walls squeezing.

He lowers his head to lick my nipple again, and my body gives one last long, deep, clenching shudder before I drop my head back to the ground.

And my legs.

And my arms.

"Oma wowza," I gasp.

Dax is grinning. I think. "Good?"

"Mmm-uh."

Later—after sleep, because I think I could be lying on a bed of nails right now and pass out cold—I might stop to think about if this was so incredible because he's the first new man to touch me in seven years.

If this is about freedom and stepping out of my shell.

Or if he's just that amazing with knowing how to touch me.

"Willow?"

A soft, gritty whisper. His voice makes my clit pulse again.

"Mm?"

"Are you—"

I don't hear the rest.

Because I'm drifting off into a dead sleep.

24

*D*AX

I'M HARD AS DIAMOND, and Willow's snoring.

Passed out cold to the world, her body so limp I could probably lift her hand and drop it and she wouldn't notice.

I'm stiff and aching, but I don't mind the way I used to when Erica, ex-wife number three, aka the blackmailer whom I finally got the upper hand with, pulled the get-off-and-pass-out routine.

Probably because Willow didn't wear herself out spending my money and bitching about my friends all day, but instead tried to save me from a band of stilt fighters.

I lift myself off her and settle on my side, hand over her bare belly, feeling it rise and fall with each breath. My feet hang off the blanket, the grass tickling my toes. Her feminine scent adds a layer of perfection to the clear, cool night.

Those gasps, her cries, her hot pussy clenching my fingers—does she have a fraction of a clue how fucking sexy she is?

It's almost impossible to not rub my aching cock against her leg.

This is what she's brought me to.

Wanting to hump her leg while she sleeps.

I won't. I do unfasten my button and yank down the zipper to give myself some breathing room though. There's a lot wrong with me, but I'm not a sick fuck who gets off on sleeping women. Still, I can't remember ever aching so bad.

For the craziest woman on the planet.

She's not my normal kind of crazy. My normal crazy is *does this dress make my ass look big, I'm only in this for what you can give me, if you fucking look at another woman I'll cut a bitch* kind of crazy.

Willow—she's *living* crazy.

She's *find the joy* crazy.

She's *just woke up* crazy.

And she's fucking *magic*.

A truck motors up the long driveway. I reach across Willow and cover her with the blanket, just in case.

As I'm tucking her tight, she curls into me and murmurs, "Good donkey."

I choke on a laugh, because I can't help it.

She snuffles and bolts upright. "Wha—who—*oh my gosh*, that was delicious."

Lights flash over her bare skin, she shrieks, and she drops flat with another shriek.

"Shh," I tell her, pulling the blanket across her again. "Nothing he hasn't seen before, princess."

"But it's still *mine*," she replies. "And it's up to me who sees it."

The truck stops and the engine rumbles down to silence, leaving us with only night insects keeping us company.

The night insects, and her soft breathing.

"Do I get to see it?" I ask.

"Tonight?"

"Tonight, tomorrow, this weekend, several times in between…"

Her fingers find my chest, and did I say I was hard as diamond?

Now I'm hard enough to crack diamonds.

"This isn't real," she whispers.

But her fingers trace lower on my chest, swirling, teasing, tickling, making my skin ache for her everywhere and my cock throb like it'll never know relief again.

"Feels fucking real," I grit out.

"I was supposed to marry someone a few days ago."

"But you didn't."

"And we both have to get back to our real lives eventually."

"You're talking too much, princess."

"Shush. This isn't easy. I don't—I don't do short-term flings with guys. But I want to do…" her fingers crest over my navel and head for the promised land "…you."

"No objections here."

"Right. This is normal for you."

There's no judgment in her voice—just a simple fact—but the statement hits me in the gut.

Not for long, though, because Willow's fist grips my cock through my boxers, and her touch is suddenly the only thing that matters. "*Fuck*, you're good at that."

She squeezes lightly and pumps me once. "This is good?"

"*Yes*." I'm kissing her before I realize I've moved, thrusting into her hand, covering the small mounds of her breasts and teasing her nipple with my thumb.

She has the world's most perfect nipples set in soft pillows of pashmina. The bumps of her ribs worry me, but she squeezes my cock again, and nothing else matters beyond touching.

Tasting.

Worshipping.

I lower my mouth to her breasts and lick her areolas. Her gasps and moans are better than any music I've ever made, that soft whimper, the plea for *more*, the catch in her breath—she's a melody that will haunt me to my dying day.

"Can I—lick—you?" she asks.

Fuck me, those words have never been more erotic. "Darlin', you can do anything you want to me."

She stills. "Like handcuffs?" she whispers.

My cock throbs, and her head dips down like she's looking at it. "Oh," she says with a giggle, "you like that idea?"

"Not usually."

"But you do tonight."

Letting this woman use my body as her playground?

I've never trusted *any* woman to tie me up and have her way with me.

But Willow—I trust her.

I didn't mean to. When she put *Trust Willow* on my bucket list, I actively intended not to trust her.

But I can't seem to help myself. She's—she's different. An odd mix of worldly and innocent and kindheartedness, and I do. I trust her.

It's fucking terrifying.

"Somebody needs to teach you how to use them right." My voice is husky and jagged in my own ears. She pushes me onto my back and straddles me while she leans over and grabs her bag.

"But," I add, "you have to catch me first."

She jerks back to me, but I'm not going far.

Not when I have the opportunity to explore her breasts. I grip her by the waist and lick a trail between them, her skin quivering under my tongue while she tightens her legs and grips my hair. Cold metal bops my shoulder.

"Oh, *g-god*, Dax, touch me," she says while she holds my head to her breasts, guiding me to her neck.

"I am touching you, princess."

I suck at the sweet spot below her ear, and she gasps. "T-touch my b-breasts."

"Manners," I chide. I add a nip at the straining tendon in her neck, and the way she squeezes her legs around me makes me so fucking close to coming my knees are shaking.

And I'm sitting on the ground.

"I want you to fucking pinch my nipples," she orders.

My hands slide up her sides to roll her nipples between my thumbs and forefingers. Even if I wanted to deny her, my body betrays me.

"Oh, yes, *yes*, Dax, *harder*."

My pulse is racing. My cock is straining. She's kissing my ear, scratching my scalp, snapping a cuff on my—

I jerk my hands away, but *fuck*, she's fast.

And I'm cuffed.

Both wrists.

She's breathing fast, her laugh triumphant.

But she doesn't laugh long.

She's too busy tilting my head up, lowering her lips to mine, and claiming my mouth.

Carefree. Wild. Eager.

Sucking on my lips, teasing my tongue, licking into my mouth.

Completely in control.

I fucking hate giving up control.

But when she breaks the kiss to lift my arms over our heads while she pushes me once again to my back, I don't give two fucks about being in control.

"Stay," she orders.

"Yes, ma'am."

She trails her fingers lightly down the length of my arms, wrists to shoulders. Her touch is feather-light, and my skin hums with craving more.

This isn't normal.

Usually my dick wants more, and that's it.

Women don't fuck me for *me*. They fuck me for *them*.

She rolls her hands over my shoulders, and I strain into her touch. My wrists jerk at the metal binding them.

"If you—if you need me to let you out—just tell me, okay?"

Christ.

She's trying to take care of *me*.

"There's no fucking way I want out."

Her hands drift lower, scraping my chest. When her fingernails rake my nipples, I buck against her, because my dick's about to blow.

"Not even if it means the sisters find you naked and cuffed to a tree in the morning?" she asks.

"Bring it, baby doll."

She giggles. It should be annoying, all the giggling, but with her, it works. She's an intoxicating mix of innocent and pervy, and I like it.

"I want to lick you," she whispers.

"I'm at your mercy." *Fuck*, I am. Completely and wholly at her mercy.

And that's before she dips her tongue to my chest and flicks it over my nipple. My hips buck off the blanket.

She scratches my other nipple while she flicks her tongue over the first again.

All the stars overhead swirl into a giant orb of light, and I have to recite the preamble to the Constitution in my head to keep from blowing my load.

"I'm going to take your pants off," she informs me.

"Thank fuck."

"Do you have protection?"

"Wallet."

She can steal my ID, my credit card, the four bucks in change I have in there, and I won't give a fuck. She could feed them to the cows for all I care.

She slides down my body and pulls at the waistband of my open jeans.

I lift my hips, she peels the fabric away, and my boner bounces free in the cool air.

"Oh," she whispers. "I think you've gotten even bigger."

Her fingers grip my bare cock and stroke, and I groan, because—

"Holy fuck, that's—"

Before I can finish, she bends and licks my head. Swirls her tongue around it, leaving a wet trail around the tip of my cock.

"Willow," I grunt.

"Is that not right?" she whispers.

"It's so fucking good I'm going to come all over your face if you don't stop," I grind out.

"Oh," she whispers. "Then I guess I should get naked before you're done."

Before I can protest that I can get myself back under control, she rises, with the Milky Way as a backdrop, and I watch her profile while she shimmies out of her jeans.

I have to swallow twice to get enough moisture back in my mouth to talk. "Or you could sit on my face," I offer.

"Oh my gosh, I couldn't do that to you."

I freeze. Because that translates to *no one's ever made that offer to me before*, and that's just fucking *wrong*.

"Oh, princess, I'm going to have to insist," I growl.

She's digging for something on the ground. I recognize the sound of foil being ripped, and then her hands are on my cock again, and everything else is forgotten. "You shush. I'm in charge."

"And you need a proper eating out."

"That sounds so deliciously dirty."

"It is, princess, and you're going to—" My words freeze, because she's cupping my balls. My eyes cross. The Milky Way becomes three different galaxies, all of them shaped like Willow's pussy.

"That's better," she murmurs, and I realize I'm making desperate gasping noises and pumping my dick into her touch.

This isn't normal. This is—

Magic.

Magic with a sweet melody and a heavy bass beat and a desperate crescendo building in my gut, spilling over into my chest and crashing through all the roadblocks and walls I've had up since I sold my soul to spend my life making music.

She slides the condom down my thick, heavy length. "I'm going to fuck you now," she whispers.

That sweet mouth. Those dirty words.

She pushes my hands back over my head while she hovers over me. "Stay," she orders.

"I want to touch your wet pussy," I growl. She pushes harder on my hands, pinning them to the ground, while she hovers over me, her center grazing the tip of my straining dick.

"I get so wet when you say *pussy*," she whispers.

"*Fuck*, I want inside you."

"Like this?" She lowers herself onto me, tight and hot, already squeezing my cock with her tight channel even though she's barely taken in my head. "Oh my god," she moans softly. "You're so big."

"More, princess." I'm not smooth, not in control. I'm bucking up into her, craving her, craving something deeper, something *more*. "I need to feel your pussy squeezing my dick."

"Tell me—you want—to fuck me," she gasps.

"I want to fuck you," I grind out. I pump up, and she presses down, taking all of me inside her. We thrust together, wild, reckless, desperate. "I want to fuck you until you can't breathe. I want to fuck you with my tongue. I want to suck on your sweet little clit. I want to fuck you with my fingers until I've memorized the feel of every inch of your pussy. I want to shove my cock so far up inside you that you see fucking stars and never come again without thinking my name."

"Dax," she gasps. Skin slaps skin while she rides me, my cock burying deeper and deeper with every thrust. She's still pinning my arms to the ground, her breasts hovering just out of reach of my mouth. She rises until she's almost pulled all the way off my cock, then pumps down, deeper and harder, faster—

"Oh god, *there*," she whimpers. She's jerking against me, squeezing me so tight I can't hold out much longer. She lifts her hips and slides back down onto me. "*There*, Dax, *oh*, that's the spot *right there*."

"Come, Willow," I order, She's so fucking tight, so fucking *good*, so fucking *right*. "Come for me *now*, princess."

She lifts her hips, slams down onto me once more, and this time, she presses hard against my pelvis while she arches her head back and cries my name once more. "*Dax*. Oh, god, Dax, *I'm coming*."

Her pussy clenches impossibly tighter around me, and I'm exploding too.

The heavens open, and fucking angels sing.

My cock pulses, spilling everything I have and more. Wave after desperate wave of release shoots out of me while I clench my ass and push as deep as I can go inside her.

I can't get deep enough.

Can't get close enough.

I want more.

So fucking much more.

She collapses on top of me while my cock's shooting off its last fireworks. Without her holding my arms down, I wrap her in a tight hug.

As much as I can while I'm still cuffed.

"*Wow*." Her breath is coming quick, and the feel of her chest pressing into mine is making my cock ache with the desperate need to get hard, *now*, fast, *again*. "That was…"

"Fucking fantastic." I press a kiss to her hair.

"Freeing," she whispers.

My heart freezes.

Right.

This *isn't* about me.

She kisses my shoulder. "I know I'm not supposed to get attached, but you're making that very difficult."

She sounds sleepy. Like one more good orgasm is going to knock her out again.

While I'm still cuffed.

I snort.

"Mm?" she lifts her head. "Sorry. Right. I'll get off you."

We get tangled, because I can't just lift one arm. And soon, even though I know I'm only a tool on her journey, she's on her back, holding my hair while I kiss her mouth.

Her neck.

Her breasts.

Her belly.

"*Dax*," she gasps when my mouth reaches her center.

I'm still cuffed.

But that doesn't stop me from making her come one more time.

And I love every fucking minute of licking her dry.

25

Dax

A COW FINDS us sometime in the middle of the night. It doesn't make a lot of noise, just settles to the ground and rubs its soft fur and thick body against my arm while it gets comfortable. I wake enough to realize if the damn thing rolls over, it'll crush both of us, so I nudge Willow to her other side and spoon her, pulling one of the blankets around her body.

Good thing she let me out of the handcuffs after that fourth orgasm.

Not that I mind being chained by Willow.

She murmurs softly in her sleep, crickets chirp, the night breeze carries in the scent of cow and grain, and the next thing I know, Sister Mary Biceps is standing over us.

And she's not alone.

"Is this him?" she asks a tall figure in black.

"Yep," a very familiar voice answers. "Lookin' just as shitty as he did the last time I saw him too." A boot kicks my foot. "Hope this one isn't a witch, jackass."

My eyes fly open. I jerk up, remember we're both naked, try to cover Willow, and—

She's gone.

"Where's Willow?" She's not on the ground. Not tangled in the blankets. Not where I left her.

Fuck me.

She's probably found a traveling circus to take her skydiving strapped to a pig or something.

"The skinny brunette?" Edison says. "She darted for the house about the time she saw us coming."

Edison.

"What the *fuck* are you doing here?" I try to scramble up, but I trip over the fucking cow that's moved to my feet. It moos indignantly, and Edison coughs.

I remember I'm naked and hope to fuck Willow was able to get her clothes on before Edison got much of a show.

Once I have the blanket around my waist, I finally make it to my feet and grab my buddy in a one-armed hug.

Forget the manly man-hug shit.

I hug him like I missed him, because I did. Edison, Danger, Oliver, and Cain—they're family.

"You okay?" he asks me gruffly.

"Yeah."

I pull away and slap him on the back. "What the fuck are you doing here?"

"What the fuck do you think?"

The nuns' van is sitting in the farmhouse driveway, and behind it is another blocky European van. Taller. Longer. Not tour bus size, but almost guaranteed to have bunks and a stocked mini-fridge. I wonder if it's a short-term rental, or if we're headed out on a mission.

"Any word from Danger?"

He flinches and drops his dark gaze to the lush grass. "Not yet."

I rub my neck and look away, counting the thick old trees in the farmer's front yard so I don't have to look at Edison and see the fear etched in his face.

Danger can't be gone.

But no one's heard from him in nine—no, ten days now.

"Brought Biscuit and your old man," Edison says. "Not that they gave me any choice in the matter."

I straighten. "Pop's here?"

"Making friends with the nuns." Edison glances at me, and an honest grin splits his features. "Nuns. Only you, Gallagher. You defile one last night, or was that—"

I cut him off with a jab to the chest. "Shut up, dickhead. How'd you find me?"

"You mean after your cell signal went dead?" He jerks his head at the group of people coming around the corner of the picturesque farmhouse. "Long story. Short of it is, we were tracking your new girlfriend too."

"She's not—"

"You're gonna shut your mouth when you're talking to me, and you're gonna do it right now, because I know who she is, and I know what you did, and I'm gonna kick your ass later when all these lovely ladies of God aren't watching."

I grab him in another hug.

Because I'm so fucking glad to see him, I don't care how much he kicks my ass.

I let him go when I realize who's coming with the nuns.

"Fuck," I mutter.

"He's worried about you, and he doesn't care what kind of shit you got into over here." Edison punches me back in the shoulder. "Don't be a jackass."

I'm more worried about the sting behind my eyeballs.

My pop's surrounded by the sisters. Sister Mary Knits-a-lot is chewing his ear off, and judging by the bewildered expression on his face, she's talking about the handcuffs. Pop's not an idiot—he knows I've done some crazy shit he doesn't want to know about on tour, and he knows I've slept with too many women—fuck, by my third wedding three years ago, he quit asking questions—but that doesn't mean either of us want to share details.

I don't want to know much about his longstanding relationship with Widow McGuire back home either.

But it damn well better not involve handcuffs.

Willow's not with the group.

Which makes greeting Pop easier, even if it's awkward doing it while wearing just a blanket around my waist. Because it's going to be simpler to explain the nudity and the nuns than it is to explain Willow. Who's probably going to be riding the rest of the way to Paris with the nuns anyway.

And I don't like that thought a single fucking bit.

For a variety of reasons.

Not the least of which is that I'm not done with whatever this thing is between us. Road trip fling? Stress relief? Reluctant friends with benefits?

I don't know.

But I know that nothing's felt so *right* as last night did.

And not just the fucking.

The talking. The sleeping. The cuddling.

Fucking *cuddling*.

Whatever this is between us, it's not normal.

My father stops a foot from me and eyes my blanket. I lift my free hand in a small greeting. "Pop."

I barely get the syllable out before he's crushing me in a hug.

He might be pushing seventy, but he's still strong as an ox and sharp as a tack.

It's just his hands that are giving out.

Fucking arthritis.

"Like to give an old man heart attacks, don't you?" he says.

His voice is choked, and I have to swallow twice before I can answer. "Just taking care of some business."

"Don't have to do it alone, you stubborn old mule." He pulls back, glances at the cow, who's now on her feet, then the nuns, and he gives me a rueful smile. "Though it looks like you picked some damn fine company."

"That I did," I agree.

"You have to do it naked?" Pop asks.

"Seems so."

"You're fucking insane," Edison mutters.

"You don't know the half of it."

A flock of chickens races around the house, squawking and darting and running into each other. Some of them try to fly.

Most of them are chasing a tall, slender, dark-haired vixen who's shrieking and tripping over her biker boots while she's trying to get away.

Huh.

Would've thought chickens would love Willow. Doesn't everything love Willow? Strangers, donkeys, men on stilts.

Me.

Fuck.

"What in the holy name of all hell is that woman doing to those chickens?" Pop asks.

"She better not fucking be another witch," Edison growls.

The cow snorts and ambles slowly toward the ruckus.

And I couldn't stop the grin spreading over my face for anything.

"Everything okay, princess?" I call.

She flips me a double bird.

Willow.

Flips me a double bird.

I double over laughing at the shock of seeing her two middle fingers waving while half the nuns gasp and half of them cross themselves. "We'll be taking her under our wing," Sister Mary Biceps informs me.

"Think she's already got too many wings," I reply. *I'm* laughing so hard I'm crying.

She flipped me off.

"Jesus Christ," Edison mutters.

Pop slaps him upside the head, gnarled knuckles and all. "Mind your manners around the nuns, boy, or I'll be talking to your parents."

Willow finally escapes the chickens. She's coated in feathers and keeps casting furtive glances to where the cow's attempting to corral the birds.

Or maybe it's just trying to be a bovine playground. It's hard to tell.

"Oh my gosh, you're Edison Rogers," Willow gasps as she finally reaches our group. "*Please* tell me Martin didn't steal all your money too. Do you have your guitar—ah. Never mind. Right. Your finger. I'm so sorry. I hope the reattachment was successful, because—"

I finally get myself under control and hook an arm around her neck. "Willow. Cut it out."

She shoves me, but not a quick *get off me* shove. This shove has some lingering *I don't want to quit touching you* to it. "Go put your clothes on. You're scandalizing poor Sister Violetta."

"This one's as bossy as number two," Pop mutters to Edison.

"So long as she doesn't practice black magic, I don't give a fuck," Edison replies. "And number two never made him laugh like that. I don't like it."

Willow grabs my pile of clothes, shoves them at my chest, and gives me the look of *you're going in timeout if you don't go get dressed.*

So I drop the blanket and start getting dressed.

Her cheeks go pink.

Half the nuns cross themselves.

Edison heaves a long-suffering sigh.

And Willow turns to Pop. "Oh my gosh. You're—oh wow, are you Dax's brother? He didn't tell me he had a brother. I'm Willow. Dax and I met under some…interesting circumstances."

Pop studies her carefully before taking her hand. "You're a flatterer, aren't you?"

She smiles at him. "People always say that to my mom, and she loves it."

He shakes her hand, but he's giving her the Chuck Willie Gallagher squint of suspicion. "You're a momma's girl?"

"She raised me. But since she got married a few years ago, we don't get to hang out quite as much. She's happy though, and that's what matters."

"You always get attacked by chickens?"

"Sheep sometimes. Rarely chickens."

"Mice and birds? Do they sing with you too?" Edison asks.

"Not like the cow did with Dax last night."

Edison finally cracks a grin. A reluctant grin, but a grin nonetheless.

Since I'm dressed again, I hook an arm around Willow's neck once more. "Funny. Real funny."

"We're behind schedule, ladies," Sister Mary Leadfoot announces. "And *I'm* driving, *with* the satellite GPS today, so we'll get there on time."

"Are you coming, Willow?" Sister Mary Sudoku asks her. "Or…?"

"You can come with us," I say. "We're headed to Paris too."

"No, we're not," Edison says.

I look at him sharply. "You have a lead on Danger?"

His eyes narrow. He doesn't, and that's not why he's saying no.

He's saying she can't come with us for all the reasons he should be saying she can't come with us.

She's Vanderweilie's ex. She's an unknown factor. She's gotten into my head.

But I don't give two fucks.

I'm not ready to let her go.

Plus, left to her own devices, with the questionable navigation skills of Sister Mary Biceps, Willow probably will try to BASE jump off the Eiffel Tower, or hitch a hot air balloon ride to Switzerland, or try to get all the way to Africa without a passport and money.

And if she's going to do all that, I fucking want to do it with her.

"We have somewhere else we have to be?" I ask.

"We're *not* doing this, Gallagher," Edison says quietly.

"We kinda have to. She's threatened me with both Berger twins popping my head off, and then letting her three Viking stepbrothers eat my entrails if I don't get her back to her mom in one piece."

Yeah, it's a stretch.

But only a small stretch.

"And how was it you found me again?" I add.

"Fuck."

"It was her friend, wasn't it?"

"Don't fucking like this," Edison mutters. Pop isn't looking too convinced either.

"Hey, princess, did you know it's Edison's birthday?" I say.

"It is?" She smiles broadly at him.

He's shaking his head. "My birthday's in—"

Before he can finish protesting that his birthday was three months ago, she's launched into "Happy Birthday." The nuns join in.

So does the cow.

By the time she's done, Edison's cursing me in his head. I've known him since we were six. I know where the scar on his temple came from. I know about the time his mom washed his mouth out with soap after he said *fuck* for the first time. And I know he didn't actually lose his virginity until he was twenty-two, despite the rumors in high school that his girlfriend started.

"Not a good reason," he mutters.

"She's my responsibility," I mutter back.

He punches me in the arm.

I probably deserve way more than that.

"Wanna see how rock stars travel, princess?" I ask Willow.

She studies me like she's trying to decide if I'm asking because I feel an obligation to keep her safe, or if it's because I want to be her friend, or if it's because I want to tie her up in the back of the bus and make her come six more times today.

The truth?

It's probably a combination of all three.

Which means Edison's right, and I should turn her care over to the nuns.

But I don't fucking want to.

"Do I get to make a guitar cry and to sign people's chests?" she asks.

Now Pop's eyeing me like I've lost my marbles too.

"Whatever you want, darlin'." I flash some good old-fashioned Texas charm at her—I'm feeling nostalgic for home with Pop being here—and offer a wink and a smile.

She rolls her eyes and huffs. "*Darlin'*?"

"Too much?"

"Too much. Especially with the sleazy wink. What do you think I am, one of your groupies? Pretty sure it's the other way around."

But there's a smile playing on her lips, like maybe, just maybe, she's forgiven me for kidnapping her and wouldn't mind hiding in one of those bunks later on.

Unless last night really was just about her bucket list.

That idea makes ice cubes settle in my chest. I shove it away, because really, what's she to me?

I've known her for five days.

Wading into dangerous territory here. I might do a lot of stupid shit, but it's never put my heart at risk.

"We have a fridge stocked with Belgian chocolate," I tell her.

"No, you don't."

"We probably do. Guarantee you Edison's brought some peanut butter cups."

Now I have her attention. "Are you serious?"

"They're his favorite."

"You also just said it's his birthday when it's not."

I open my mouth.

And close it.

She smiles broader. "But I've always wanted to sing for a rock star. So thank you for the chance."

"*I'm* a rock star."

She waves a hand. "You don't count anymore." Then she turns to Sister Mary Biceps. "Thank you so much for the ride yesterday."

"It was our pleasure, dear child," Sister Mary Biceps replies. "We're always happy to help lost sheep."

"We'd be honored to take you the rest of the way to Paris," Sister Mary Knits-a-lot adds.

Willow shakes her head, and then she tugs the ring off her left hand and presses it into Sister Mary Biceps's hand. "Can you please do me one last favor and find a good use for this?"

"Willow—"

"I grew up too poor to just throw a diamond ring away. Sell it and use it to help someone or pay for gas or *something*. Please?"

The nuns all surround her in a group hug, some still protesting, some thanking her for her generosity, some offering to pray for her.

Edison's watching with his chin dangling. "I don't want to know what you've done the last few days, do I?"

"Nope."

Willow breaks free about the time I sense Edison's ready to grab me and force me into the van without her. "I need to keep Dax in line," she says to the nuns, "and I'm not sure his dad and his friend are completely up to the task. They're jetlagged."

"Rock stars don't get jetlagged," Edison tells her.

"Oh, *pfft*. You'll be passed out in an hour."

I almost warn her off, because I know what's coming.

Edison's going to bet her. And he hates losing bets.

But she wants an adventure.

I'll let her have an adventure.

Bonus if it means I get another few hours in her company.

26

WILLOW

DAX WAS RIGHT.

They have peanut butter cups in the mini tour bus. And a little dinette. And coach chairs for looking out the front window at the scenery. And bunks in back.

I'm traveling with almost half of Half Cocked Heroes, *plus* Dax's dad. We're on our way to Paris. Edison Rogers keeps scowling at me. Dax keeps trying to make me eat more, but I know he's actually just looking for excuses to touch my elbow or talk to me, which is both thrilling and a little scary.

I was supposed to get married last weekend. To someone else. Who stole Dax's money.

Getting emotionally attached isn't smart.

And I'm not a good enough liar to convince myself that all I want from him is a few more rounds of insanely awesome sex.

So instead, I'm concentrating on the journey today. And the fact that their driver's name is Biscuit.

Biscuit Cooper-Jones.

Every day of this trip gets better and better.

"What's the weirdest thing you've ever seen on the road?" I ask Biscuit. I'm sitting behind him, munching on some cheese that's basically the best cheese I've ever had in my mouth, and I don't know if that's because Eloise was right about what multiple orgasms can do for your life, or if it's because rock stars can afford really high-end cheese, or if it's because Europeans just do cheese better, but whatever it is, I'm going to keep eating this cheese.

And then have more peanut butter cups.

It's a delicate sugar-to-protein balance.

And I'm probably going to keep accidentally letting my hands rest on Dax's thigh, or glancing at his tattoos, because I have no idea if they're going to just drop me in Paris and go on with whatever else they have to do, or if Dax will stick around when he finds out I want to look up skydiving companies and see if I can get a ride.

Biscuit points a finger at a passing yellow road sign that features what appears to be a toddler on his back. "See that there? That sign about not changing your baby's nappies on the side of the road?"

"Mm-hmm," I answer around a mouthful of cheese.

"That doesn't even come close to the weirdest shit we ever seen. Once we were in—where was it, Dax? Nebraska? Iowa? One of them midwestern states—and we passed a giant rubber duck riding a banana."

"Like a Bratwurst Wagon-size duck? Bigger? Smaller?"

"Way bigger," Dax says. He smirks. "And what do you know about the Bratwurst Wagon?"

"My friend Sia lost her virginity in one."

"She's not the only one," Dax says, jerking a head toward Edison, who throws a drumstick at his skull.

Dax easily ducks it, and his affectionate grin back at his friend makes my heart squeeze.

This isn't the same man I woke up handcuffed to on a fishing boat four days ago.

He still has the haggard look of a man worried about his friends, but whatever desperation drove him to Stölland seems to have lessened.

And I haven't even told him that Eloise texted with the news that she thinks Martin's uncle's company is stashing client funds at an offshore account in the Cayman Islands, and that Martin's cell phone seems to indicate he's somewhere in Europe too.

With cash.

Because his credit cards haven't been used at all, unless he has secret credit cards Eloise can't find.

She scares me sometimes.

"What about the time we almost missed our show in Denver because of that chocolate syrup spill?" Edison says.

"Or the time Oliver got all his clothes stolen when he disappeared with those women at the hookah bar?" Dax adds.

"All y'all's crazy," Biscuit says with a grin that clearly says he enjoys the heck out of being part of their crazy.

Dax's dad doesn't add anything, because he's nodding off at the little dinette table. He seems relieved to be back with Dax, which is making me worry about my mom.

I hope she's not freaking out about my trip.

Edison ambles to the seat on my other side, so I'm sandwiched between him and Dax. His finger's still wrapped in a bandage. I heard it was an accident with a fishing knife, but the more important part was that it means he can't play for weeks.

He's about Dax's height but bulkier, with dirty blond hair and dark brown eyes. He's in a light polo and cargo shorts where Dax is in a tight black T-shirt and jeans, but both men are shoeless.

They look at each other over my head and seem to have a silent conversation. Both their noses and lips are twitching, not to mention some serious eyebrow action going on.

"Are they always like this, or is it just for my entertainment?" I ask Biscuit.

"They're always up to no good," Biscuit replies.

Dax shoves another piece of cheese at me. "Eat. You're too skinny."

"Don't be talking 'bout women and their weight, man." Biscuit shakes his head while he steers the small bus onto a major highway. "Never ends well no matter what you think you're saying."

"Eat. Your body needs the energy," he corrects.

His gaze dips down my body. I flush. Not because I'm embarrassed, but apparently because my skin is just as reactive to his attention as other parts of me.

I probably should've ridden with the nuns.

But I wasn't ready to say goodbye.

I'm still not.

And though we didn't exactly have the "let's be fuck buddies for a few days and then go our separate ways" conversation, we both know that's exactly what last night was about.

"Bad idea, idiot," Edison mutters to Dax.

"Bad ideas are my entire game plan this week," I tell him.

"They'd be yours, too, if you'd just barely escaped marrying someone you weren't in love with."

"Bad ideas are the reason Dax has gotten married three times already," Edison replies.

Dax lifts a water bottle in a toast. "True story. Also the reason you—"

"So you sing," Edison says to me, cutting Dax off before he can get to what I suspect will be a juicy story.

I let him get away with it, because *he's Edison Rogers*. I saw a YouTube video of him once where he played *both* parts of "Dueling Banjos" *and* somehow took all the twang out of it to make it sound like a badass metal song.

"I'm in an all-girl boy band cover band. We play juice bars," I tell him.

His lips part.

"It's not exactly playing shirtless for thousands of women who want to have my babies, but we have fun," I add.

"You—"

"Yeah, she's for real." Dax squeezes my knee, and a flush creeps over my whole body at the note of pride in his voice. "Hard to believe, but she is."

"Do you know black magic?" Edison asks me.

"Is that a band?"

He looks at Dax again. I glance at Dax too.

No humor there now.

"Ever hire anyone to do any blackmail?" Edison continues.

Oh. I see. I'm getting The Questions. "I do occasionally refuse to let my preschoolers have cookies until they've put their toys away and washed their hands with soap and water. And once I threatened to light Eloise's hair on fire if she didn't quit tapping the beat to 'It's a Small World' during rehearsals."

"That's not blackmail."

"It's the best I've got. Did somebody curse you guys or something? Because Eloise said something about a witch the other day too."

More silent communications over my head. Edison finally looks away and pulls out of his seat, disappearing behind us.

I glance at Dax.

His hand drifts higher up my leg so that he's getting close to being able to touch my kitty with his thumb.

He doesn't say anything, but that simple gesture says he knows I'm not a witch.

I think.

Or possibly that he's glad I'm here.

Which is silly, because he has one of his best friends, a crew member he clearly cares about, and his dad here.

And I know they brought copies of his passport, so he's basically set.

He doesn't need me too. Eloise, maybe, but not me.

And honestly, after trying to be what Martin needed for so many years, I'm in no position to try to be some kind of savior for another man.

Especially one who knows this whatever-it-is between us ends when we go our separate ways.

"Ever thought about seeing the catacombs in Paris?" he asks me.

I sit straighter. "Are they creepy?"

"Probably."

"Did a witch curse you?"

"No."

"She cursed him good," Biscuit tells me. "He took her home, told her goodbye the next morning, and she put the hex on him. Next thing we know, the whole band's dropping like flies."

"Except you," Dax says dryly to his bus driver.

"Live a good life, got no reason to worry about hexes."

"Good karma's important," I agree. "That's why I try not to fucking cuss so much."

Biscuit hoots. Dax barks out a surprised laugh and squeezes my thigh. Edison sighs.

And Mr. Gallagher snorts himself awake with a *hmm?*

"Dax got himself good and cursed," Biscuit says. "Slept with the wrong woman, he did."

"Always does," Edison chimes in.

Dax tosses dirty socks at him. Edison throws back a closed cup of yogurt. The van bumps over something and lurches, Biscuit curses, and horns scream around us. Everything rattles and shakes, Dax flings an arm in front of me, bracing me against the seat while I grip his leg with one hand and the bottom edge of the seat with the other. Edison grabs the back of my seat while Biscuit white-knuckles the steering wheel and guides the small bus to the edge of the road.

When we stop, all four of the men are on their feet, hopping into shoes and heading out the door to inspect the damage.

"What's that you were saying about your karma?" I hear Dax say to Biscuit. The tension's back in his voice.

"You shut your trap, boy. We drove all the way from Amsterdam without a lick of trouble until *you* got in the bus."

Their voices fade, and I'm left alone inside.

I could go outside with them, but I've never owned an automobile in my life and I'd be one more person gaping at whatever's wrong.

Or, I can stay in here, and I can snoop through the bus on my own.

Which feels way more wrong than it would've four days ago.

So instead, after I take a quick peek outside to see the men all standing over some box that Biscuit apparently ran over, I text Eloise.

It's a good compromise.

Plus, she'll probably encourage the snooping.

Willow: Okay, dish on this witch thing, because Dax isn't telling.

Eloise: You want the *National Enquirer* version, or possibly the more official version gleaned through means you don't want to hear about?

Willow: Both. I love gossip.

Eloise: Girl, I am so proud of you. Okay. Here's the deal. The *National Enquirer* says Dax's mom was actually an alien love child of Bigfoot and that purple people-eater thing, and once he reached his thirty-fourth birthday, he was destined to be cursed until he fell in love.

Willow: Oh, I love a good cursing until you're cured by love. But I don't believe the alien thing.

Eloise: And here I thought you were making progress.

Willow: I slept naked under the stars last night.

Eloise: Cool. Did Dax's mom come visit from her home planet of Trimoridor?

Willow: Yes, and she blessed our secret love child too.

Eloise: I am so turned on right now.

Willow: I might be too if you tell me the real witch story.

Eloise: Liar.

Willow: Okay, fine. I'm really not into you that way, but I love you in so many other ways, and I might even one day name a baby something that starts with E in honor of you. As a middle name.

Eloise: Your middle name starts with E.

Willow: Total coincidence. Are you going to tell me, or do I need to tell Sia about the glitter you put in her shampoo bottle?

Eloise: Fine. I'll tell you. But only because I hate fuckers who pretend to be witches.

I wait...and I wait...and I wait...but Eloise doesn't text back. I peek out the door again. Edison's stomping down the road like he needs to cool off. Dax is pressing his palms into his eye sockets, his lips twitching. Biscuit's on the phone, talking loudly, which most likely means whoever's on the other end can't understand either English or his thick Southern accent. And Mr. Gallagher is squatting beside the front of the bus, reaching out with large, gnarled knuckles to brush his fingertips over what appears to be a hole over a blown tire.

There are long pink and purple rubber things scattered all over the ground, leading to a ripped box. That must've been what—

Oh. *Oh*!

I squelch a giggle.

We ran over a box of dildos.

We ran over a box of dildos.

Dax drops his hands and takes a knee next to his dad. He's snickering. The two of them point at the damage on the bus, two generations of Gallagher men tackling a problem together while they laugh about *running over a box of dildos*.

He glances up and catches me watching. "Know anything about changing tires?"

I shake my head.

His lips twitch harder. "Know anything about phallic litter?"

His dad shoves him, and he topples sideways onto three dildos. He rolls, grabs one, and holds it up to the light. "So this is what they settle for in France?"

It sparkles like there's glitter inside the silicone. Mr. Gallagher snags it from him and tosses it toward a crushed box. He glances at Dax, his eyes take on a small twinkle, and he shakes his head despite the grin forming at the edges of his lips. "Didn't I teach you not to wag your dildos at the ladies?"

"You did your best, old man."

They're adorable.

And I suddenly miss my mom.

Hardcore.

"C'mon, princess," Dax says to me. "Someone's gotta Cinderella this mess. Might as well be you."

Did he just—

He did.

Oh, he's going to pay for that.

I step out of the bus, bend down, and grab a thick purple dildo. "This mess?" I say.

His grin widens. "That mess. Hold still, darlin'. I need a picture." He reaches into his pocket like he's reaching for his phone—which isn't there, because it's charging inside the bus—and so I do exactly what Sia, and Eloise, and probably Parker would do in this situation.

I launch that dildo straight at his head.

27

DAX

TWO WEEKS AGO, if you'd told me I'd be having a dildo fight around a broken down bus on the side of the road outside Paris, I would've told you to get off the fucking drugs.

Instead, I'm leaning around the chewed-up wheel well, peeking out to see if Willow's about to throw anything, two pink sparkly dildos in hand, contemplating if I can add this to her bucket list for me just to mark it off.

I'd bet my last penny she's going to add it to her list.

My nose barely makes it past the safety of the van when a glittery purple schlong-rocket grazes my face.

"I got you!" Willow shrieks.

"Here, Miss Willow, I got you six more," Biscuit says. They're hunkered down at the back of the van, Biscuit refilling Willow's ammo, Edison camping out with them only because he says he doesn't want to be on my team, which really means he's still trying to figure out what Willow wants from me.

And I can't remember the last time I've laughed so hard.

Pop's shaking his head. "Back in my day, we just threw water condoms," he says. "Dildos were made of wood. Too hard to throw those suckers and left too much of a dent if they got you in the head. Not cheap and made in China either."

I lean out again, and a dildo bounces off the side of the bus.

"Gonna get us all arrested for indecent public exposure," Pop muses.

"You're in the clear. No dildos in your hands."

"I'm never in the clear with you," Pop says, but he's smiling that *good to see you happy, son*, smile, and I can't help smiling back.

"Thanks for coming, Pop."

"I'd come for you anywhere. You know that."

Of everyone in my life, yeah, I should know that. But I haven't been home enough the past few years. Been working too hard. Playing too hard.

Forgetting that I *do* have people who love me just for me and still would even if I were broke.

It's a small list—Pop, Edison and Danger—*fuck*, we need to find him—and Oliver and Cain.

And I'm broke.

But I don't feel so empty about it anymore.

I lean around the bus and toss a dildo. Willow shrieks with laughter. "Were you trying to hit a cow in the next county?"

"Does France even have counties?" I call back.

"You might as well just give up now. You're going to lose. Like you always do."

She probably has a point. And I don't actually mind. "Big talk for someone who ran out of clean underwear yesterday."

"None of us want to know how you know that," Edison yells.

The flashing lights and screeching siren of the French highway patrol interrupts us. And when I realize Willow's here without any ID or a passport, I drop my dildo bombs and head to the back of the bus.

This isn't going to be fun.

28

Here I am, standing on the side of the road outside Paris, clutching two dildos to my chest, ready to go to jail—I'll have to add that to my bucket list so I can scratch it off—when the most remarkable thing happens.

Edison produces a copy of the front page of my passport.

I gasp. "Where did you get that?"

He grunts while he hands it over to the gendarme. "I don't ever want to meet your friend. *Ever*. Understood? She's freaky."

"So, not even if she was a bridesmaid when me and Dax get married?"

All four men choke. Even the French policewoman gives me a lifted brow.

And I laugh so hard I have to lean against the bus. "Ohmygosh," I gasp. "Your faces."

"Shut up and get on the bus," Edison grumbles.

Maybe because it looks like we've started cleaning up the dildo mess, or maybe because it's clear the bus accident wasn't related to criminal activity, the gendarme lady dismisses me and Mr. Gallagher. Edison has some rudimentary French skills, so he's staying to translate. Dax is dismissed too, but he has this responsibility complex and insists on staying with his driver and bandmate.

"What's your story, darlin'?" Mr. Gallagher asks me while we gather more dildos, because let's be honest, I'm not going to sit in a bus when I could be helping, and apparently he isn't either.

"I'm a runaway bride gone wild," I tell him.

It's not exactly the truth. Or maybe it is. I guess we'll see how much of my newfound fearlessness sticks when we—when *I* get home.

I've been trying not to think about going home.

I'm not ready.

"You weren't fixin' to get hitched to my son, were you?"

"Nope. Just the guy who stole all his money. What about you? What's your story?"

He shoots me a look that clearly says I'm off my rocker, because his story is obviously that he's Dax Gallagher's dad, and he wouldn't be here picking up dildos off the side of the road if he hadn't come along to track Dax down.

But to my surprise, he actually answers the question.

"Fell in love with a firecracker of a girl long after I'd given up. Thought she loved me back, but two weeks after Dax was born, she took off to pursue some Hollywood dreams. Raised him up best I could, let him go when he was old enough, and now I just worry. Supposed to get easier when they get older, but it doesn't. Worries just get bigger."

I really need to call my mom. She's been pretty patient the last few days, but given how much I worried about her when she moved to Stölland, when I knew where she was and who she was with, I can only imagine how many antacids she must be popping now.

"You gettin' ideas about my boy?" Mr. Gallagher asks me as he piles more dildos into the box. I'd insist he should let me do it all— his hands look like they ache—but if he's anything like his son, he won't appreciate the thought.

Instead, I smile at him. "I've had lots of ideas, ranging from ringing his neck to hugging him"—and more—"and I've had a lot of fun the last few days, but we both have our real lives to get back to. He's been very kind to watch out for me. I don't get out in the world on my own like this very much."

He peers at me like he's deciding if I'm telling the truth or not.

I think I am.

But there's a part of me that knows my heart got a little attached under the stars last night.

As much as this trip is about breaking free, though, my heart isn't up for grabs. I was supposed to get married four days ago. I'm not going to fall for some rock star just because he gave me a few orgasms and showed me his soft underbelly.

Mr. Gallagher must decide he can trust me, because as we work, he tells me a few stories about messes Dax made when he was little. At school, at home, in Mr. Gallagher's workshop. He tells me about the first time Dax picked up a guitar, about the talent show where he sang "My Ding-a-Ling," and about when his dog went missing when he was thirteen.

I'm starting to get suspicious about Mr. Gallagher's intentions when Dax and Edison join us. "All good," Dax tells me. "Just have to wait on a tow."

"Called for another ride too," Edison adds. "So now we just wait. Nice job with the dildo pile. You could do this full-time."

"You're just jealous that you didn't get to touch all the rubber wieners," I reply with a sweet smile.

"At least she's different," Edison tells Dax, who's choking back a laugh once again.

He's going to be okay.

He has his family here now.

He disappears into the bus, and a minute later emerges with a guitar. "So now we wait," he says. "What was it you said your favorite song was, princess? Something boy bandish?"

"Fucking hell," Edison mutters.

Dax hits the guitar strings, and I instantly recognize the first chords of Hanson's "MMMBop." I clap my hands. Edison groans. And Dax starts laughing. "You know this one," he says.

I answer by launching into the first verse right on key.

And when we hit the chorus, Dax joins me.

Smiling. Laughing. The bad boy rock star playing fun boy band songs, staring into my eyes the entire time.

It's magic.

Perfection.

And it doesn't end after one song.

By the time the tow truck arrives, we've been singing for close to an hour, and we're causing a scene. Cars have pulled over. People are taping us on their phones, laughing at the crazy Americans rocking out to boy band songs. Even Edison and Biscuit and Mr. Gallagher have joined in.

We've done a kick line. I gave everyone a show when Dax didn't think I'd know the words—or moves—to Sir Mix-a-Lot's "Baby Got Back." And I don't want this to ever end.

But the gendarme are arriving again, a new bus pulls up, and we get down to the business of moving everything out of one bus and into another.

We're nearly done when I find myself alone with Dax in the new bus. He tugs me into the back and drops the curtain separating the bunks from the dinette and the seats. "You're fucking incredible, do you know that?" he murmurs while he nibbles at my ear.

My skin lights up like Times Square, my nipples tighten, and I lean into his hard body, because I can't resist. I might never get this chance again. "Thank you." His whiskers tickle my hair when I press a kiss to the side of his neck. "Thank you for everything."

"Pretty sure that's supposed to be my line, princess."

"You're only saying that because I put it on your bucket list."

He laughs, a deep rumble that makes my whole body shiver in anticipation.

"Dude, if you're taking her clothes off, I'm going to fucking kill you," Edison calls from up front.

"You're too late," I call back. "He has me naked and he's ravishing me right now with his massive crotch weasel. Go away."

"Crotch weasel?" A hard bulge sprouts against my belly. "Did you just call it a *crotch weasel*?"

"I think I'm getting my metaphors confused. It made sense in my head."

"He's not doing it right if you can still talk," Edison replies.

"Fuck," Dax mutters.

"Apparently later," I whisper. I squeeze his butt—*wow*, that's some solid muscle—and step back.

He snags me by the waist and pulls me in for a kiss.

A long, slow, deep, *everything* kiss.

Like he's laying claim. Thanking me back. Or possibly just horny.

I'm feeling that horny buzz myself.

The curtain rips open. "Quit mauling her, you animal. We're ready to go."

I get one last swipe of my tongue in before I pull back.

"You're a tease," Dax murmurs.

"I'm learning."

"Christ." But he laughs, adjusts himself, and then snags a pillow from the nearest bunk and throws it at Edison. "Let's get out of here."

When I turn to head back up front, he taps my butt. "We're not done yet, princess," he whispers.

I shiver.

It's a good shiver.

And I hope he's not wrong.

29

Dax

I'M ALMOST DISAPPOINTED when we arrive safely in Paris. No random flying farm animals crashed through the windshield, no naked protests slowed traffic, and no alien signals fried the electronics system on the bus.

Edison isn't happy with my plan to take Willow to the Eiffel Tower before we head to the embassy to get lost in the red tape of having new passports issued, but he's given up arguing. We've just pulled into a parking garage when Willow gasps. Her phone dings, my phone dings, and Biscuit swears.

The bus screeches to a hard stop in the middle of the lane.

Because there are two giants stepping into our path, blocking us from continuing into the garage.

"Holy fuck, is that the Berger twins?" Edison says reverently.

I grasp Willow's hand.

She's not going. She still has shit to do. Hot air balloon rides. Skinny dipping in the Mediterranean. Riding a camel.

A dark-haired Viking wrenches open the door while two more Viking princes join the Berger twins in blocking Biscuit from pulling all the way into the parking garage.

Willow gasps again. Her hand tightens in mine, but only briefly before she's pulling away.

"I'll run 'em over, boss," Biscuit says.

"No, *stop!*" Willow cries. She flies out of her seat and tackles the Viking forcing his way onto the bus. "Colden! Stop. They're *friends*. How did you—never mind. Eloise. Right."

"You fucking *disappeared*," he growls. His gaze lands on me and promises everything from pummeling in my head to ripping my nut sack off, and my respect for him inches up.

"I *called*," she says. "And I texted. And I'm *fine*."

The other princes and the Berger twins are crowding into the bus now. "Which one do we need to beat first?" the louder of the twins demands. He looks between me and Edison. "Too bad for you fuckers you're not boy banders. Then we might be gentle."

"*Stop*," Willow orders again. "Don't make me get the spiders out."

"*Fuck*."

"And I'll pluck your sheep naked if you try anything," she adds to the prince. "Ares, get these guys out of here. Please. Before I never sing any more New Kids on the Block with you *ever again*."

The second Berger twin's eyes go round, and he grabs two of the princes by the belt loops and pulls them out of the bus's door and back to the concrete wall. They thrash and twist, but he doesn't let go. The first twin retreats, but the third prince doesn't. "She's coming with us," he growls at me.

"She's going to do whatever the *fuck* she wants to do," Willow announces.

It's a struggle to not laugh when she cusses, though the fear exploding in my chest helps keep my amusement in check. If anything, that's sheer panic threatening to bubble out.

She's not done here yet. *She's not done*.

The prince's eyebrows shoot up to his hairline. "Did you just say *fuck*?"

She crosses her arms and glares at him. "I'll fucking say whatever the fuck I fucking want to." Her cheeks go pink. "Oh, *shit*, it's getting bad. They're going to fucking fire me at work."

"Would you boys *please* stop behaving like Neanderthals?" a new voice says.

Willow straightens. "Mom? *Mom!*"

She mows over the prince on her dash out the door, and Edison and I both move to watch her throw herself at a tall woman with dark hair and blue eyes who emerges from a large white van parked in the nearest spot. Three other women crowd around them, all talking at once.

I recognize the shortest of the bunch.

"Is that—"

"The notorious Eloise," I finish for Edison.

Who was probably tracking our entire journey today and guessed where Willow wanted to go.

The woman's freaky.

With the obstructions gone, Biscuit finishes parking the bus. He couldn't get it in here if it were a normal tour bus, but he takes two spaces and calls it even. Edison, Pop, and I all climb out.

Willow's rattling off a story a mile a minute, shielded from view by the three princes, two Berger twins, and a dark-haired muscular dude with some sparkle in his hair and chin cleft.

Can't judge.

I've been into weird shit a time or two in my life too.

"Dax, come meet my mom," Willow calls. "She wants to say thanks for you keeping me from going skydiving yesterday."

"That was all the nuns," I reply, watching her closely. She's still going skydiving…isn't she?

"But the tattoo is totally his fault," Willow announces.

All of the women—I swear they're multiplying—look at my arms.

All of them men scowl like they're considering skinning me alive.

"We're fucking outnumbered," Edison mutters.

"They're not going to hurt you," Willow tells him. "Because if they do, I'll run away and join the circus."

She grins broadly.

None of her friends grin back.

Except Eloise. The pixie chick holds out a fist. "I knew you had some badass hiding in there."

They bump fists, and once again, I'm checking a smile.

It's the most terrified smile I've ever smiled.

I catch Willow's eye.

She gnaws on her bottom lip and drops her gaze.

Like she's retreating. Right there. Morphing back into the woman who thought it would be a good idea to marry fucking Vanderweilie.

"By the way, I solved your problem," Eloise tells me.

I tear my eyes from Willow, but only for a second. "You found Danger?"

"You got his money back?" Edison says.

"Actually, I sent a very official looking cease-and-desist order to that girl you fucked in your tour bus that might've included some very incriminating photos of her and someone else I can't publicly name, but whose wife would hate to see them. So whatever goes wrong in your life now, it's all your own fault."

It's always been my own fault. But I didn't know how to solve it. Still don't, though some ideas are taking shape.

I'm going to have to leap. Professionally. Personally. Emotionally.

You're scary as fuck," the louder Berger twin tells Eloise.

"I've been telling you that for months," the glitter-hair guy replies.

"She's perfect," one of the women announces.

"Maybe not *perfect*, but definitely memorable," another one says.

"Fuck, yeah." Eloise eyeballs the dark-haired prince and purrs while she licks her lips.

"You need a keeper," he tells her.

"Oh my gosh, I missed you guys." Willow dives into another group hug, still not meeting my eyes. "Let's go get our pictures taken at the top of the Eiffel Tower!"

"What about Danger?" I ask quietly.

Willow's eyes go wide. "Oh my gosh, yes. What about Danger? And Martin?"

My eyeball twitches.

"Martin can go fuck himself," one of the women say.

A collective murmur of agreement goes up from the group.

"The Martin situation will sort itself out," Eloise says. She winks at me. "Maybe sooner rather than later if you introduce me to Oliver."

Willow pokes her. "Stop hitting on everything with two legs."

"I do like them better with three…"

"*Eloise.*"

She lifts her slender shoulders. "What? I do. You should too. Oh, and I found Danger. But I'm not allowed to tell you where he is."

My heart climbs into my throat. Edison surges forward, but gets blocked by the ape squad. "Where is he?" Edison demands.

She holds out her phone. "Proof of life." A video starts.

There's Danger.

Rolling his eyes, in his favorite gray Guinness shirt, his hair cropped military short, bleeding heart tattoo half-showing under his sleeve. He holds up a paper. "Yo. It's me. That's yesterday's ads for some grocery store. You need to see a date? Fine." He moves the paper closer to the camera. I see ads for discount watermelon and corn, and then yesterday's date. "I left a note with my old man. Guess you didn't get the message. I'm good. Have some shit I need to take care of. I'll be back. Whatever this crazy chick says, it's only half true, and probably not the half you think, because god only knows what she'll dream up to tell you. But quit worrying. I'm fine. Okay? Okay. Dax, none of this is your fault. Ignore the crazy. Make your music. We'll get the fucker who took our money. We'll get back on top. Just a phase, man. We got this. I'll be back. Soon. Just…stuff."

The video stops with Danger leaning into the camera, shutting off the video, so all we can see is his neck.

I'm so fucking relieved he's okay I almost can't talk. "What else do you know?" I force out.

"That you should say *thank you*," she prompts.

"Thank you," I say.

Pop claps me on the shoulder. Willow smiles at me. And *fuck*, there goes my breath again.

She didn't do the heavy lifting, but she found someone who could.

"Thank you," I tell her.

"No, thank you," she replies.

Like *I* did something.

I didn't do anything.

Her breaking free? That was all her.

"We should get to the embassy," Edison says.

The dark-haired prince pulls something out of his back pocket and hands it over. "For this?" he says.

My passport.

I almost don't want to take it.

But it doesn't matter what I want. Willow's back with her crew. Her tribe. The people who will make sure that if she jumps out of a plane, she's picking a company with a solid reputation and that her parachute's been checked a dozen times over.

"You got a lead on Vanderweilie?" Edison asks Eloise.

"No, but every checkpoint in Europe knows to watch out for a man fitting his description and transporting nuclear materials," she replies with a shrug. "He'll turn up. Probably soon. Especially since he's probably traveling with a fake ID."

"I worry about your friends," Willow's mom says to her.

"She's harmless unless you piss her off," Willow replies. She clamps a hand over her mouth. "I mean *tick* her off. Sorry, Mom."

"She lives with us," the less beefy of the taller princes says to Willow. "She's become quite immune."

"I still can't believe you're *all* here," Willow says.

"You *disappeared*." One of the women slips her arm through Willow's elbow. "Of course we're all here. And since we're here, let's go see that tower."

"We should absolutely go see the tower," Willow agrees. She glances at me, but there's far more hesitation than I've ever seen on her. "Do you guys want to come along? Or did you…have other places to be?"

It's a loaded question.

Do you still want to see me?

Yeah, I fucking still want to see her. No, I don't want to let her go.

But despite getting a few answers, my life is stuck in limbo. I don't know when we're going back out on tour again. We need to find Danger. I don't give two shits if he thinks he needs to do whatever he's doing *all by himself.*

No one should ever be alone.

Even for *I need to do this myself* shit.

"We're going skydiving," I tell her. "You should come."

Her eyes widen. She shoots a glance at her mom, whose eyes are bulging.

And right there, while we're all watching, I swear Willow shrinks two inches and something inside her dies. "Make sure you triple-check your parachutes," she tells me. "And have fun. Maybe I'll see pictures online later."

I wasn't going skydiving, but I fucking am now. "You should come," I repeat.

She's going to say no.

She's going to deflate back into what she thinks everyone else wants her to be, and it's fucking pissing me off.

"You should *live*," I add.

The men are getting riled. The women curious. The queen tightens her grip around Willow's shoulders.

"Thank you for watching out for Willow," she says to me.

"She watched out for me."

I hook a thumb at the bus and look at Willow again. She won't make eye contact.

"You want your stuff?" I ask.

"Got your phone, ma'am," Biscuit says. "And that camera you had. And your souvenir dildo."

And now she's turning red as a beet.

Like she wasn't in a meadow last night asking me to fuck her.

"Th-thank you," she stammers while one of the princes takes her stuff, though they have a silent battle over who has to touch the dildo.

"What about your list?" I'm getting more pissed by the minute.

This isn't Willow. The woman huddling back to safety, hiding behind her friends *isn't* Willow.

Not the Willow I know.

"Keep it," she whispers.

Fuck.

I step toward her, because I'm not done.

But the two Berger twins crowd closer, along with their glitter-hair friend, and the beefier of the two brown-haired princes joins them in being a wall between me and Willow.

"*Stop*, you guys." She pushes through them and wraps her arms around my shoulders. "Thank you. For everything. And good luck."

I squeeze.

Hard.

I don't want to forget this. Not the way she smells like sunshine and freedom, not the slide of her fingers down my neck, not the delicate feel of her bones. "Eat something," I order. "Cuss a little. Sing a lot. Go fucking skydiving. And call me if you ever need anything."

Fuck, I'm getting a lump in my throat.

I was supposed to trade her four days ago for my money.

Now, fuck the money.

I just want to take her home and show her it's okay to keep living.

But I've already kidnapped the woman once.

I won't do it again.

She pulls back, and I tell myself it's just my imagination that her eyes are shiny and her voice wobbly. "Everything will work out for you. It will. And if I ever see Martin again, I'll give him an extra kick just for you."

She presses a kiss to her fingers, then touches my cheek with them. "Bye, Dax." She waves to Edison, Biscuit, and Pop. "So nice to meet you all. Take good care of him, and try not to run over any more dildos, okay?"

Edison claps my shoulder while we watch them walk away. "Best this way," he tells me.

I shake my head.

Doesn't feel like it.

But she doesn't need me.

Except I think she might.

Almost as much as I'm starting to need her.

30

Two weeks to the day after I was supposed to become Mrs. Martin Sampson Vanderweilie the Fourth, all of my friends are gathered in the basement of Sia and Chase's Manhattan brownstone just a block off Central Park. This is less man cave and more band practice room, since this is where Eloise, Parker, Sia, and I have our rehearsals a couple times a week. Mom's here. My band is here. Manning and Gracie and the baby are here. The Berger twins are here, along with their girlfriends. Parker's boyfriend, Knox, is here.

Everyone's here.

But I still feel like someone's missing.

And it's not because Martin used to join us all the time either.

He didn't. Which should've been one more clue in a long string of clues that we shouldn't have been so close to getting married.

I love my friends, but I don't want to be here tonight.

I want to be out hang gliding upstate, over the Hudson Valley.

Mostly because Dax texted me a link to a company that offers hang gliding tours in the Hudson Valley last night, and now I can't stop thinking about it.

I realize I've zoned out again when Mom puts her hand to my forehead. "Are you sure you're not coming down with something?"

"Just processing," I tell her.

It's the same excuse I've been using for ten days now, and I'm almost starting to believe it.

But if they think I'm processing the end of my relationship with Martin, they're wrong.

I'm processing my grand adventure.

And it keeps coming back to the same thing.

Every night since we've been back in the States, while Mom and I have been staying in Sia and Chase's guest rooms, I've been sneaking out to a studio apartment in SoHo that Dax is borrowing from a friend.

And we've been banging like bunnies.

We don't talk about Martin. Or Dax's missing money. Or my band. Or his band. Or his friend Danger, who hasn't returned.

I don't like to say *missing*.

We mostly just get naked, jump each other, and then wonder what the Sisters are up to, if that cow still wanders aimlessly about the Belgian countryside, and what happened to that box of dildos.

Other than the three Dax rescued and keeps in the apartment to pull out when he wants to remind me that the sex toys are no match for his natural endowments.

We also laugh.

A lot.

He asks me to go skydiving.

And I say no.

I remember how tightly Mom hugged me when the entire gang showed up in Paris to find me.

And the guilt at knowing that they wouldn't have all come after me if they hadn't been so worried.

I don't like worrying my Mom. Or my friends.

But I'm starting to feel suffocated, whereas before, I've always felt just plain *loved*.

"You know what we need?" Eloise says.

Most of the group groans.

"What?" I ask her.

"Karaoke night," she replies.

My shoulders sag.

She should've suggested all of us head out to get matching tattoos. Or that we all go streaking through Central Park and hope one of the hot cops catches us.

"Dibs on 'Manic Monday,'" Sia calls.

"No fucking way," Zeus replies. "You always get 'Manic Monday.'"

"Rock paper scissors for it!" Ares's girlfriend, Felicity, calls. Except she does it without moving her lips because she's a ventriloquist, which is both freaky and cool at the same time.

Plus, since Ares rarely talks, it works really well.

Also, apparently karaoke night is happening in the basement.

Not out in public.

Mom's watching me again. So is Ares's emotional support monkey, who was kind of an accidental pet, but also totally works for Ares.

I rise. "Bathroom," I say to Mom. "Be right back."

Her eyes narrow like she knows I don't actually have to pee.

But the walls are closing in tonight.

I've always loved hanging out with my friends. Our band, their goofball antics—they've always been my walk on the wild side.

Now, it's not enough.

I still love them. Dearly. They're family.

I close the bathroom door and lean against it. Whoever owned this place before Chase bought it had some weird fetishes, and the entire bathroom looks like a jungle. The sink has fake ivory tusks for handles, and the water pours out of a faucet shaped like an elephant's trunk. The sink basin is painted so that it looks like a coiled snake. The floor is marble, the walls papered with jungle foliage, and when you lift the lid on the black toilet, the tiger painted on it growls.

For real. There's a sound box in the toilet.

I snap a picture of the tiger and text it to Dax. *Think of this next time you're licking my tattoo.*

I don't expect an answer—he told me last week when he messaged me about being in town that he was here for meetings with his record label and management and to meet with some of his favorite songwriters. Plus, since everyone was freaking out about him being missing, along with the photos and stories surfacing from Europe that made him look a little off-center—the stilt fighter pictures were especially not flattering—he's been making some public appearances with A-list movie stars and prominent musicians.

Signing autographs.

Posing for pictures with random fans.

Smiling.

Buying drinks for the bar.

Giving everyone a show like there's nothing wrong.

I hate the games he's playing.

Not that I'm any better.

My phone vibrates

Dax: I can't unsee that.

Willow: You're not standing two feet from it.

Dax: You should leave. I'll send a car.

Willow: I can't leave. My mom's flying back to Stölland tomorrow.

There's silence.

I don't need to see his face to know what he's thinking.

Then invite me over.

Not an option.

For one, if I invite him over, then everyone will think we're a couple, and he'll start getting invited to do couple things, and I don't want to be a couple.

For two, I actually kinda do want to be a couple. But I know I shouldn't. Because my life is a little topsy-turvy, and his is just plain crazy, and I don't feel like I should be trusted with major life decisions.

My phone buzzes again.

Dax: You don't find yourself in routines and normalcy and comfort. You find yourself when you jump.

This time, I don't reply.

Because I know he's right, but I don't know if I'm ready.

There are some leaps you can't take back.

Would my friends stand by me no matter what?

Without a doubt. They're not only the most generous women I've ever known, they're also the craziest. They won't judge. They'd probably leap with me.

But I don't want to disappoint my mom, or make her life any harder.

She's settled in really well in Stölland. And she hasn't just settled.

She's gotten involved. She sits on boards. She takes on royal speaking engagements. She kisses babies and charms parliamentarians and fights for the rights of working mothers.

She's making an actual difference in the lives of the people of an entire *country*.

And King Tor needs her.

I didn't know him before—obviously—but I've seen old videos and heard stories from my stepbrothers.

He's a better ruler with her by his side.

I know Mom loves me.

I know she wants me to be happy.

And I don't want to be the cause of undue stress in her life.

I'll leap, I promise myself.

Once I'm more settled into my new life.

31

DAX

"You're fucking insane."

Not the first time Edison's said that to me in the last two weeks, and it won't be the last. Mostly because he's right.

I've boarded the crazy train, and I'm not getting off anytime soon.

Yeah, I fake it well in public—picking battles is important, and if the label wants me to have lunch out with an A-lister, fine—but I'm completely consumed with doing the one thing Willow won't do.

I'm leaping.

That bucket list?

It's grown.

Edison's pacing the sidewalk outside a consulate in Midtown early Sunday morning. I'm just leaning against the fence.

Waiting for a queen, whom I have on good authority is inside before her flight back to Stölland this afternoon.

No biggie.

Finally, he stops and looks me dead in the eye. "What's so different about this one?"

Fair question. "She'd like me even if I wasn't Dax Gallagher."

He presses his fingers into his eyeballs. "You can't know that."

"I'm broke, the band's in limbo, and you can't go much lower than trying to kidnap someone for ransom. She's seen me at my worst. She knows I might never be at my best again. But she keeps coming back."

"Your dick still works. She's not doing this for nothing."

"Shut. The fuck. Up." I hate that he might have a point.

Except this is Willow. The woman who's refusing any money from her stepfather to get her set up in an apartment, because she wants to do it on her own. The woman who hasn't posted a single picture of me online in the last ten days, though I know she snapped plenty of pictures on her camera.

The woman who hasn't asked me for a single thing except that I make her feel good.

And she gives as good as she gets.

Every time.

Got the cuff marks on my wrists again to prove it.

But more than that—she's given me inspiration. Hope. Belief.

In a time when I wouldn't have thought it was possible.

All by doing the one thing no one else would do.

She offered to help when no one else would.

"Gentlemen." A haughty quasi-British voice speaks behind us. We turn, and there's an armed guard eyeing us both from behind the sharp-tipped wrought iron gate. "Please move along."

"I need to speak with the queen."

Not even an eyeball twitch out of this one. "Move *along*, gentlemen."

Edison, who once dropped trou and pissed on a stop sign as a *fuck you* to a cop who was giving us shit about public drunkenness, grabs me by the collar. "We're going."

I pull the notebook from under my arm and refuse to budge. "This is her daughter's," I tell the guard. "Willow's. She left it with me in Europe. Just wanted to give it back."

He studies me, and I know he recognizes me.

Not sure if it's because I'm Dax Gallagher, or because I'm the man who kidnapped the queen's daughter.

He takes the notebook. "Move. Along. Sir."

I shrug. "Sure. We'll go get a cup of coffee." I point to a java hut across the street.

We walk to the end of the block and use the crosswalk.

"You're fucking insane," Edison says again.

I buy him a cup of coffee with some change I found in the cushions of the apartment I'm bumming off a friend. We settle into two seats in the back near the doorway to the kitchen. I'm fully bearded now, and with a hat on, mostly unrecognizable when I cover my arms, but we learned a long time ago that escape routes and clear visibility to the door are important, and it's not a habit I expect either of us to break in our lifetimes.

While we drink our coffee, we both pull out our phones. My email, texts, and voicemails aren't interesting. Willow hasn't replied to me since I challenged her to jump last night. Danger hasn't texted back to any of my daily messages, and the detective Edison hired can't figure out how the fuck Eloise got that video of him.

I'm about to shut off my phone when a new text message arrives.

Speak of the devil. It's Eloise.

She's getting more boring by the day. I thought I could count on you to do something more than just bang her. You're dead to me now.

I lower my coffee cup and frown. A shiver slinks down my spine and takes root in my gut.

She's not wrong. Not that I'd ever call Willow *boring*. But she's not *living* anymore either.

"What now?" Edison asks.

I shake my head.

I can't live Willow's life for her. Can't make her do all those things she said she wants to do.

Except it's tearing my heart out of my chest at the idea of her never riding a camel or going on a safari or learning to scuba dive.

I can't give her any of that right now, but I can work my fucking ass off to get back to where I once was so I can.

No.

To get farther than I once was. Fuck dropping ticket and album sales. Fuck what the label wants.

We're going back to our roots.

Back to what shot us to fame in the first place.

Back to the music we love.

To what we were born to do. No more holding back.

I shoot Eloise a text back while Edison watches.

As soon as I hit send, there's movement across the street at the consulate.

Three guards and a tall, dark-haired woman in sunglasses are stepping out of the building.

I nod toward them, and Edison follows my gaze.

Five minutes later, Willow's mom takes the seat across from me.

Her blue eyes are curious, her posture relaxed for royalty, but there's no mistaking the mama bear attitude.

She extends a hand. "Mr. Gallagher."

"Your majesty."

Her nose wrinkles. Like daughter, like mother. "Sylvie is fine, please. I was hoping we'd have an opportunity to chat."

Edison squeezes his eyes shut. I can hear what he's thinking.

You're about to get arrested, dumbass.

Sylvie cuts a look at him. "Please excuse us for a moment, Mr. Rogers."

"Do I need to call a lawyer?"

She smiles, and *fuck*, I miss Willow.

She left my bed early yesterday morning, and I miss her already.

"He should be safe for now," she tells Edison.

Edison grabs my empty cup and wanders to the counter.

"Do you know the one thing I never asked Martin?"

"If he was a douchecanoe who liked to fuck people over?"

Her brow quirks. "No, but I'll be certain to tell my stepsons you've passed the creative cussing test."

"That's a relief."

Now she's holding back a smile. Her ears twitch like Willow's do when she's doing the same thing.

"I never asked him when he first knew he loved her."

In the farmer's yard in Belgium, when she toppled over laughing after she got me with that zinger, agreeing that I was a terrible person.

I feel my eyes go wide.

Because *fuck*.

I'm in love with Willow Honeycutt.

I'm not here as her friend.

I'm not here as her lover.

I'm here as a man head over heels in love with a woman who's hiding from who she could be.

Her mother smiles softly. "You know."

"She's not happy." *This* is why I'm here. "Not like she could be."

"And you want to make her happy."

"I—"

Do I?

Of course I do.

But more important— "I want her to *be* happy. I want *everyone* to want her to be happy. And that means she needs *you* to tell her it's okay to go jump out of a fucking airplane if she wants to jump out of a fucking airplane."

Sylvie straightens, and there it is—that fear.

The fear that's held Willow back from *living*.

It's a flash, and she hides it fast, but her pupils dilated and her mouth tightened and I could all but *hear* her saying *no*.

"You wouldn't stop the princes."

She squeezes her eyes shut for a moment.

"I would not," she concedes dryly. "But their father would."

"You know she's not happy."

"I also know she's been sneaking out every night to visit you."

"Can't blame her. I'm a catch."

Sylvie laughs, and for the first time since she walked into the coffee shop, I draw a full breath.

"I'm not here for me." I don't think I'm here for me. Maybe I am. "I just think she needs to know that you're not going to fall apart if she decides to go BASE jumping or skydiving or rock climbing."

"Or running around the country chasing a rock band?" she prompts.

I hold my hands up. "Not here for me," I repeat.

She pulls the notebook from her bag and pushes it across the table to me. "This isn't mine to give to her."

I push it back. "She won't do half of this unless you tell her it's okay."

She folds her arms.

I grin. "Or unless I kidnap her again."

Her eye twitches. "She's been quite insistent that she voluntarily got on that boat with you."

"And I haven't told a soul that she handcuffed me and forced me into a van full of nuns, so I guess we're even."

Now both her eyelids are twitching.

"You want to see her with another Vanderweilie?" I ask.

"I want to see her happy."

I shove the notebook closer to her. "Then tell her to live. She won't listen to me. Maybe she'll listen to you."

She rises. After a moment's hesitation, she takes the notebook with her. "This was much easier when all she wanted was tickets to boy band concerts."

"At least she's moving up in the world."

I get another look like the one Danger's mom used to give us when we'd swear the Baker boys were the ones who ran through her flowers on their bikes.

But her expression softens. "You know Willow was with Martin for seven years."

"I've gone through three divorces. I know what *not love* looks like. And I'd rather be her rebound than be nothing at all."

"That's...strangely romantic."

"It's a gift."

She's chuckling as she walks away.

I don't always do the right thing.

But I try sometimes.

Remains to be seen if this one will be a hit or a miss.

32

WILLOW

ELOISE IS NOT NEARLY AS CONSIDERATE a kidnapper as Dax was.

For starters, she's making me listen to "Escape"—you know, the piña colada song?—on repeat. Also, she's making me ride in her Hummer—yes, Eloise, who's barely five feet tall, is driving a *Hummer* around Manhattan—and she's as bad as a taxi driver, except worse, because at least taxi drivers are trained for this, whereas Eloise can barely see over the wheel and seems to think she's just playing MarioKart.

I should be thrilled, because this *is* an adventure, but I'm actually legitimately scared that I might not get out of this Hummer alive.

But she has peanut butter cups, so at least there's that.

"I didn't think we were playing tonight," I tell her as she careens into a turn and I grasp desperately for the oh-shit handle.

"Last-minute gig," she says. "And then I might have to go underground."

"What? Why? For how long? What about the twins' wedding? And Parker and Knox?"

"Don't get me started on *Knox*." The Hummer rocks as Eloise steers it down a steep entrance to a parking garage. "He should've minded his own fucking business."

"Because we'd love you any different for knowing that you have the resources to take care of yourself and some mad computer skills?"

"Yes."

She slams on the brakes before we bust through the traffic arm at the ticket booth. Eloise has to put the beast in park and climb half out the window to grab the ticket. Once the arm lifts, she punches the gas, and we fly into the garage.

"Is this thing going to fit in any of the spots down here? And also, I'm freaking related to royalty and Sia's engaged to a billionaire. Of course we're not going to love you any different."

The tires squeal, and for a split second, I think she's going to pull a donut, but instead, we end up jerking forward in our seatbelts when she slams us into a parking spot built for a compact car.

"Eloise. Seriously. I can't open my door. I'm going to hit this Smart car next to me."

"We're climbing out the back, bitches!"

"Aren't your drums back there?"

"Willow. This is a fucking *Hummer*. I could get the whole fucking band in my trunk and still have space left over for both of Sia's brothers to bang each other."

"Okay, first, gross, and second, while I can almost see your point, I don't think that's actually physically possible."

Seriously, how can you *not* love Eloise?

She's crazy.

And sometimes wrong, but in a good way.

We climb out the back—she's right, we can get around her drum set—and I help her lug everything up to the main level, where we're apparently playing a victory party in a gym for a local softball league champion team.

Sia and Parker meet us in the weight room.

It's not as weird as it sounds. We've warmed up in some really odd places before.

"HCH Fans? What kind of a team name is that?" Sia asks. "Like *huch fans* or something?"

"Maybe they're the…high cholesterol…hottie fans?" Parker guesses.

Knox, who carried in her guitar, presses a kiss to her hair and makes a strangled noise like he's trying not to laugh.

"Hard core hell fans?" Sia guesses.

"Half cow hippie fans?" I suggest.

"*Half cow hippie fans?*" All of my friends crack up, and I give myself a silent pat on the back for being funny.

I'm rarely the funny one.

The *don't do that* one, yes.

The funny, crazy, zany one, no.

"Come on, you backstabbing agent of no good," Eloise says to Knox. "Help me set up my drums."

"Don't beat him too badly," Parker tells her. "I have plans for him later."

"Yeah, you and your unicorn blanket," Eloise grumbles.

"You want one? I know where to find patterns and directions for crocheting," Knox tells her as they lug her boxes out the door.

"She's going to hate that," Sia says with a grin.

"He knows," Parker replies with a matching grin.

She pulls her guitar out of her case, and the three of us warm up. Eloise comes back in, I take a trip out to check the mics, and then we finalize the set list and gossip and catch up while we wait for show-time. A couple minutes before we're due to take the stage, the crowd in the gym across the hall suddenly roars.

We all share a look.

"Trophy presentation?" I guess.

"Must be one hell of a trophy," Sia replies.

The door to the weight room swings open, and a perky brunette with long hair tied up in a loopy bun, athletic shorts, and a loose HCH Fans jersey tank over a sports bra sticks her head in. "Yous guys ready?" She's grinning so hard, my cheeks hurt for her.

"Let's rock 'n' roll," Eloise says.

We follow her across the hallway to the basketball courts and come in behind the stage, which is actually corkboard laid over the courts with black curtains on a collapsible rack as a backdrop. We step out from behind the curtains, and there must be at least two hundred people packed into the bleachers.

There's actually a rope separating us from the crowd. There's no way this is just *one* team. This has to be the entire league.

They erupt in cheers. Cameras flash. Phones aim at us, like we're being taped, which isn't actually so unusual. We've been together a while, and we do have something of a fan club.

And—oh, this is a surprise.

There are a local news anchor and cameraman too.

"Who *are* these people?" Parker whispers to me while Sia and Eloise take their places at the keyboard and drums respectively.

"I don't know," I whisper back.

I head to the front mic, smiling and waving, while Parker goes stage right with her guitar to the mic set up there.

More cheers.

Jeez, I'm glad we finalized our set list instead of winging it like we did at that May the Fourth party we played for the Widows Of Star Wars Club last month.

"Hey, wow," I say into the mic. The acoustics are terrible in here, so my voice bounces back at me, but we've been performing together for years. It doesn't bother me. I'm getting that sizzle in my veins again that I love—the adventure of playing for a crowd. "We heard you all are some serious winners."

The crowd roars.

Of course they do. Everyone wants to be a winner.

"So let's have some fun and celebrate!" I cry.

That's Eloise's cue. She hits out a beat, and though it's not a boy band song, we launch into a cover of Katy Perry's "Roar."

Seems appropriate for a victory party.

And I swear, I can feel my tattoo roaring too.

My tiger's been caged up. Dax is right.

I'm falling into old habits. Hiding behind the excuse that I need to figure out who I am without Martin, when the truth is, I'm being a chicken.

I'm lying to myself again.

I should be grateful for what I have.

I have a comfortable life doing a job I enjoy.

I get my kicks by singing with the band.

I do love singing, but this isn't an *adventure*. It's *safe*.

It's something I'm good at.

Not something I have to stretch for.

I want to stretch.

And I know it'll probably give Mom some extra gray hairs if she hears I went skydiving, but *I want to go.*

I want to go hang gliding over the Hudson Valley.

I want to go white water rafting.

I want to meet fun and crazy people. Set sail around the world.

I want to make love under the stars in the Rockies. And in

Morocco. And—well, pretty much anywhere I can convince Dax to go with me, because I can't picture any of this without him there.

He might call it kidnapping, but I did get on that boat on my own. And I did it because I wanted an adventure.

I did it for me.

But I wouldn't have done it without him.

We roll seamlessly into some classic New Kids on the Block, and the crowd screams. I haven't seen Zeus and Ares—I'm pretty sure they left New York this morning around the same time as my mom, since both their girlfriends have to work back home tomorrow—so if the crowd's expecting our show to be crashed by the NHL's twin tanks, they're going to be disappointed.

Except they're screaming louder.

And higher.

And—oh my gosh, I think that woman in front just fainted—no, wait, she's getting up, but she's crying. And—holy shit, that's my mom.

I stumble over the lyrics, because *why is my mom here*?

She smiles at me—*everything's okay, I just couldn't leave you yet*—and tears prickle my eyes.

I don't want to worry her.

But I can't hold myself back anymore either.

Parker covers for me while I get a quick grip on myself. I pick back up in the chorus, and we're doing all the old moves from their video, when another voice—no, *three* new voices pick up on the mic.

"Getting too old for moves like that, old man."

"Speak for yourself, fingers."

"You two keep arguing. I'm going to dance."

The crowd is screaming.

Sia gasps and completely stops playing.

Parker's dazed.

My lungs freeze.

Only Eloise is still banging away.

Dax and Edison are here.

And so is Levi Fucking Wilson.

Former Bro Code member, current pop king of the entire world.

Sia still uses a comforter with his picture on it.

Which is why she's sort of hyperventilating.

Dax settles a guitar strap over his shoulder, grins at me, and stops next to Parker. He jerks his chin at the mic. "Mind sharing this?"

She gapes up at him for a minute. "You're going to have to bend over."

Her eyes go wide as she clearly processes what she just said. "Ohmygod, I didn't—"

"You heard the lady, Gallagher," Levi says. "Bend over."

Everyone roars.

My mom's smiling and sighing like she does when my stepbrothers get together. Off to the side, Knox and Chase share a fist bump. Apparently they were in on our surprise guests.

Eloise is *still* drumming.

HCH Fans.

Oh, jeez. Of course.

Half Cocked Heroes Fans.

"Are you crashing my band?" I ask Dax.

His eyes land on mine, my heart swells, and when he grins, I completely lose my breath.

He's *mine*.

He's not easy. He comes with complications. But he's *mine*.

"Yep," he says.

I wave a hand at him. "I've seen videos of you in concert. You're not dressed right."

"Miss Honeycutt, are you asking me to strip?"

The crowd goes utterly insane.

My boss is going to see video of this and I'm probably going to have one of those come-to-Jesus talks when I go back to work in the morning. She's from Alabama. I'm very familiar with come-to-Jesus talks.

"I'm not asking." I smile. "I'm telling. And Levi Wilson, get your butt over there by Sia. You're gonna have to cover for us on the keyboards."

Dax pulls his shirt off and tosses it to my mom, who hands it off to the woman in the front row who's crying.

The noise is deafening.

And that's before Dax stalks across the stage to join me.

He's a natural in front of a crowd. Confident. In charge. Larger than life.

And sexy as fuck with his pants slung low on his slim hips, his dragons shifting over his solid chest while he moves, his eyes locked on mine.

I pull my mic away. "You did this, didn't you?" We weren't supposed to perform anywhere tonight.

He leans into my ear, the intoxicating scent of raw male and fresh air and leather tickles my nose, my panties go damp, and my whole body lights up from my toenails to the tips of my split ends. "Your friend did this, and I'm going to love every last minute."

I glance back at Eloise.

She is *still* drumming. Tongue hanging out, head banging, piercings glinting in the harsh light.

He starts to pull away, but I grip him by the arm and pull him back. "When we're done, can you steal a motorcycle and take me away?"

He doesn't answer.

Not with words anyway.

But judging by the way he cradles my face and claims my mouth and presses his hard body to mine, I'm going to assume that's a yes.

33

*D*AX

I'VE BEEN DOING this rock 'n' roll thing for long enough that I've forgotten one basic truth.

Change isn't just *good*.

It's artistically necessary.

Tonight, playing for the smallest crowd I've played in years, with a woman who has completely and utterly bewitched me singing by my side, I know what I need to do to grow.

And it doesn't matter if I never get my money back.

It doesn't matter if they never catch Vanderweilie.

It doesn't matter how long it takes Danger to get back to us—so long as the fucker stays in touch, because I'll fucking kill him if he doesn't.

It's never too late to start over.

And I'm starting over. Tonight. Right now. While I'm singing, watching Willow, who's watching me, because apparently she can't take her eyes off me any more than I can take my eyes off her.

Until we roll into the chorus on "All Yours," which has always been one of my favorite ballads that Half Cocked Heroes has ever done.

We're cruising through, and just before we get to *I've got my heart all over you*, we both freeze.

Only for a millisecond.

Just long enough to come to a silent agreement.

You in?

Oh, fuck yes.

For the record—that *fuck* came from Willow.

"And I've got...my...*fart* all oooo-ver you," we both croon together.

Edison loses it and drops his guitar. He's getting good at playing despite his not yet healed finger. Willow's guitarist snort-laughs into the mic. Her keyboardist jams her hands down on all the keys at once.

"Fuck *yeah*," Eloise yells over the music.

"Dude...you should see a doctor about that," Levi says.

He's still jamming on his guitar.

And the crowd—they're my favorite kind of crazy. Laughing and screaming and cheering and chanting.

And that's before the Berger twins crash onto the stage, both of them howling the chorus, changed words and all.

They make a sandwich out of Willow and me, and the four of us close out the song together.

This is the part of rock 'n' roll we've been missing.

The *fun* part.

We do two encores, because we're fucking rock stars and that's what we do.

And then, finally, I'm dragging Willow out of the gym.

We make it about ten feet before three guards and a queen block our path.

"Mom," Willow whispers. "I thought you went back."

Sylvie pulls her into a hug. "Someone convinced me to stay a little longer."

"I'm going skydiving," Willow blurts.

Sylvie visibly tightens her hug. "Check your parachute a dozen or two times, okay? And *have fun*, but be safe. And just call when you're done."

"And white water rafting. And camel racing. And—"

"Willow. Oh, my sweet girl." Sylvie pulls back and brushes Willow's hair out of her face. "Don't hold yourself back. You're only young once. Go see the world. Have adventures." She winces. "Sleep with rock stars, but use protection."

Willow blushes. "I don't want to make anything harder for you."

"I'll let you know when you get close to topping anything your stepbrothers have done," Sylvie replies dryly.

"I can help with that," I offer.

"I know," Sylvie says on a sigh. But she's smiling. A little. "Go be free," she tells Willow. "Enjoy yourself. Don't hold back for me. Okay?"

"I love you, Mom."

"I love you too, baby girl."

I have to clear my throat and blink a few times while they hug each other.

"Go on home," Willow tells her mom. "I'll come visit soon. And I know King Tor misses you like crazy."

Sylvie looks at me. "Don't make me send Magnus after you."

The tallest, beefiest of her three guards eyes me like he'd enjoy gutting me like a fish.

"Mom. I can handle him." Willow releases Sylvie and grabs my hand. "If nothing else, I know how to chain him up."

"There are some things you can still keep to yourself."

Willow laughs, and it's better music than everything we've done for the last ninety minutes.

"One last thing." Sylvie pulls out Willow's notebook. "Fill this up. And please don't ever show it to me again."

Willow's laughing while she gives her mom one last hug. "Promise."

"Come on," she says to me. "You promised me a stolen motorcycle."

I mouth *Not stolen* to the guards while we dash down the hall. I stop in a locker room just long enough to grab my jacket and a spare shirt. The crowd will be out soon, and there's still an entire city between me and getting Willow naked.

She squeals when we hit the parking garage and I lead her to my Ducati. "Seriously?"

I pass her a helmet. "Hop on, princess. We're going on an adventure."

34

I DON'T KNOW how long we're on the road, but I don't care.

With my arms wrapped around Dax, my thighs pressed against him, the wind whipping around us while he navigates us out of the city, I'm in complete bliss. Eventually civilization falls away, leaving the moon to guide us.

Wherever we're going, I'm pretty certain I'll be missing work tomorrow.

This morning, I probably would've had a near heart attack at the idea of taking a fake sick day. Right now, though, nothing has ever felt so right.

Finally, Dax turns us off onto a backcountry road in a forest so thick the moon isn't penetrating the canopy overhead. We ride along for a ways more until we arrive at a small unoccupied campground well off the main road. Scents of wood smoke and citronella suggest we're not entirely alone, but other than the chirp of crickets and the gurgling of a nearby stream, all is quiet.

We both pull off our helmets, and Dax helps me off the bike. Before I can utter a word, he's kissing me.

Hard, but not crushing.

Deep.

Thorough.

I whimper into his mouth, the stroke of his tongue sending lightning through my veins. I claw at his shirt, he paws at mine, and soon we're both half-naked, desperately tugging at each other's jeans.

"I could sing with you every night, and every night, you'd put me to fucking shame," he says while he licks and nips his way down my chest and belly.

"Oh, no, *you're* the talented one," I gasp as his fingers slip under my waistband.

"Lies," he declares into my belly button.

He snags something from the bike behind me, then turns us both, guiding me with one arm wrapped around my butt, and I realize he's laying out a blanket behind me.

I run my fingers through his hair, scratching his scalp, feeling him fumble with his task behind me. "Dax Gallagher, you were going to kidnap me again, weren't you?"

"Whatever it took, princess. Lay down, baby doll. I'm gonna make you scream."

"Make me," I whisper.

He lifts his head, and in the moonlight filtering through the trees, I see a smile.

An *oh, I'm going to enjoy this* smile. "Make you, hm?"

The skin on his ears is so soft. So many soft parts to him, hidden under the hard body and black ink. "Make me," I repeat.

He circles my waist with his hands, then pushes my pants down, one hip at a time. I shift to help him, because let's be honest here, I'm all in favor of getting naked as fast as possible. The summer air swirls about my hips, then my thighs.

He kisses my belly button again. His lips drift lower while he tugs my jeans past my knees, and soon he's kissing the small scrap of satin right above my clit. "Oh, god, *yes*, Dax," I moan.

"Go skydiving with me tomorrow," he whispers against the fabric. His hot breath tickles my sensitive nub, and I arch my hips toward his face. "Promise me, Willow. Say it."

"I'll go skydiving with you tomorrow," I gasp.

He rewards me by sucking at my clit through my panties.

"Oh, *yes*, Dax, *more*."

His fingers trace the seams at the apex of my thighs. I'm not going to be able to stand much longer. "And we'll join the mile high club before we jump."

My pussy surges, that thick, desperate need coiling hard and fast. "*Yes*," I gasp.

He slides my panties down my hips and licks my center. I grip his hair, panting, gasping, holding him closer, sensations rocketing over my skin while he sucks and nips and teases my clit and my pussy. My legs are trembling, my core throbbing, his every touch, every stroke of his tongue driving me higher and tighter until my knees give out as powerful wave after wave of release explodes through me.

He catches me, guiding me down, still with his face buried between my legs, coaxing my orgasm deeper, stronger. My toes curl and my vision blurs at the edges.

"Thank you," I'm panting. "Thank you."

He doesn't let go until the last of the tremors have finally faded and my entire body has gone limp. But it's not enough.

I'm still empty.

"I need you inside me," I whisper. "Dax, I need you *now*."

"Fuck, Willow." He kisses my belly just under my navel. "You're delicious. You make me so fucking hard."

"Take me," I order.

He slips two fingers into my channel. I gasp and arch into his touch, even though I would've sworn a minute ago that I was as boneless as a jellyfish.

"So fucking delicious," he whispers against my quivering belly while he thrusts his fingers in and out, everything deep inside me coiling hard, his lips and tongue teasing their way up my ribs until he's nibbling on my nipples and fucking me with his fingers and urging me on with encouraging hums and grunts.

My skin is lit up like it's powered by fireflies, my breasts heavy and tingling and straining into his mouth, my hips pumping out an ancient rhythm while I chant his name until I'm climaxing *again*, squeezing and clenching his fingers while he adds one more, stretching me and hitting that *ohmygod* magic spot over and over.

"*Dax*," I gasp.

"Give me more, princess." He sucks my nipple, nips it with his teeth, I clench impossibly tighter and wetter and deeper, and an entire supernova bursts behind my eyelids. "That's it, baby doll."

I don't realize how much I'm straining into my release until I collapse all the way back onto the blanket. It's scratchy—wool, thick and durable—and I love the roughness.

"M-more?" I stammer.

Because I haven't been full enough yet.

"More what, princess?" He's moving up my body, kissing and licking his way to my collarbone. His fingers, wet with my juices, tracing my tiger tattoo. "Tell me what you want."

"I want *you*." I'm out of breath, but I still *want*.

"Right here, Willow. I'm right here."

"Make love to me with your body, Dax," I whisper. "I don't want you to *fuck* me. I want you to *love* me."

He lifts his head. "Willow. Princess, I do."

Everything stills.

The insects. The brook. The summer breeze.

The earth and the stars and the moon.

"Dax—"

He pulls himself even with me, so his head is bent close to mine, and he strokes my hair. "I love you, Willow. I love your courage. I love your loyalty. I love that crazy sense of adventure you keep hiding. I love your heart. I love your spirit. I love *you*."

My heart spirals into a gallop, and I don't know if it's joy or panic. "I don't want to get married," I blurt.

He chuckles and brushes a kiss to my ear. "I don't need to get married to love you. I just need—I *want* you. More Willow. All the time. I miss talking to you. I miss watching you with other people. I miss the way you blush when you say *fuck*. But if all you want is to keep sneaking to my place to screw around, that's what I'll give you. I'll be here, princess. I'll be here as long as you want me to be. For whatever you want me to be."

"Why…why would you do that for *me*?"

"Willow." His breath comes out ragged. "Because you're the only person I've ever known who would ask that." He takes my hand and pulls it to his chest, where his heart is beating strong and steady and fast. "Nobody remembers *this* anymore. But you—you've seen me at my worst. My lowest. And you held out a hand and pulled me up, with nothing to gain for yourself. I don't care if I never get my money back. I'd rather have you."

I gasp softly. "But I'm just—"

"Perfect." He cradles my hand in his and buries his face in my neck. "Imperfectly perfect."

"Dax," I whisper, because I can barely talk for the pounding of my heart and the way my lungs want to burst out of my chest.

"I don't have a lot to offer you, but I'm game for dashing around the world without a clue where we're going next if you are."

I laugh through tears. "You're crazy."

"You're *my* kind of crazy."

"Yes. You're my kind of crazy."

He laughs into my neck, tickling me and igniting my nerve endings all over again. "I wasn't correcting you, princess."

"Well, of course not."

He laughs again, and I start to, but then he licks a trail up to my ear, and my body instantly responds to his touch. I curl into him and hook my legs around his hips. "More," I whimper.

His hard length nudges my entrance, and I gasp in sheer pleasure again. "*More.*"

"I love when you tell me what you want."

"I want *you.* All of you."

He presses deeper, and *oh,* nothing has ever fit so right as he fits inside me. And it's not just the exquisite pleasure of his heavy length spiraling me so fast toward climax again. It's the combination of his thrust with the way he claims my mouth. It's the way he links his fingers through mine and pins my arms to the ground.

I'm not just *full.*

I'm *complete.*

Physically.

Emotionally.

Musically.

Oh, there's music.

Sweet, heavenly music. Beating in the rhythm of our hearts, the syncing of our breaths, the frantic rising tempo of our hips pumping together.

It's too soon to love him.

But it's *not.*

I wrench out of his kiss and grip his hair, and I leap. "Dax," I gasp.

"Fuck, I love when you say my name."

"I love *you.*"

"Willow—"

"I—love—*you,*" I gasp while the first tremors shake my core. "You. Only you."

"Oh, fuck, Willow, I'm—"

He cuts himself off with a groan as he strains into me, and the dam bursts one more time, my channel clamping hard around him while his cock spasms inside me and my body gives its all for one last release.

I don't want him to come alone.

I don't ever want him to come alone.

He grinds into me once more, neck straining, head back, before he drops his face to my neck again. He scoots off me onto his side and pulls me close. "Willow," he murmurs into my hair.

Wrapping my arms around him is easier than breathing.

More necessary than breathing.

"Thank you for showing me the world," I whisper.

"Thank you for being my world."

I smile against his chest and stroke a lazy hand over his smooth, hot back. I'm getting sleepy.

"I do love you," I say through a yawn. "It's not just the sex talking."

He tightens his grip around me. "Wouldn't care if it was."

"Yes, you would."

"Whatever it takes to keep you coming back for more."

"Well, I want more for you than for someone to love you just for the sex."

"And that's exactly why I love you, princess."

35

Dax

AN IRRITATING BUZZING wakes me out of a sound sleep, and it takes me a minute to remember where I am.

Sunlight filters through the trees, I'm butt-ass naked in the grass, and Willow's wrapped up in the blanket, sleeping peacefully. The buzzing is coming from my pants.

Which are somewhere.

They spin into focus by my bike, so I amble to my feet and snag them. The phone's rolled to voicemail before I dig it out of my pocket. Takes me a minute to hop into my jeans—slept too hard last night, and my body wants to get back to it. About the time I settle on the ground beside Willow again, the voicemail notification buzzes.

I'd ignore it, except it's a Texas area code.

And it's not Pop's number.

I'm instantly awake, because if something's happened to Pop—

"Dax?" Willow rolls over and sits up beside me. She has grass and leaves in her hair, the blanket droops to expose one very pretty rosy nipple, but I'm so intent on dialing up voicemail I barely notice. "Everything okay?"

Her hand settles on my back while a male voice I don't recognize comes on the speaker. "Mr. Gallagher, this is Red Sorenson, president of Sorghum State Bank. Apologies for missing you at the bank on

Saturday. Not quite sure how that happened, since I usually like to handle wealth management accounts like yours personally, but none-theless, I wanted to call and tell you how happy we are to have your business here. Nice that you're bringing it home. The wife and I have always been big fans. Big fans. If you're available to drop by today, we'll be happy to get you your ATM card. Seems you didn't take it with you. Again, Red Sorenson. President, Sorghum State Bank."

He rattles off his number and hangs up.

Willow gapes at me with those pretty blue eyes only half-awake, rosy lips parted, whisker burn on her neck.

"What was that?" I ask her.

She blinks twice, those dark lashes flirting with her cheeks. "I don't have a clue. Do you want to figure it out, or do you want to fuck me?"

I toss the phone over my shoulder and tackle her, because is that even a question?

She's laughing and stroking my skin and kissing me, and I'm taking her skydiving today—or maybe tomorrow, since I have no desire to leave this little alcove right here and there's nothing in the world like making love to a woman in the sparkling sunshine of a summer morning.

We're both out of breath and bonelessly satisfied when her phone starts buzzing.

"You want that?" I ask her.

"Nuh-uh." She curls into me, then stiffens. "Oh, crud monkeys. That could be the preschool."

"Crud monkeys, huh?"

She points a hushing finger at me as she flies off the blanket and lunges for her pile of clothes. I don't mind the view of her sweet ass as she digs for her phone, though I still worry about the notches of her spine.

I need to get this woman some breakfast.

Something *besides* her eating me.

"Oh," she says. Her dark hair brushes her shoulders as she turns to look at me. "That wasn't the preschool. I should probably call them, but…" She tucks her hair behind her ear and holds the phone out to me. "I think this was for you."

I pull her whole hand instead of taking the phone, and she crawls back, shaking her head, but smiling. "You—"

"Love touching you." Once I have her settled in my lap, I look at the message.

It's from Eloise.

It's my email address—my private email address that only seven people in the entire world have—and a random string of characters.

"Is that your email password?" Willow asks.

I shake my head.

And I'm getting a creepy-crawly feeling down my back. "Your friend is nuts, isn't she?"

"Actually, I think she's probably more lonely and afraid of being misunderstood."

I pull up a browser on my own phone, search the Sorghum State Bank back home, and use Eloise's email and password.

And suddenly I'm logged into an account.

Willow chokes.

I go a little dizzy too, because that number is about twenty million higher than what it should be.

"What did she do?" Willow whispers.

Before I can utter a sound, her phone dings again with another message from Eloise.

Tell Mr. Rockstar that his former financial advisor is now downing his antacids in a Canadian prison. Ditching this phone. Catch you on the island.

She sucks in a breath. "No. Oh, no no no, you don't—" She types out a quick message and sends it, but it hangs up, and eventually comes up as undeliverable.

"Dang it," she mutters.

"Did she—"

"Disappear? Maybe."

"What's the island?"

"Zeus and Ares's wedding." She's typing again, a group message with Sia and Parker, looks like.

"To each other?" I ask.

She whips her head up, eyes wide, and— "Oh, you—"

And once more, I'm in my favorite spot in the world.

Under Willow. Out in the fresh air. "You are *trouble*," she informs me.

Primly.

"Damn straight, princess."

She kisses me again, laughing, cradling my head. "So much trouble."

"I love you," I tell her.

Her eyes light up, crinkling in the corners because she's smiling so big, and my heart swells hard and fast.

I'd do anything for this woman.

Anything.

"I love you too," she whispers. "You and your trouble and your crazy life."

"You ready for an adventure, princess?"

"More than ready."

"Then call your ass in sick. We're going to go find us some fun."

And eventually—once we're both dressed again, with a few more orgasms thrown in first—we do.

And we're just getting started.

EPILOGUE

WILLOW

I AM NOT GOING to chicken out.

I am not going to chicken out.

I am not going to—"*Ooh!*"

Dax just pinched my butt.

We're at something like ten thousand feet in the air. The plane's small, made smaller by the fact that there are six skydiving instructors squeezed onto the benches lining the sides of the plane with Dax, me, my stepbrothers, and Dax's bandmate, Oliver.

And I'm going to jump out of it in mere minutes.

I eyeball Dax.

He gives me a fake-innocent grin that makes my nipples shiver.

In a good way, of course.

You got this, princess.

I square my shoulders. Dang right I do. This is going to rock even more than watching him and Edison and Oliver writing songs for a new album they're working on.

On Dax's other side, Colden punches him in the arm. "Hands off," he growls.

"Too little, too late," Manning tells his brother cheerfully.

Colden turns a glower on him.

Manning grins broader.

Gunnar shoves him. "Quit taunting the sheep beast."

"Sylvie shall have all our heads," Colden replies.

"Viggo and Sophie will be in good hands if we all perish," Manning assures him. Cheerfully.

"We shan't perish." Gunnar's getting cross. Not a good sign before he jumps out of a plane at ten thousand feet. "Shall we, gentlemen?" he adds to our skydiving instructors.

None of us have done this before—I mean, not enough for any of us to go solo. We're all to be strapped to a diving partner who will supposedly make sure we don't panic and forget to pull the chute.

"We're going to fucking *live*," Dax murmurs to me. "And then I'm going to eat that sweet pussy until you're begging for mercy."

Okay, yeah, this is all happening. I open my mouth to answer, but my tongue has done that thing it does when Dax is whispering promises of things he wants to do to my body, and I'm incapable of coherent words.

Which is why it's good that my instructor stands at this exact moment. "Time to hook up."

A herd of rabid dragonflies sprouts in my belly.

But it's not fear.

No, it's anticipation.

I'm about to soar like a bird through the open atmosphere. Completely free and untethered—except to my instructor, I mean.

I'd rather be tethered to Dax, but if I was, we might try something funny like kissing in mid-air and miss the cues to deploy our chutes and probably crash to the ground with our hands down each other's pants or something.

He presses a kiss to my temple. "Go on, princess, before I pull you into the airplane bathroom and have my way with you here."

Much as I love airplane sex with Dax—and private flights between New York, Texas, and LA that enable *comfortable* airplane sex with Dax—I'm not sure it could deter me from jumping out of this plane.

"It's okay, Dax," I tell him. "You can do this. You don't have to be scared."

His lips quirk up, and an amused light brightens his eyes. "I liked you better when you were handcuffed and terrified."

"No, you didn't."

We're both grinning now. He leans in for another kiss, and

Colden shoulders between us, which leaves Dax's lips smearing Colden's cheek.

"You two are quite nauseating," my stepbrother grumbles as he wipes his cheek.

I tackle him in a hug and press sloppy kisses all over his other cheek until he pushes me away.

"If the Sisters Mary could see you now." Dax is raking an approving gaze up and down my body. I might've gained a couple pounds in the few weeks since we became official, and he seems to approve.

"You'll meet me on the ground?" I ask him.

"Wild horses couldn't stop me."

"I didn't know watching you wrestle wild horses was an option. We'll have to do that next time." All those lean muscles getting hot, sweat dripping over his tattoos...yeah, a girl could enjoy watching that.

"You ready, ma'am?" my instructor asks.

"I was born ready," I tell him.

Dax is smiling again.

I'm kinda madly in love with his smile. It's so much more natural than that defeated scowl he wore most of the way through Europe.

We all get hooked up to our instructors, and I end up sandwiched between Dax and Manning as we line up for the jump. The instructors are reminding us of everything we need to know as we're about to launch ourselves out of a perfectly good plane to freefall through the sky.

I check the harness that I'm strapped into.

Dax catches my eye in the small space, and he winks. *You got this, princess.*

He says he's taking me to Australia to dive the Great Barrier Reef this winter. And to Morocco to ride a camel.

I've informed him I don't need his charity, and I can earn my way, thank you very much.

So he has me helping him with lyrics for his new album.

And I might even cave and agree to sing back-up on one or two of his songs. I don't know that I want to give up teaching preschool—that's its own kind of fun and adventure—and I love my girlfriends too much to ditch our boy band cover band, but I still wouldn't turn down a chance to be on a real album, or to have a guest appearance or two at a stadium show.

Hello, thrill.

Plus, I'll miss Dax when he's touring.

We'll have to work that out.

And we will.

"Go time," one of the instructors yells.

Manning grins back at me. "Best idea yet, Willow," he calls. "Can't wait to see what you come up with next."

He's rigged the pro hockey championship cup into a special harness around his shoulders and waist. His team, the Thrusters, won it this year, and he decided that he wanted to bring it along today. He has a GoPro rigged up, and Colden, for all his grumblings, has another. I'm positive Colden misses having Manning around in Stölland, even though he'd deny it.

"Are you going to jump or what?" I call back to him.

He and his instructor give us a thumbs-up, and suddenly they're gone.

Whoosh.

Out the door. Flying to the earth below.

Oh. My. Gosh.

This is going to rock.

"Ready, princess?" Dax calls to me.

"Fuck, yeah!" I yell back.

We give the plane a thumbs-up, I lean out the door to the earth lingering thousands of feet below us, my heart gives a hiccup, and I let go.

I just let go.

I scream—in joy, I promise—as the rush of air promises me that I'm not just dangling in midair. My cheeks are flapping, and I force myself to let go of my death grip on my harness to stretch my arms out.

"Great job," my instructor yells. "Just enjoy it, Willow."

Manning is below me to my right, the battered cup still glinting in the sunlight. Colden is almost even with him, and the two of them are waving at each other and pumping their fists and being general goofballs.

Something to my left catches my eye, and I realize Dax is floating too.

I wave at him.

He's gripping his harness so tight I can almost see the white of his knuckles. His legs are straight as boards, not relaxed and flowing like his instructor's. "Dax," I call.

Of course he doesn't hear me.

He doesn't see me either. I'm pretty sure his eyes are clenched tight.

No smile. No joy.

"Dax," I whisper as the air rushes around us and the world becomes a little larger beneath us.

This man.

He jumped out of an airplane *for me*. So I'd go. Because when we couldn't get reservations before now, I almost bailed.

But he wouldn't let me.

And he's terrified.

An unexpected lump forms in my throat, and it has nothing to do with the beauty of the trees and valleys beneath us, and everything to do with being this loved.

My stepbrothers wanted to do this badly enough that they all ditched their royal guards.

Dax, though—he's doing this for me.

His head twists toward me, and I see his eyes blink open.

I smile at him. *I love you.* And I blow him a kiss. *Thank you.*

The poor man. He's green around the gills, but he blows me a kiss back. And then grips his harness again.

I flap my arms. *Let go. It's awesome.*

I get the Dax Gallagher Dubious Eyeball, and I laugh despite the worry growing in the pit of my stomach. If he's okay enough to side-eye me, he's not going to totally freak.

"Chute opening," my instructor tells me.

"I could fall like this all day," I call back to him.

"Couple more jumps, and you can train to go solo."

I'm *so* training to go solo. "Can I start today?"

He laughs, there's a jerk, and suddenly the fall slows and we straighten vertically.

Manning and Colden below are both having their chutes opened too. Gunnar's joined them, three Stöllandic princes just falling from the sky over upstate New York. Oliver's pulling his chute beyond Dax, who's also going more vertical as his canopy deploys.

He scrubs his hands over his face. There's too much space between us. I want to hug him, though I know crossing chutes probably isn't a good idea. And I want to kiss him for doing this for me.

Beyond him, Oliver's floating down. I like Oliver. He's given me the least amount of crap of all the guys in Half Cocked Heroes.

And not in an *I'm not giving you shit because I secretly don't like you* kind of way. He asks about the kids at school and genuinely listens. Probably because he has sisters. He has practice.

Dax is glancing around now. Probably having his parachute open is reassuring. He looks my way again, and this time, it's a very sheepish grin spreading over his pale features.

He's adorable.

Sexy and headstrong and talented and loyal and adorable.

The descent to the earth takes not nearly long enough, but as soon as I'm free of my tethers, I dash across the field to where Dax has landed. He's on his feet by the time I get there, but he doesn't stay on his feet when I throw myself at him.

We tumble to the ground while I pepper his jaw with kisses. "You —crazy—should've—told me—I love you."

He cradles my head and sucks my lip between his teeth, and I quit talking in favor of kissing him.

Later, I'll tell him how much I enjoyed soaring over the earth.

Right now, I'm too busy enjoying *him*.

ABOUT THE AUTHOR

Pippa Grant is a stay-at-home mom and housewife who loves to escape into sexy, funny stories way more than she likes perpetually cleaning toothpaste out of sinks and off toilet handles. When she's not reading, writing, sleeping, or trying to prepare her adorable demon spawn to be productive members of society, she's fantasizing about chocolate chip cookies.

Find Pippa at…
www.pippagrant.com
pippa@pippagrant.com

COPYRIGHT

9 781940 517759